To Aunty, Hap

I hope you en

as I have.

Martin

"Read not to contradict and confute,
nor to believe and take for granted,
nor to find talk and discourse, but
to weigh and consider."

Francis Bacon,
"Advancement of Learning"
Book I.

16

The Pleasures of **Gaelic** Poetry

Edited by Seán Mac Réamoinn

Allen Lane

Allen Lane
Penguin Books Ltd
536 King's Road
London SW10 0UH

First published 1982

ISBN 0 7139 12847

Designed by Anthony Froshaug
Set in Linotron Bembo
by Western Printing Services Ltd, Bristol
Printed in Great Britain
by Richard Clay (The Chaucer Press) Ltd, Bungay, Suffolk

Acknowledgements

The publishers wish to thank the following for permission to use the poems quoted in this volume.

The Dolmen Press/I Gcomhar le Bord na Gaelige for 'Beatha an Scoláire', 'Ar Maidin a Mhacaoimh Óig', 'Adoramus te, Christe', 'Is Mairg Nár Chrean le Maitheas Saoghalta', 'Seirbhíseach Seirgthe Iogair Srónach Seasc', 'Do Shiúlaigh Mise an Mhumhain Mhín', 'Gile na Gile', 'Mac an Cheannaí', 'Cabhair ni Ghairfead' (original texts and translations), 'Taisigh agat Féin do Phóg', 'Ní Bhfuighe mise Bás Duit' (original texts); published in *An Duanaire*, Baile Atha Cliath, 1981.

Canongate Publishing Ltd for poems by Sorley MacLean, 'Calbharaigh', 'Conchobhar', 'Hallaig', 'Eadh is Fein as Sar-Fhein', 'Aig Uaigh Yeats', 'A' Bheinn Air Chall' (original texts and translations); published in *Reothairt is Contraigh: Spring Tide and Neap Tide – Selected Poems (1932–1972)*, Dun Eideann, 1977.

An Clochomhar TTA for poems by Máirtín Ó Direáin, 'Fuaire', 'Mothú Feirge', 'Eala-Bhean', 'Cranna Foirtil' (original texts); published in *Danta 1939–1979*, Baile Atha Cliath, 1980. For the translations we thank *International Poetry Review* (Spring 1979, volume 5, number 1), Greensboro, North Carolina, U.S.A.

Sairséal O Marcaigh TTA for 'Na Leamhain', 'Seanmóintí', 'A Theanga Seo Leath-Liom', 'Tulyar', 'An Lacha', 'Catchollú' (original texts); published in *Brosna*, Baile Atha Cliath, 1980. The translations are by C. W. C. Quin.

The Dublin Institute for Advanced Studies for 'The Child is Born in Prison', 'The Shannon' (original texts). For the translation of 'The Shannon' by Robin Flower, published in *The Irish Tradition*, 1947, we thank the Oxford University Press.

Routledge & Kegan Paul Ltd for the translation of 'Trust No Man', published in *A Celtic Miscellany*, London, 1951.

The Irish Times for the translation of 'Envoi', published in *Poems from Ireland*, Baile Atha Cliath, 1944.

Allen Figgis and Co. Ltd. for the translation of 'The Kiss', published in *The Oxford Book of Irish Verse*, Oxford, 1955.

7

Gill–MacMillan for 'The Hermitage', 'Winter', 'Cill Aodáin' (original texts and translations), published in *Kings, Lords and Commons*, Baile Atha Cliath, 1970.

The Dolmen Press for 'Is Mo Chen in Maiten Bán', 'Och, a Long' (original texts and translations), published in *Medieval Irish Lyrics*, Baile Atha Cliath, 1967.

Faber & Faber Ltd for 'Against Blame of Women', 'Under Sorrow's Sign' (translations), published in *The Faber Book of Irish Verse*, London, 1977.

Oxford University Press for 'Fil Súil Nglais', published in *Early Irish Lyrics*, Baile Atha Cliath, 1956.

Unless otherwise stated, translations from Gaelic have been made by the individual essayists.

Introduction by Seán Mac Réamoinn

The scope and purpose of this book are, we hope, sufficiently indicated by its title. It provides neither a history nor a comprehensive critical survey of its subject; the essayists differ widely in their approach, and, besides, more than a few important names and even periods are not touched on at all. As in the case of the original broadcast talks (an adult education series on Irish radio) on which the book is based, all the contributors were invited to discuss a poet or a kind of poetry of their own choice, to share their own pleasures of discovery as guides in a series of explorations of a fascinating but all too little known literature.

The 'Gaelic' of the title is the language of Ireland which became also one of the languages of Scotland. Gaelic literature shares with that of Welsh the distinction of being the oldest in any European vernacular. Apart from the great prose epics, which include verse passages of remarkable antiquity, some of our early lyrics and religious poems can be dated back to the seventh century – and there are fragments which may be older still. Gaelic poetry has never ceased to flourish, though not since the eighteenth century has there been such a flowering as in the last forty or fifty years, in the work of two or three poets of quite exceptional power. One of these is in fact a Scot, Somhairle Mac Gill-Eain (Sorley MacLean), whose verse is the subject of the essay 'A Northern Vision'; apart from this piece, all our contributors confine themselves to Irish poets and poetry. But down to the seventeenth century the heritage was held in common, and for at least four centuries a common literary language was used by poets from Kerry to Skye. This 'classical' language can be regarded as belonging to the 'Early Modern' period, even if it may present difficulties to the twentieth-century reader (but then *mutatis mutandis* the same is true of Chaucer). More difficult still, of course, is the Old and Middle Irish of the earlier verse, represented in some of the examples cited in Seamus Heaney's essay.

The appreciation of poetry, any poetry, is rare enough: a minority pleasure. It is sadly true that even in Ireland (or Scotland) the pleasures of Gaelic poetry are still more rarely known. The problem is of course basically one of language: not merely those difficulties of detail just referred to, or that of mutual comprehension between the now quite divergent Irish and Scottish 'dialects', but the great and overwhelming difficulty that the language itself is dying. It has been dying for over three hundred years, ever since it became de-institutionalized with the final collapse of the old Gaelic social order in the seventeenth century. (I am thinking mainly of Ireland here – the process was delayed a little in parts of Scotland.) However, despite the erosive effects of intense colonization ('plantation') and the growth of small cities and towns as centres of Anglicization, the great majority of the Irish remained Gaelic-speaking right through the eighteenth century. Even in the first half of the nineteenth century, the two languages were not far from being on equal terms as to strength of numbers in a wildly over-populated country. The Great Famine (1847–8) and consequent mass emigrations helped to solve the population problem, and in a new demographic situation the language went into a sharp decline. It might well have died peacefully, but for the uncovenanted mercy that a number of ineffectual attempts to arrest the process were subsumed and transformed into what became a great popular movement – the Gaelic League – founded in 1893, and led by an unlikely prophet, Douglas Hyde, the son of a country clergyman of colonial stock. Hyde's great aim was the 'De-Anglicization of Ireland' and the restoration of the Gaelic vernacular. In this task he and the League patently failed. But it can be said that from this movement most of what has happened in Ireland in the present century, for good or ill, directly or indirectly derives: 'I have said again and again,' said P. H. Pearse, 'that when the Gaelic League was founded the Irish revolution began.'

The most tangible result of that 'revolution' has been of course the setting-up of an independent Irish state, and successive Irish governments have, over the past sixty years, maintained the conservation of the language and the cultivation of things Gaelic as a 'national aim'. Irish is taught in all schools, there is a complex support system for various cultural enterprises involving the language, and special social and economic provisions for those (by now marginal) areas where Irish survives as a vernacular.

But putting time's chariot into reverse is a tricky business, and never more so than where language and culture are concerned. While language is usually the dominant and crucial factor in shaping a culture – and certainly was in Ireland – it is itself affected, enriched or attenuated, made to flower or decline (even sometimes to die) by the weight and pressure of a host of other elements, material and psychological alike, some of which we have only very recently come to recognize as being of 'cultural' significance.

That the poetry of a little-known language should lack a wide international audience is only to be expected; that it should also be little appreciated even among those with a knowledge of Gaelic, either inherited or acquired, may perhaps be understood for reasons I have suggested. For it is not merely a matter of understanding the words, but of in some way partaking of the social and psychological presuppositions of Gaelic culture. In all poetry the meaning lies as much between the lines as in them. And there is another problem which derives from this. What meaning, function, or area of resonance is given in the Gaelic (or in any) culture to the word *poetry* itself? Socio-cultural change even *within* a tradition, without any question of another language, can create difficulties here: someone brought up on Shelley and Keats may find Auden or Eliot hard to take. He will certainly be slow to recognize La Fontaine's fables as poetry in any real sense. And Irish birth and education in the second half of the twentieth century give no 'Open Sesame!' to a thousand years of Gaelic poetry – or even to the work of contemporary writers.

So much for difficulties. The aim of this book, as I have said, is not to discourage but to provide an informed introduction to a *hortus occlusus* and to its rare variety of flowerings. A thorough course in Irish studies is hardly necessary in order to begin to taste the pleasures within; after all, many of us have come to appreciate artists working in unfamiliar idioms from other countries and cultures, some of them very exotic indeed. This usually happens through the mediation of a critic, a translator of more than usual sensitivity – even through the encouragement of a friend who has discovered the delight behind the alien mask, whether of language or of style. And it is surely of heartening significance that, with one or two exceptions, all our essayists (including the editor) have themselves been explorers from without, who learned Irish as a second language and so discovered a hidden heritage.

Before briefly plotting the course of this second shared exploration, a few general remarks may be helpful. First of all, it is well to remember that while we think of poetry as necessarily involving writing and reading, paper and print, Irish poets and their audiences got on quite well for lengthy periods without any of these. Verse was *made* rather than spoken or sung, and listened to rather than read. It was of course usually committed to manuscript after composition, and such texts were copied, circulated, and incorporated in collections, private or communal. In saying this I am telescoping and generalizing: it is also true that oral and manuscript transmission of poetry was at one time normal in other countries and cultures. But it went on much longer here than in many other places because, in the first centuries of printing, the native culture had little access to the process of book-production. The art and craft of the scribe lingered on in parts of Ireland, north and south, until quite late in the last century, as did the commissioning, presentation and exchange of manuscripts as much prized *objets d'art*. I am reminded of the Armenian belief (symbol of a not dissimilar cultural history) that anyone who copied and passed on a manuscript had a sure passport to heaven, however scarlet his sins!

I have referred to verse being either spoken or sung. This has had two lasting effects: the first being that poetry and music remained close allies to the point of some lexical ambiguity – *amhrán* can mean either a verse-form or a song; *ceol*, the usual word for music, may in Ulster be used of a spoken poem; and *abair amhrán!* ('say a song!') is a common phrase of encouragement to the native *virtuoso*. The other effect of the poetry–music alliance is that folk-song and oral literature have not always been clearly distinguished.

This is ambiguous territory anywhere, and nowhere more so than in Ireland. There is a long tradition of professionalism in Gaelic poetry: something very real in the centuries of patronage, and the attitude, if not the rewards, survived long after. So long that when, some twenty-five years ago, I was in County Galway researching local traditions about the poet Anthony Raftery (1784–1835), I came quite suddenly up against it. Talking to a farmer in a hay-field who entertained me with many of Raftery's *amhráin*, but also with verses by other hands – some anonymous – I asked him what was the difference between the poet Raftery and these others:

'Oh,' he said, 'these were only *fir tíre* (countrymen): Raftery was a poet.'

'And how would you know?' I asked. 'How do you tell a great poet?'

He leaned on his hay-fork and thought for a moment.

'Better words,' he said, 'better placed . . . the way you'd be building a wall and you'd know where to put the bricks . . .'

A good answer, putting a premium on skill, but perhaps unconsciously relating excellence to a tradition of such skill, inherited by blood or academic succession. Poetic inheritance by blood is indeed part of the story: many of the professional poets of the classical period were of certain specific families – as were the lawyers and medical men, in the days when every local chieftain had his professional court.

Even after the completion of the process of de-institutionalization, in the Ireland of the Penal Laws that followed the final defeat of Limerick (1691) the making of verse was regarded as a social craft or service. Indeed it is interesting to note that a people utterly denuded of institutions of law, the arts and education sought to forge for themselves structures based on the practice of poetry. The story of these *Cúirteanna Filíochta* ('Courts of Poetry') which grew up here and there in the eighteenth century belongs to literary history and we cannot tell it properly here; but it was, above all, thanks to these that later generations could once again discover the pleasures of a past sophistication.

The tradition of *Amhráin na nDaoine* (the 'Songs of the People') grew alongside, and was the bread and butter of Irish culture in the eighteenth and nineteenth centuries. The songs are still sung, either spontaneously, out of living oral memory in Gaelic-speaking areas, or, thanks to the work of the collectors, from Charlotte Brook to Ciarán MacMathúna, at a near-authentic second hand. Of course, the border lines between these and the poetry of the 'poets' is blurred – both draw ultimately on the same sources, but they are *different*.

And so to plot our course. Following this introduction, there are ten essays on ten different subjects, and a final summing-up, coda or postscript. Of the ten, four deal with themes and kinds of verse, the

15

other six with individual poets – three of the past, three of today. After these essays is appended a selection of additional poems – in bilingual texts – as illustration to what has gone before.

'The God in the Tree' is the title of the first exploration. Our guide is the Ulster poet Seamus Heaney, and he looks at what is one of the most immediately attractive chapters of our literary history, and one of the earliest. (I should say we will be keeping a roughly chronological order in the series, beginning in the Old Irish period and coming down to the nineteen-seventies.) Seamus Heaney's subject is our early nature poetry, a body of verse of remarkable beauty and charm which has kept its freshness down through the centuries. The adjective 'Franciscan' has been applied to it, and although it predates the Canticle of the Sun by some hundreds of years, a sense of joy and delight in God's physical creation is one of its most strikingly attractive characteristics. But there are depths of reflection in it, of self-knowledge and sometimes of pain, which give it dimensions which a thousand years later a Wordsworth or a Yeats might recognize . . .

In his remarkable 'Lament for Pádraig Ó Conaire' the poet F. R. Higgins imagines the shade of the twentieth-century novelist and writer of short stories, who was his close friend, finding his own private heaven in:

An ale-house overflowing with wise Gaelic
That's braced in vigour to the bardic mind.

It's a fine image, and one utterly right for the subject. For Ó Conaire did, I believe, inherit something of the 'bardic mind' . . . But here I must go easy.

No words relative to our ancient culture are better known than *bard* and *bardic*. Few are more often misunderstood. The basic word, descriptive of the practitioner of a creative or performing art, has precise meaning in Irish, and indeed in Welsh; in English it has been hopelessly subjected to pseudo-antiquarian and romantic misinterpretations, and these misinterpretations have, alas, found their way too often back home. In our second essay, which bears the title 'The Bardic Mind', the late Professor David Greene lifts for us not only this veil of confusion, but also a curtain more difficult to penetrate. I mean the inherent difficulty that we have today in understanding what the poets of the Gaelic middle ages were really about. There is a considerable corpus of their verse available; classical in its strictness of form, as in the severe limits of its emotional range, highly professional in its provenance – the work of craftsmen who served a long apprenticeship before graduating to full poetic stature – it is a particularly hard kind of nut for the uninformed reader of today to set about cracking. What was the mind of the long bardic generations who dominated Irish poetry until the seventeenth century; who were the men of this mind? In answering these questions Professor Greene may well help us to appreciate some of the subtler pleasures of Gaelic poetry. More fundamentally, he may help us put into perspective a school, a discipline, an *art*, which was and is classical also in the sense that it remained a norm to be followed and imitated, or else reacted against – even rejected – long after the collapse of the world in which it was formed and flourished.

I have, in speaking of bardic poetry, used the phrase 'the severe limits of its emotional range'. In fact, Professor Greene shows, towards the end of his essay, how these limits were at times strained and breached, as personal feeling broke through. And, indeed, alongside the professional poetry of late medieval Ireland, there is one particular body of verse which is by common consent one of the great pleasures of our literature. I mean that unique treasure, born of a happy fusion of two traditions, the Gaelic and the French-Provençal, which we call the *Dánta Grá*, the Poems of Love. These poems are the aristocratic and rightly sophisticated equivalents of the love songs of the countryside: the men who made them were – as well as the professionals, 'off-duty' as it were – the cultivated gentry of Anglo-Norman stock now Gaelicized, 'more Irish than the Irish', but mindful of their remote ancestral world of trouvere and troubadour, of high gallantry and the courts of love. The last and best-remembered of them was Piaras Feiritéar of Kerry, a very parfit gentle knight, born late into a most ungentle time, and who died a most ungentle death at the hands of Cromwell's governor. In our third essay, Eiléan Ní Chuilleanáin, who lectures in English literature and makes her own poetry in English, reflects on this part of her literary heritage, and extends her consideration to love in a wider sense, and to the poetry of friendship.

Piaras Feiritéar died under Cromwell; his great contemporary Daibhí Ó Bruadair lived to see the Williamite settlement achieved, and with it, the apparent final conquest of the Gaelic nation. Ó Bruadair was a giant, an artist and craftsman of great power and of long and sustained output. Had he flourished in the fifteenth or the sixteenth century, instead of the seventeenth, he would have been one of the great professional poets of his day. In the event, he comes to us out of the ruins of the old Gaelic world, and makes his way through the convulsive sequence of events which swept the fragmented nation along, from the high hopes of the Confederation of Kilkenny with the Stuart star in the ascendant, to fall in the Williamite victories of Aughrim, the Boyne and Limerick. And as the landscape darkens his voice grows ever more powerful as he 'rages against the dying of the light'. He is not an easy poet, but he richly repays the demands he makes on the reader. Michael Hartnett, a young Irish poet who turned from English to Gaelic, and whose recent writing has been nourished in the Limerick countryside where Ó Bruadair spent most of his life, tells of *his* personal struggle to break through a rock-like mind and art, in 'Wrestling with Ó Bruadair'.

And then we move to another name, perhaps the best-known and probably the greatest in the canon of our literature between Kinsale and our own time. This is Aogán Ó Rathaille of Kerry, father of the Munster school of the eighteenth century, but of unique national stature and significance. He speaks for a people broken and bereft of all human comfort and dignity, and if his voice offers little comfort, the dignity is superb in its rhetoric; but more, there is memory and there is hope. To the fire and rage of Ó Bruadair is added a music strong and dark, but sometimes lit by a vision of bright beauty as in his masterpiece 'Gile na Gile', the supreme example of that genre of Irish poetry where the vision-woman images a nation transfigured and triumphant. But although the matter of Ireland is Ó Rathaille's great theme, joy and grief on a more personal scale have their own place in his poetry. Aogán Ó Rathaille and his work form the subject of a remarkable essay by the Dublin poet and critic John Jordan.

One of the unmistakable characteristics of Irish verse, what makes it I suppose most obviously Irish, is a recurrent use of place names, and this on two levels. There are the legendary names of

Ireland itself – *Banba*, *Ardmhágh Fáil*, *Fód Feidhlim*, *Inis Ealga*, and the rest – as well as the famous and holy places: Teamhair or Tara, Eamhain Macha, the Boyne river. And beyond these, there are a thousand other names of rivers and mountains, church and castle sites, townlands and *tuatha*, from Inis Eoghain to Sceilg Mhichil. As a matter of fact, *dinnseanchas*, the lore of places, was one of the classic divisions of our ancient literature. But, far beyond this specific concern, the literature in prose and verse has carried these names for a thousand years and more, with each name an echo of ancient memory, or of recent adventure. Passion and mood are given a local habitation as often as action and incident; places are as often a part of the telling as are people. An Ulster writer of today, Benedict Kiely, whose own work shares this characteristic, writes on 'A Sense of Place'.

Perhaps the most famous description of an Irish landscape is the evocation of early morning by the shores of Loch Gréine in Clare which forms the prologue to Brian Merriman's 'Cúirt an Mheán Oíche', the Midnight Court. Every schoolboy knew it at a time (not so very long ago) when the poem itself was not regarded as suitable for young – or even older – eyes. The Irish Censorship Board never got around to banning the original, but Frank O'Connor's splendid translation was, quite disgracefully, put on their list. It's no longer there, I'm glad to say, and the poem has also been translated by, among others, Arland Ussher, the late Earl of Longford, David Marcus, Patrick Power and C. W. C. Quin. Canon Quin – Cosslett Ó Cuinn as he is widely known – contributes an essay on Merriman and his poem. I say *poem*, rather than poems, because, with the exception of one or two doubtfully attributed short compositions, this great comic poet was a man of one book. It did not, in fact, become a book in our common meaning of the word until it was first printed some eighty years ago. But it had a long life before that in manuscript, and in the oral tradition of North Munster – and there were manuscript translations also before the ones already mentioned. Since it was first written just two centuries ago it has been enormously popular.

'Cúirt an Mheán Oíche' has been described, and properly so, as 'Rabelaisian' – but not just in the commonest, most superficial use of the term. I believe the first time the word was used in its profounder sense about certain Irish writers (including Merriman) was in a perceptive essay by Seán Ó Ríordáin, the Cork poet who died in 1976. A full assessment of Ó Ríordáin's work and that of his contemporary Máirtín Ó Direáin can only come in the perspective of time – and of course we may hope that Dr Ó Direáin has still much more to give us. They are however, by acclamation, the two major Gaelic poets of our time – in Ireland at least. For from Scotland the work of Somhairle Mac Gill-Eain comes as a challenge, and a great and surprising delight, to many who thought perhaps that the old language of the Highlands and Hebrides had no longer within it the potential to be a vehicle for a poetry expressive of, and responsive to, the complex sensibilities of the contemporary world. How wrong such an impression would be is triumphantly apparent in Mac Gill-Eain's verse – as, indeed, it is clear in Ó Ríordáin's and Ó Direáin's own achievements – a refutation of anyone so misinformed as to doubt the vigour and continuity of the Gaelic poetic tradition, or the ability of its practitioners at once to reflect and transcend it with their vision and their craft.

There are, I may add, in this country (and in Scotland) other distinguished modern poets writing in Gaelic; it would be invidious to name names. I must however mention two of them: Professor Seán Ó Tuama and Micheál Ó hUanacháin, who write here respectively about Ó Ríordáin and Ó Direáin. John Montague, an Ulster poet who works in English, introduces us to his Scottish contemporary Mac Gill-Eain.

The final essay is by another Irish poet Thomas Kinsella. He writes in English, and some years ago gave us a splendid translation of the prose epic *Táin Bó Cuailnge*. His coda or colophon to this book takes the form of a very personal account of his own rediscovery of the Gaelic poetic heritage, and of the pleasure he has derived from certain poems which he describes as 'occasional', but regards nevertheless as occupying a central position within the tradition.

I had occasion earlier to quote from F. R. Higgins' poem on Ó Conaire. He goes on to say of the bardic 'ale-house':

> And there his thoughts will find their own forefathers
> In minds to whom our heights of race belong
> Crafty men, who'd rib a ship or turn
> The secret joinery of song.

Perhaps, when all is said and done, it is in such an encounter that we may find the deepest of the pleasures of Gaelic poetry.

The brief selection of poems which follows the essays, while in no way exhaustive, or even properly representative of the Gaelic tradition, is intended to provide further reading for those who have shared our essayists' pleasure in their chosen periods and authors. It may also provide a slight shift of perspective in choice both of the original poems and of translations.

For those who would wish to explore more widely and deeply we would recommend the collections detailed in the list of acknowledgements on pages 7–8.

Seamus Heaney
The God in the Tree

Early Irish nature poems have been praised and translated often. Their unique cleanliness of line has been commented on. The tang and clarity of a pristine world full of woods and water and birdsong seems to be present in the tang of the words. Little jabs of delight in the elemental are communicated by them in a note that is hard to describe. Perhaps Wordsworth's phrase, 'surprised by joy', comes near to catching the way some of them combine suddenness and richness – certainly it would do as a title for these eight lines, twenty-two syllables in all, which have etched themselves in the memory of generations, and in English go under the title 'The Blackbird of Belfast Lough'. In the original the language is old and tough with its age, but as always in this poetry, it has an edge to it:

Int én bec	The small bird
ro léic feit	let a chirp
do rind guip	from its beak:
glanbuide;	I heard
fo-ceird faíd	woodnotes, whin-
os Loch Laíg	gold, sudden.
lon do chraíb	The Lagan
chrannmuige.	blackbird!

In its precision and suggestiveness, this art has been compared with the art of the Japanese haiku, and the comparison is a good one. Basho's frog plopping into its pool in seventeenth-century Japan makes no more durable or exact music than Belfast's blackbird clearing its throat over the lough almost a thousand years earlier.

Equally memorable, compact and concrete are the lines beginning 'Scél lem duíb', lines that have all the brightness and hardness of a raindrop winking on a thorn. The poem shows us how accurately Flann O'Brien characterized early Irish verse-craft when he spoke about its 'steel-pen exactness'; and this is what he was intent on catching in his version, where the authentic chill of winter and the bittersweet weather of a northern winter pierce into the marrow of the quatrains:

Scél lem duíb:	Here's a song –
dordaid dam,	stags give tongue
snigid gaim,	winter snows
ro-faíth sam;	summer goes
gáeth ard uar,	High cold blow
ísel grían,	sun is low
gair a rith,	brief his day
ruirthech rían;	seas give spray
rorúad ráth,	Fern clumps redden
ro-cleth cruth,	shapes are hidden
ro-gab gnáth	wildgeese raise
gingrann guth;	wonted cries.
ro-gab uacht	Cold now girds
etti én,	wings of birds
aigre ré:	icy time –
é mo scél.	that's my rhyme.

I can think of only a few poets in English whose words give us the sharp tooth of winter anywhere as incisively as that: the medieval poet of *Sir Gawain and the Green Knight* managed it beautifully, and so did Shakespeare, and Thomas Hardy. That line in *King Lear* – 'still through the sharp hawthorn blows the cold wind' – has the *frisson* of the bare and shivering flesh about it, but a touch like that is unusual in English verse. It almost seems that since the Norman conquest, the temperature of English language has been subtly raised by a warm front coming up from the Mediterranean. But the Irish language did not undergo the same Romance influences, and indeed early Irish nature poetry registers certain sensations, and makes a springwater music out of certain feelings, in ways unmatched in any other European language. Kuno Meyer, the great pioneering scholar and translator of Celtic languages, alluded to this distinctive feature when he wrote: 'These poems occupy a unique position in the literature of the world. To seek out and watch and love Nature, in its tiniest phenomena as in its grandest, was given to no people so early and so fully as the Celt.' And Kenneth Hurlstone Jackson expanded upon that perception in his delightful anthology, *A Celtic Miscellany*:

Comparing these poems with the medieval European lyric is like comparing the emotions of an imaginative adolescent who has just grown up to realize the beauty of nature, with those of an old man who has been familiar with it for a lifetime and is no longer able to think of it except in literary terms . . . The truth is that in its earlier period Celtic literature did not belong at all to the common culture of the rest of Europe; nor did it ever become more than partly influenced by it.

On the margin of a ninth-century manuscript, from the monastery of St Gall in Switzerland, we get another glimpse of nature, through the rinsed eyes of Celtic Christianity, in 'Dom-farcai Fidbaidae Fál', translated by James Carney:

> A wall of forest looms above
> and sweetly the blackbird sings:
> All the birds make melody
> over me and my books and
> things
>
> There sings to me the cuckoo
> from bush-citadels in grey hood.
> God's doom! May the Lord
> protect me
> writing well, under the great
> wood.

This poem has been called 'The Scribe in the Woods' and in it we can see the imagination taking its colouring from two very different elements. On the one hand, there is the *pagus*, the pagan wilderness, green, full-throated, unrestrained; on the other hand there is the lined book, the Christian *disciplina*, the sense of a spiritual principle and a religious calling that transcends the almost carnal lushness of nature itself. The writer is as much hermit as scribe, and it is within this anchorite tradition of the early Irish church that early Irish nature poetry develops. Moreover, P. L. Henry, in his learned and thrilling study of *The Early English and Celtic Lyric*, links this praise poetry with another kind of poem which is its corollary and opposite, a kind we might characterize as penitential poetry. Both spring from a way of life at once simple and ascetic, the tensions of asceticism finding voice in the penitential verse, and the cheerier nature lyrics springing from the solitary's direct experience of the changing seasons.

These two strains are often dramatized vividly in the later 'Fenian' poetry when St Patrick, the newly arrived missionary who comes along to disrupt the old heroic order, argues with Oisín, the unregenerate natural man. Patrick praises the cloister with its music of massbell and plainsong, Oisín catalogues the more full-blooded and noisier joys of the hunt or the battle. In Irish, a whole system of such poems had been elaborated by the thirteenth century, and continued to develop in subsequent centuries, when a convention of celebrating specific places also emerged. This love of place, and lamentation at exile from a cherished territory, is another typical strain in the Celtic sensibility, and one poem will here have to represent the whole extensive genre. I choose Oisín's praise of Ben Bulben, translated from a fifteenth- or sixteenth-century original, partly because it is an early appearance in literature of the mountain which W. B. Yeats was to impose upon the imagination of the modern world by his own famous celebration of its dominant presence in the Sligo landscape. The 'son of Calpurnius' is, of course, St Patrick:

> Benn Boilbin that is sad to-day,
> peak that was shapely and best
>   of form,
> at that time, son of Calpurnius,
> it was lovely to be upon its
>   crest.
>
> Many were the dogs and the
>   ghillies,
> the cry of the bugle and the
>   hound,
> and the mighty heroes that were
>   upon your rampart,
> O high peak of the contests.

It was haunted by cranes in the
     night
and heath-fowl on its moors,
with the tuning of small birds
it was delightful to be listening
     to them.

The cry of the hounds in its
     glens,
the wonderful echo,
and each of the Fianna
with lovely dogs on the leash.

Many in the woods were the
     gleaners
from the fair women of the
     Fianna
its berries of sweet taste,
raspberries and blackberries.

Mellow purple blaeberries,
tender cress and cuckoo-flower;
and the curly-haired fair-headed
     maidens,
sweet was the sound of their
     singing . . .

We were on this hill
seven companies of the Fianna;
to-night my friends are few,
and is not my tale pitiful to you.

Scholars might classify this as an elegiac poem as much as a poem of
place, and it does indeed have a backward look which gives it a more
modern tone, a more alienated stance; but in the first flush of the
hermit poetry six or seven centuries before this poem was written, it
is not the tears of things but the joy, the lifting eye and heart, that we
respond to. We are nearer the first world in that first poetry, nearer
to the innocent eye and tongue of Adam as he named the creatures.
These next stanzas, for example, come from a poem put into the
mouth of a seventh-century anchorite from Connacht called Mar-
bhán; even this literal version conveys the exhilaration of the feeling:

An excellent spring, a cup of noble water to drink; watercresses
sprout, yew berries, ivy bushes as big as a man.

Tame swine lie down around it, goats, boars, wild swine, grazing
deer, a badger's brood . . .

A bush of rowan, black sloes of the dark blackthorn; plenty of
food, acorns, spare berries, pennywort, milk.

A clutch of eggs, honey, produce of wild onions, God has sent it;
sweet apples, red whortleberries, crowberries . . .

A heavy bowlful, goodly hazel nuts, early young corn, brown
acorns, manes of briars, fine sweet tangle . . .

Though you delight in your own enjoyments, greater than all
wealth, for my part I am grateful for what is given me from my
dear Christ.

And so it goes on, the hermit's rhapsody, full of the primeval
energies of the druid's grove. And that word 'druid', of course, calls
up a world older and darker and greener than the world of early
Christian Ireland, although some authorities would have it that the
role of the *file*, the official poet in historic times, was continuous
with the role of the druid in archaic times. I must say I like that
possibility a lot because the root of the word 'druid' is related to
doire, the oak grove, and through that the poet is connected with the
mysteries of the grove, and the poetic imagination is linked with the
barbaric life of the wood, with Oisín rather than with Patrick.

And this is where I want to turn to my title, the god in the tree.
Poetry of any power is always deeper than its declared meaning. The
secret between the words, the binding element, is often a psychic
force that is elusive, archaic and only half-apprehended by maker
and audience. For example, in the context of monasticism, the god
of my title would be the Christian deity, the giver of life, sustainer of
nature, creator Father and redeemer Son. But there was another god
in the tree, impalpable perhaps but still indigenous, less doctrinally
defined than the god of the monasteries but more intuitively
apprehended. The powers of the Celtic otherworld hovered there.
Ian Finlay, in his *Introduction to Celtic Art*, has noted that it was not

until the Romans dominated Gaul and reduced it to a province that the Gaulish or Celtic gods were reduced to the likenesses of living men and women; before that, the deities remained shrouded in the living matrices of stones and trees, immanent in the natural world. Indeed, when we think of all the taboos and awe surrounding the fairy thorn in the Irish countryside until very recently, and of the pilgrimages which still go on in many parts of Ireland to the ancient holy wells, there is no problem about acknowledging the reality and truth of Finlay's statements. So I want to suggest that this early poetry is sustained by a deep unconscious affiliation to the old mysteries of the grove, even while ardently proclaiming its fidelity to the new religion. After all, there is no reason why literature should not bear these traces as well as architecture; the old religion kept budding out on the roofs of cathedrals all over Europe, in the shape of those roof-bosses which art historians call 'green men' or 'foliate heads', human faces growing out of and into leaves and acorns and branches.

And those green men remind me of another foliate head, another wood-lover and tree-hugger, a picker of herbs and drinker from wells: I am thinking, of course, of Mad Sweeney, that literary creation who is the hero of a sequence of poems that bears his name, and who was at once the enemy and the captive of the monastic tradition. In the story, Sweeney is a petty king who is cursed by St Ronan to be turned into a bird and to live a life of expiation exposed to the hardships and delights of the seasons until, at the end, he is retrieved for the church by St Moling, who also records his history and his poems. One of these poems is clearly very old, continuous with archaic lore, but rendered literary and dainty by long familiarity. This is Sweeney's praise of the trees themselves, another paean to nature's abundance, another thanksgiving, another testimony to the nimbus of the woods in the Celtic imagination:

> The bushy leafy oaktree
> is highest in the wood,
> the forking shooting hazel
> has nests of hazel-nut.

The alder is my darling,
all thornless in the gap,
some milk of human kindness
coursing in its sap.

The blackthorn is a jaggy creel
stippled with dark sloes,
green watercress is thatch on
    wells
where the drinking blackbird
    goes.

Sweetest of the leafy stalks,
the vetches strew the pathway,
the oyster-grass is my delight
and the wild strawberry.

Ever-generous apple-trees
rain big showers when shaken;
scarlet berries clot like blood
on mountain rowan.

Briars curl in sideways,
arch a stickle back,
draw blood, and curl up
    innocent
to sneak the next attack.

The yew tree in each churchyard
wraps night in its dark hood.
Ivy is a shadowy
genius of the wood.

Holly rears its windbreak,
a door in winter's face;
life-blood on a spear-shaft
darkens the grain of ash.

Birch tree, smooth and blessed,
delicious to the breeze,
high twigs plait and crown it
the queen of trees.

The aspen pales
and whispers, hesitates:
a thousand frightened scuts
race in its leaves.

But what disturbs me
more than anything
is an oak rod, always
testing its thong.

That is only one of Sweeney's frequent outbursts where his imagination is beautifully entangled with the vegetation and the weathers and animals of the countryside, and it will have to stand for scores of similar poems from the sixth to the sixteenth century, all of them attesting to the god in the tree as a source of poetic inspiration. And over a thousand years one may find verses which, but for the evidence of linguistic development, would be hard to date with any certainty. The spontaneity that we find in the earliest poems does of course become conventionalized in time, and yet even the works of poets far removed from the first clear vision of 'the scribe in the woods' seem to retain something of the shock of revelation.

I have not attempted a chronology, nor given an inclusive catalogue of the poems. Anybody interested will find much help and pleasure in the works of Robin Flower, Kuno Meyer, K. H. Jackson, Gerard Murphy, Frank O'Connor, David Greene and James Carney; in anthologies of Irish verse by John Montague and Brendan Kennelly; and in surveys of the Celtic world by writers such as Nora Chadwick, Myles Dillon and Alwyn Rhys. I confined myself here to poems that have had an enhancing effect on my own imagination and have tried to account for the peculiar nature of that effect. And I want to end with a moment which, I feel, is relevant to all that we have been considering, a moment that was a kind of small epiphany. This was eleven years ago, at Gallarus Oratory, on the Dingle Peninsula in County Kerry – an early Christian stone oratory, about the size of a large turf-stack. Inside, in the dark hutch of the stone, it felt as if one were sustaining a great pressure, bowing under, like the generations of monks who must have bowed down in meditation and reparation on that floor. I felt the weight of Christianity in all its rebuking aspects, its calls to self-denial and self-abnegation, its humbling of the proud flesh and insolent spirit. But coming out of the cold heart of the stone, into the sunlight and the dazzle of grass and sea, I felt a lift in my heart, a surge towards happiness that must have been experienced over and over again by those monks as they crossed that same threshold centuries ago. And it is this surge towards praise – this sudden apprehension of the world as light, as illumination – this is what remains central to our first nature poetry and this makes it a unique inheritance.

David Greene
The Bardic Mind

In ordinary English usage 'bard' is nothing more than a high-flown word for a poet; Shakespeare has been called the Bard of Avon for over a hundred years, and this has in turn given rise to the word 'bardolatry', meaning an excessive devotion to that great poet. But Shakespeare's contemporary Edmund Spenser, who knew Ireland well, would never have called an English poet a bard; as he put it very clearly: 'there is amongst the Irish a kind of people called bards, which are to them instead of poets, whose profession is to set forth the praises or dispraises of men in their poems or rhyme'. By Spenser's time the word 'profession' was being applied to the practice of divinity, law and medicine, so he was telling his readers that the Irish bards were professional men in that sense of the word, the basic element of which is, of course, that they earned their living in this way. The bards themselves knew well that they lived by selling poems of praise, though like members of other learned professions, they preferred to put things differently. They liked to think of their relations with their patrons as an exchange of gifts between equals; both of the words for a poem, *dán* and *duan* basically mean 'gift' and it seems likely that the word for the payment, *duais*, is also related. There was no doubt about the value of the gifts the bards received; land, cattle, horses, swords, jewellery are all mentioned by the bards themselves in the hope of stimulating further generosity – but what had they to offer in return? Undying fame, was their answer; a name which would be remembered when all the transitory rewards given for it had long crumbled into dust. The greater the patron, the more reckless his gifts to the bards; as early as the seventh century one of them said about a Munster king *is mairg séntu dianaid rí, céinmair tír dianid búachaill*, 'woe to the treasures of which he is king, happy the land of which he is shepherd'. And, as we see, his name has lived for over a thousand years, if only in books read by scholars.

The bard as a professional man existed among all the Celtic peoples, and we know of him in Ireland from the beginning of our literature. He comes into special prominence at the beginning of the thirteenth century for two different, but closely linked reasons. The first of these is the fact that by that time not only the Anglo-Norman invaders, but the native Irish too, were patronizing the monastic orders which had come in from the European mainland, and the native monastic system had been abandoned. It was in the native monasteries that all our early literature had been developed and preserved, and when they ceased to exist the continuation of the tradition was left to laymen and, more precisely, to that section of the laity who were both educated in that tradition and had a solid economic foundation – the bards.

The economic foundation was the wealth they received from their patrons, and that brings us to the second reason for their importance at this period. Those patrons rightly saw the Anglo-Norman invasion as a deadly threat to their way of life; the native lords needed more than ever the assurance of continuity and stability which the praises of the bards could give them. The invaders knew this perfectly well – as one of Spenser's contemporaries put it: 'these people can be very hurtful to the commonwealth, for they chiefly maintain the rebels' – and during the Elizabethan campaigns which put an end to the native Irish order the bards were especially marked out for liquidation.

When we talk about bardic verse, what we mean are the poems composed by these professional men in the four centuries between 1200 and 1600, in a standardized language and metres which they learned during a seven-year training period, and which they were thus able to maintain unchanged for the whole of that period. That training was above all in technical skills; when Spenser had some of their poems translated he found that they lacked 'the goodly ornaments of poetry', by which he presumably meant the personal lyric element dear to Renaissance men. He did admit, however, that the poems were 'sprinkled with some pretty flowers of their own natural device . . . the which it is a great pity to see so good an ornament abused to the gracing of wickedness and vice'.

The wickedness and vice consisted, of course, in supporting the Irish way of life, and does not shock us today. But bardic poetry could be shocking to a nineteenth-century Irish nationalist, too. We find John O'Donovan, one of the greatest of our native scholars of that time, deploring the tone of the lament which Giolla Brighde Mac Con Midhe wrote on the death of Brian Ó Néill in battle against the Normans in 1260. He does not like the boasting about the

victories of the O'Neills over other Irish princes, and is outraged by
the pride and pleasure shown by the poet in recalling the fact that
they possessed a set of chess-men made from the bones of Lein-
stermen – 'Rather a barbaric boast in 1260!', he exclaims, and
concludes: 'The only fact referred to, worthy of an Irish prince of
the house of Neill, or which could be considered national glory, is
the carrying off the hostages and the tribute of the Danes of Dublin.
Not a single victory over the English is referred to, and the bard had
nothing to say on that subject except that they had achieved nothing
in Ulster until they slew his hero.' O'Donovan misses the real point,
which is that Giolla Brighde had nothing against the English except
precisely that they had killed Brian, his patron. No doubt he was
aware that the very existence of the English in Ireland threatened the
Gaelic relationship of poet and patron, but he was very far from
working that awareness into the kind of Daniel O'Connell nationalism that John O'Donovan expected to find him expressing. And he
was to some extent justified, for things went quite well with the
bards for quite a long time. More than a hundred years after Brian
had been killed, one of the greatest of them, Gofraidh Fionn Ó
Dálaigh, addressed a fulsome poem to Muiris Óg, later to be Earl of
Desmond and of course a Fitzgerald, of a Norman family which had
been thoroughly Gaelicized culturally, while maintaining at least a
fitful allegiance to the English Crown. Muiris is on a visit to the
English court and Gofraidh begins:

Iongnadh dhúinn reacht re rígh Saxan
na slógh meanmnach,
tré bheith aige go mear muirnioch
don gheal ghreadhnach.

Strange that I should rage
against the King of England, of
the gallant hosts, because he
keeps with him the bright
joyous one in mirth and revelry.

Dalta ríogh Saxan Sior Muiris,
maith a chaomhna,
trén ina mhúr mac an iarla,
slat úr aobhdha.

Sir Muiris (Maurice) is the
fosterling of the King of
England, he is well protected;
the Earl's son is secure in his
place, the fresh lovely lad.

What does the modern reader find in these poems, which are
clearly not addressed to him? Well, in the first place, the marvellous

39

technical command of language and felicity of phrase which comes from long training in a very old literary tradition. What Spenser called 'the pretty flowers' of this verse do not survive unwithered in translation, but often the images are striking enough to hold our attention today. In that lament on Brian Ó Néill, for example, Giolla Brighde speaks of the superiority of the foreigners' arms and armour – and these two stanzas, both ending in *iaruinn*, 'iron', carry over something of their weight into the English translation:

Na Goill ó Lundain a-le,	The foreigners from London, the
na pobail ó Phort Láirge,	people from Waterford, they
tagaid 'na mbróin ghealghlais ghuirm	come in a bright blue-black
'na n-eanghais óir is iaruinn.	mass, in a medley of gold and
	iron.
Leattrom do chuirsead an cath,	It was unequally that they
Goill agus Gaoidhil Teamhrach:	fought the battle, the foreigners
léinte caolshróill fa chloinn gCuinn	and the Irish of Tara – the
is Goill 'nu n-aonbhróin iaruinn.	Children of Conn (the O'Neills)
	in shirts of fine cloth and the
	foreigners in one mass of iron.

Secondly, the bards had taken over from the church the idea of driving home their points by telling an apposite story. No doubt these stories pleased their patrons, and the audiences before whom the poems were delivered, and no doubt, too, the bards enjoyed the stories more than the more conventional phrases of the praise poems. We find Gofraidh Fionn, in his poem lamenting the absence of Muiris at the English court, going on in a passage of extraordinary technical virtuosity to compare the very undistinguished Muiris with Lugh Ioldánach, the Apollo of the Irish pantheon. Here are the verses which describe Lugh leaping over the wall of Tara, so as not to break the prohibition on opening the gates after nightfall:

Níor mhill geasa	He did not break the
ghrianáin Teamhra an teaghlaigh	prohibitions of the palace of
airmdheirg;	Tara, of the red weaponed
tug céim ar gcúl	household; he stepped back, he
rug léim isan mhúr don maighleirg.	sprang from the sloping plain
	into the fort.

40

Ní bhrisfeadh ar bhailg ós abhainn	The light brisk leap of his
d'aighthibh ógbhonn,	graceful feet, smooth, soft and
léim áith éadtrom	brown-shod, would not have
a dhá dhéagbhonn réidh mbláith	broken a bubble upon the river
mbrógdhonn.	with the tips of youthful soles.

This part of the poem is a variation on a theme which would have been well known to all the listeners, full of rhyme and alliteration and yet as light and airy as the heroic leap it describes. For the modern reader the impact of the passage is greatly lessened by the bathos of the resumption of the comparison between Lugh and Muiris:

Cosmhail cuairt Logha ó lios Eamhna	Alike are the journey of Lugh
d'fhoghluim ghairg-gníomh,	from the court of Eamhain, to
is cuairt Muiris go lios Lonndún	learn fierce deeds, and the
d'fhios an ardríogh.	journey of Muiris to the court of
	London, to visit the high-king.

So, for the great majority of the praise poems, we have to pick out the bits that appeal to modern taste; taken in their entirety they have little appeal. But fortunately the bards did occasionally produce work with a more individual voice and therefore nearer the modern concept of a poem – I say 'occasionally' because not very much of it survives, but there may have been more of it than we suspect; its chances of survival were poor, since it would not be inscribed into the patron's poem book. We know that some of the bards wrote love poems, because we have a few love poems composed in the strict metres which only a trained bard could handle; these will be discussed in another chapter. What I want to point out here is that the later bards made use of the language of love poetry to describe the relationship between themselves and their patrons, the poet being seen as the woman and the patron as the man. One of these poems, indeed, uses such erotic imagery that not only a series of translators, but a number of eminent scholars took it to be a love poem, until my colleague James Carney pointed out their error. The bard is visiting the house of Aodh Ó Ruairc (Hugh O'Rourke), in which Tomás Ó Coisdealbhaigh (Thomas Costello) is a guest, and is invited to praise both; he speaks as though he were O'Rourke's wife, in danger of falling in love with Costello. Here are some verses in Frank O'Connor's translation:

> Here's pretty conduct, Hugh
>   O'Rourke,
> Great son of Brian, blossoming
>   bough,
> Noblest son of noblest kin,
> What do you say of Costello
>   now?
>
> If you are still the man I loved
> Hurry and aid me while you
>   can,
> Do you not see him at my side,
> A walking ghost? What ails you,
>   man?
>
> Brian's son, goal of my song,
> If any thought of losing me
> Grieve you, strong pillar of my
>   love,
> Beseech this man to let me
>   be . . .

The conceit is maintained right through the thirty-two verses, in which, as Robin Flower put it, the lover has the lodgement of half a verse in the husband's portion. It is, therefore, with a farewell to the lover that the poem ends:

> And now God bless you and
>   begone,
> The time has come for you to
>   go,
> For all the grief of parting I
> could never grieve my husband
>   so.

Silence my darling! This is he!
Go now, although my heart
    should crack!
Silence! Begone! What shall I
    do?
My love! Oh, God! Do not
    look back!

A poem like that shows that the bardic tradition was not as hidebound as it sometimes seems to us; it might have come to terms with the Renaissance if the course of history had been favourable. But even without these outside influences we sometimes find the bards speaking from their hearts on the great themes of human existence, and I take birth and death as my two examples. The first of them is from Giolla Brighde, the thirteenth-century poet with whom we began, who offers his poem as a gift to God, and asks in return for a child to replace an only son who has died. The translation is by Frank O'Connor:

Cuire bláth tre bharr an fheadha,
Athair mhóir – mairg nach tuig! –
bláth tre bharr na gcrannsa, a
   Choimdhe,
clann damh-sa gár dhoilghe dhuid? . . .

You can bend the woods with
   blossom,
What is there you cannot do?
All the branches burst with
   leafage,
What's a little child to you?. . .

Mo dhá itche, a Airdrí nimhe,
neamh an céidní chuingheas mé;
madh áil lat is lór a rádha:
mac i lógh mo dhána, a Dhé.

God I ask for two things only,
Heaven when my life is done,
Payment as befits a poet –
For my poem pay a son.

That is in one sense a conventional bardic poem, in that the bard names the price he wants for his poem. When a bard composed a lament for a dead patron, we may take it that he got good payment from the heirs, even if the matter is not mentioned in the poem itself. But bards had wives and children, and it was quite natural that, when those dear to them died, they should use the craft by which they earned their living to lament them without fee or reward. We have a few of these poems, and what is perhaps the best of them

43

survives only in one very bad manuscript, written in Scotland in the sixteenth century; even Osborn Bergin was not able to reconstruct it fully, but he gave us sixteen verses, of which I give five here. The author was the thirteenth-century Muireadhach Albanach Ó Dálaigh, one of the great masters of the bardic style.

M'anam do sgar riomsa a-raoir,
calann ghlan dob ionnsa i n-uaigh,
rugadh bruinne maordha mín
is aonbhlá lín uime uainn . . .

My soul parted from me last night; a pure body that was dear is in the grave; a gentle stately bosom has been taken from me with one linen shroud about it.

Truagh leam an leabasa thiar,
mo pheall seadasa dhá snámh;
tárramair corp seada saor
is folt claon, a leaba, id lár.

It is sad for me to see yonder bed, my long couch drenched with tears; I once had a long noble body with wavy hair on you, o bed.

Do bhí duine go ndreich moill
ina luighe ar leith mo phill;
gan bharamhail acht bláth cuill
don sgáth duinn bhanamhail bhinn . . .

There was a woman with a gentle face lying on one side of my couch; her dark womanly sweet form could be compared only to the flower of the hazel.

Gé tú, nocha n-oilim ann,
ar sgaradh dár roghrádh rom
do do thoirinn ar gcnú chorr
falamh lom an domhan donn . . .

Though I am alive, I no longer exist since my smooth hazel-nut has fallen; since my dear love parted from me, the dark world is empty and bare.

Ionmhain lámh bhog do bhí sonn,
a Rí na gclog is na gceall;
uch! an lámh nachar logh mionn
crádh liom gan a cor fám cheann.

Dear is the soft hand that was here, O king of bells and churchyards; alas, the hand that never betrayed, it is a torment to me that it is not placed under my head.

No translation can convey the combination of intense personal feeling with supreme technical virtuosity; in a poem like this we catch a glimpse of how bardic poetry might have developed, given a happier environment. As things turned out, however, the bards continued to sell their conventional praises until their patrons melted away during the disasters of the seventeenth century, until there was no one left to buy a poem.

Eiléan Ní Chuilleanáin
Love and Friendship

Is é bheir mo chroí 'na ghual
An grá fuar do bhíos ag mnáibh.

What makes my heart burn like
coal is the cold love women
have.

The unexpected adjective, 'cold', in those lines from a poem by
Piaras Feiritéar gives a slight cold shock; the paradox, the burning
and the cold, is also the paradox of a body of Gaelic love poetry
composed between the fourteenth and the early eighteenth century.
It has both energy and mystery: the energy of the poets, who face
emotional experience with directness and determination; and a mystery which has nothing to do with vagueness but owes much to
control: the poems expose just as much as the poet permits – they
have a reticence, a quality of anonymity that gives them half their
strength. But the modern reader, who connects love poetry with
sincerity rather than reserve, has sometimes felt that this was indeed
'grá fuar'. He has gone looking for passion in the interweavings of
graceful compliment but has flushed out, it seemed, only hyperbo-
lical praise, undifferentiated between poet and poet, between one
girl and another; and in the search for the accents of true feeling he
has had to fall back on the strong sense of self-preservation that is
sometimes so vigorously expressed:

> O woman, shapely as the swan,
> On your account I shall not die:
> The men you've slain – a trivial
>   clan –
> Were less than I.
>
> I ask me shall I die for these –
> For blossom teeth and scarlet
>   lips –
> And shall that delicate
>   swan-shape
> Bring me eclipse?

Pádraic Colum conveys one of the strongest gestures of the original

– the stress on words meaning 'I': *mise, me féin*. The poet ends with self-assertion:

> O woman, shapely as the swan,
> In a cunning house hard-reared
>   was I:
> O bosom white, O well-shaped
>   palm,
> I shall not die!

We end up with a much stronger notion of the poet than of the lady; her blossom teeth and delicate swan shape are *de rigueur* features for any woman to whom a poem of this sort gets written.

But the poet is present by virtue of his art, by the deliberate strategy he has selected. His irony and wit display themselves and through them we are aware of the vigour of his personality. A witty strategy of this sort can give a poem its individuality however commonplace its descriptive material; it is the backbone of the work. In 'Aoibhinn, a Leabhráin, do Thriall', for example, the idea of the book's journey to see the lady, that the poet is jealous of his own gift, is not just an 'excuse' for describing her, it gives the poem its special shape.

Not all the poems are as pointed as these, of course, but the conditions of the genre ensure that it is by the excellence of deliberate art that they achieve their success. In folksong, a phrase, even a cliché, may strike home almost by accident; while in these poems the phrase or image is always subordinate to the idea of the whole. They were written, it seems, for an audience who appreciated irony and intellectual games rather than one that looked in poetry for a way of emotionally letting off steam. The phrase which Colum translates 'In a cunning house hard-reared was I' means literally 'I was brought up by a clever person' – '*Do hoileadh mé ag duine glic*'. The poet, it may be, is appealing to the values of a whole class, instilled in childhood, its ingrained response to cleverness and virtuosity. The lady is a virtuoso in her line of destroying men; he responds with the weapons of art. We recognize what poet and lady have in common as well as what separates them.

Who wrote the poems? We often have no names, or doubtful

names; the conventions of form, metre and phrase are so strong that even when we know a name the poem retains a sort of anonymity, and might seem to be the product of the whole age rather than of a single writer.

The names that are mentioned are all aristocratic or bardic; they belong to a world of powerful people who were also sometimes scholars and poets in their own right, but at any rate were bound in an ancient and indissoluble relationship with the traditional bardic class. As Professor Greene has shown, the bard looked to the chieftain for support and protection and repaid him with poems praising his greatness and generosity. But we may assume that the patron, even if chosen for his power to keep the poet alive, had a poetic function too: as the original and perfect audience. We may, without too much exaggeration, think of the poem as a collaboration between the poet and the patron – who provided inspiration and reward and who saw the poem recorded for posterity. The *duanaire* or poem book kept by great families is the reason for the survival of so much bardic verse.

We may reasonably speculate that, in their off-duty hours, a bard and a chieftain may have shared the kind of cultivated, relaxed society that the Italian writer Castiglione describes in his *Book of the Courtier*: four evenings in the early sixteenth century in the house of an Italian prince who can't have been all that different from his contemporary, the great Earl of Kildare. Half highwaymen, half politicians, the courtiers and ecclesiastics would pause in the evenings, discuss the latest news from their friends Michelangelo and Leonardo da Vinci, compliment the ladies of the court and occasionally dash off a poem in praise of their beauty or in reproach of their unkindness. In such a group, the poets shed their professionalism and the princes their dominance; both appear as gifted amateurs. An unfortunate consequence is that the love poetry produced in such circumstances, being informal, may go unrecorded.

In Italian or Irish (or even in English at the court of Henry VIII where something very similar was going on) the poems are unofficial and thus are not recorded as carefully as the long panegyric in bardic idiom – or in Humanistic Latin – which it was somebody's job to write down and keep. So the love poetry of the early modern period is preserved by chance, and by chance we sometimes have the name of the author and sometimes not. It doesn't seem to make a great deal of difference. Whether the author is professional bard, a chieftain of pure Gaelic stock or a blow-in of a mere four centuries naturalization like Piaras Feiritéar, the *Dánta Grá* form a homogeneous body of work, which shows the strength of tradition rather than giving opportunity to the individual talent. There's a starkness in the language, the plainness of poetry that is nearly anonymous, which reminds one of the great Scottish border ballads. The poems are impossible to translate without complicating, but Máire Cruise O'Brien comes pretty close:

Taisigh agad féin do phóg,
a inghean óg is geal déad;
ar do phóg ní bhfaghaim blas,
congaibh uaim a-mach do bhéal!

Keep to yourself your kisses,
Bright teeth and parted lip,
Keep your mouth away from
   me,
I have no mind for your kiss.

Póg is romhilse ná mil
fuaras ó mhnaoi fhir tré ghrádh;
blas ar phóig eile dá héis
ní bhfagha mé go dtí an brách.

A kiss more sweet than honey
From the wife of another man
Has left without taste all kisses
That were since the world
   began.

Go bhfaicear an bhean-soin féin
do thoil ÉinMhic Dé na ngrás,
ní charabh bean tsean ná óg
ós í a póg atá mar tá.

Till, and please God I may –
I see that woman again –
Her kiss being as it was –
I ask no other till then.

The hardest line to translate is the second: '*a inghean óg is geal déad*'. In a poem about sex that detail about the white teeth is the only physical detail, just as the remembered kiss is the only physical event. The white teeth are a conventional feature, a kiss is an isolated gesture; but in this poem both are alive with perilous significance. Perhaps all the more so because the poet's main statement is a negative one: rejecting a kiss in the present because he can't escape from the memory of one in the past. The use of the negative adds to the deliberate mystery of the poetry; like a single line in a drawing which lets us see exactly what the artist wants us to, leaving the rest in blackness, the choice of one gesture increases our sense of how much we do not know. Again, this is hard to translate.

Frank O'Connor translates the third line of this quatrain, which means: 'although they are not mouth to mouth' as 'as though they lingered in a kiss' – the negative would sound awkward in English.

Atáid dias is tigh-se a-nocht
Ar nách ceileann rosg a rún;
gion go bhfuilid béal re béal,
is géar géar silleadh a súl.

That's from a poem by Niall Mór Mac Muireadaich: 'Soraidh Slán Don Oíche Aréir', also about love in secret, gestures living in the memory. A less lucky poet praises the woman who cares so little for him that she wouldn't throw a stone on his grave:

Sí mo shearc
bean nár fhágaibh ionnam neart,
bean nach léigfeadh im dhiaidh, och,
bean nách cuirfeadh cloch im leacht.

The twentieth-century reader may find attraction in this economy of information, especially as compared with the bardic poems produced by the same society, which are full of names, historical allusions, placenames and genealogy which we would need to look up. Many readers of poetry prefer the poem that can be most easily detached from its original setting and credited with 'modernity' of feeling. The romantic is pleased by declarations of undying passion, the amateur of toughness enjoys the gaiety, the determination, wit and sometimes savagery. Is it worthwhile pointing out that the Roman poet Ovid wrote instructions for lovers about how to communicate by glances, or that a reason for the shortage of names in the poems may be the medieval convention that love must always be a secret, that secrecy and discretion are in fact the first virtues of the lover? So we arrive at the question of how much these Gaelic poems are influenced by changes in fashion in Europe – and especially the growth of love poetry which takes place from the twelfth century on, apparently under the influence of Arabic, filtered through Spain and Sicily and spread around the continent in its Provençal version. T. F. O'Rahilly, who first collected the *Dánta Grá*, observed in his introduction to the book that 'Love is always the same'. But by 1926 Robin Flower was pointing out that these poems are about a certain kind of love, 'the learned and fantastic love of European tradition'. Other scholars, notably Seán Ó Tuama, have considered the relationship of the poems to different strands of that European tradition.

The problem is made no easier by the many disagreements among literary historians about what it was that happened in Europe. But there does exist a large body of vernacular poetry speaking of love in a way rather new to twelfth-century people, which is known as 'amour courtois' – courtly love. Its origins appear to have been connected with international cultural movements, and its influence was certainly international. It would seem to have reached both England and Ireland in the later Middle Ages. Features which we now regard as essential to conventional love poetry were first invented by the Courtly Love poets: the idea of love as the supreme theme, eternal fidelity, the worship of the woman, the notion of love as a disease with recognizable symptoms. We find these in the *Dánta Grá*; we also find the courtly poets' insistence on secrecy and their fear of tale-tellers and calumny. We do not find the idea of the poet being the lady's 'servant' nor any suggestion that love has a mystically ennobling effect on the lover; the Irish poet-lover is noticeably less humble and less other-worldly than his continental counterpart. Although he praises the lady extravagantly, calls her a goddess or a fairy queen, we do not feel that there is a great distance separating her from him: she is not a superior being. It has been observed that Irish folksongs also owe much to the Provençal patterns, but that they stress aspects – for example, the connection between love and spring – which seem not to interest the aristocratic poets.

All this suggests that the aristocratic love poem in Ireland, like the popular love song, has its roots in a large and varied intellectual world, the international culture of the late Middle Ages. We often praise an individual poet for taking what he needs from a tradition while retaining his personal spirit; here it seems we have a body of poets consciously or unconsciously doing the same thing. The poets of Europe in the fourteenth and fifteenth centuries were capable of being down-to-earth, satirical, pious, precious and derivative as well as high-minded and devoted. They wrote poems in dispraise of women and love as well as in their favour. While the *Dánta Grá* appear first in the late fourteenth century many examples belong to a much later period, when social and political conditions had changed greatly. So when Piaras Feiritéar contrasts his burning heart with the coldness of women, he may be referring to one strand of the Courtly Love tradition, the Petrarchan cult of paradox; but that no more involves him with Petrarchan mysticism than it does his contemporaries – and, in a sense, political allies – the English Cavalier poets. Feiritéar, like Waller or Carew, can take an ancient compliment or reproach and turn it to something easy, modern, witty and yet courteous. So we seem to have a special variation on an international theme, with peculiar limitations and virtues; more interested in irony and play on words than in music, more in human nature than the beauties of the countryside. More, for example, than most of its English contemporaries, it is archaic, aristocratic and introspective.

It is entirely credible that many of the aristocratic poets spoke or understood French. It is also true that in Celtic languages generally, and especially in Irish, the theme of love was already well established in the early Middle Ages. Again, the vocabulary of extravagant compliment to the lady and extravagant despair on the poet's part, even the sense that the whole business might all be a game, can be matched with European counterparts, but also with the early Irish myths and the style in which they were told.

In the early Irish stories we have long, detailed descriptions of superbly beautiful women; we have passionate interpolated lyrics (such as those in the tale of Liadin and Cuirthir). There is also a hardness which we might recognize:

> . . . But they saw a young grown girl in front of them. She had yellow hair. She wore a speckled cloak fastened around her with a gold pin, a red-embroidered hooded tunic and sandals with gold clasps. Her brow was broad, her jaw narrow, her two eyebrows pitch black, with delicate dark lashes casting shadows half way down her cheeks.

– a refusal to rely on anything vague or suggestive, the ability to give a picture that is clear, yet remains enigmatic – which may remind us of the swan-shaped lady. Perhaps for us the most interesting thing is that the Gaelic poet of the fifteenth or sixteenth century, especially if he was an aristocrat, had a good chance of being bilingual, like his modern counterpart, though his second language might be English, French or Latin. In a love poem he does not need to show off his erudition, but he may refer in passing to Ovid, to the Bible, to the tale of Deirdre or to Aesop's fables; the tale of the fox and the stork is located in the countryside of North Cork – with the stork, unknown in Ireland, transformed into a heron.

Cumann do cheangail an corr
agus sionnach Brí Ghobhann;
do gheall an sionnach don gcorr
nách brisfeadh choidhche an cumann.

The moral is that he and his lady have the same relationship as fox and stork, and she is the beast of prey: '*ise an sionnach, mise an corr*'. Now there, I think, there is a trace of the European tradition in which the woman is not only adored and pursued but also abused for her cruelty in not yielding to the poet.

In some other languages, the arrival of foreign influences meant that native forms of verse disappeared in favour of the ones that had become internationally current, like the rondeau or the sonnet. In Ireland there is no trace of that happening. In general, the *Dánta Grá* are written in the less difficult bardic metres: suitable to the amateur status of the gentleman-poet and to the stress placed especially in the Renaissance on the 'natural', 'easy' qualities of love poetry, on *sprezzatura* as Castiglione calls it. As with such English poets as Walter Raleigh, the simplicity of form and comparative plainness of expression is appropriate to the gentleman, elaboration and fantastic conceits to the professional poet. The fact that love poetry is written in the traditional metres suggests that, to the Gaelic poet, love was not something entirely cut off from the other parts of life, from politics or morality or eating and drinking. One poet reassures us:

Do chongaibh mé m'fheóil is m'fhuil
do ghrádh ainnre an chuirp mar ghéis
ithim mórán, do-ním suan,
in gach ceól is buan mo spéis.

Is teó an teine ná mo chneas,
Dá mbeinn fá eas do bheinn fuar;
Dá ndeacha duine seang slán,
Do-ghéabha mé bás go luath.

He feels well, eats plenty – in fact he's putting on weight – enjoys listening to music and is convinced that love is doing him good. Perhaps it's a bit of a jump from that light-hearted character to the famous, bitter poem, 'A bhean lán de stuaim'; but there too there's the coexistence of one man's predicament with ordinary wisdom, the wisdom of proverbs – no sense that love happens out of time and place, rather that reality grows sharper as love makes us more aware of it:

A bhean lán de stuaim,
cuinnibh uaim do lámh;
ní fear gníomha sinn,
cé taoi tinn dár ngrádh.

Woman full of wile
Take your hand away,
Nothing tempts me now,
Sick for love you pray.

Féach ar liath dom fholt,
féach mo chorp gan lúth,
féach ar thraoch dem fhuil, –
créad re bhfuil do thnúth?

But my hair is grey
And my flesh is weak,
All my blood gone cold –
What is it you seek?

Ná saoil mé go saobh,
arís ná claon do cheann;
bíodh ar ngrádh gan ghníomh
go bráth, a shíodh sheang.

Do not think me mad,
Do not hang your head,
Slender witch let love
Live in thought not deed.

Druid do bhéal óm bhéal, –
doiligh an sgéal do chor;
ná bíom cneas re cneas,
tig ón dteas an tol.

Take your mouth from mine, –
Kissing's bitterer still,
Flesh from flesh must part
Lest of warmth come will.

Do chúl craobhach cas,
Do rosg glas mar dhrúcht,
Do chíoch chruinngheal bhláith,
thairngeas mian gach súl.

Your twined branching hair,
Your grey eye dew-bright,
Your rich rounded breast
Turn to lust the sight.

Gach gníomh acht gníomh cuirp,	But for the wild bed
is luighe id chuilt shuain,	And the body's flame,
do-dhéanainn tréd ghrádh,	Woman full of wile
a bhean lán de stuaim.	My love is still the same.

Frank O'Connor's version of the poem is great until the last stanza: that blend of vehemence and regret, of resignation and hairsplitting – '*Gach gníomh ach gníomh cuirp*' – is too delicate to be translated. By reproducing the syllable-counting metre, rendering each line exactly and individually, he shows the poem as a succession of almost independent exclamations which still add up to a deliberately-constructed complex: the second quatrain, and the second last, for example, contain contrasting portraits of the poet and the lady; the word '*gníomh*' is used, in each case with powerful irony, in the first quatrain and the last. A poem like that appears to put all its cards on the table and still it keeps its secret.

What impresses me most strongly about '*A bhean lán do stuaim*' is that this is poetry of the will. The words proclaim an absolute determination rather than analysing the state of mind of the poet. In the poems of Isobel Campbell, Countess of Argyll, the angry, impatient will is in the foreground:

An fear-soin dá dtugas grádh,	That man I gave my love to
's nach féadtar a rádh ós aird,	whose name must be a secret
dá gcuire sé mise i bpéin,	if he gives me any trouble
go madh dó féin bhus céad mairg.	may he have good cause to
	lament.

In another poem she talks about her will '*Mo mhian*' and, in the last line, '*ar riar*' – '*our will*' so that one senses a definition of love that means simply the uniting of two strong wills.

Isobel Campbell is of course a Scottish poet – reminding us that Gaelic culture and civilization and the range of the bardic and aristo-cratic world was not confined to the island of Ireland. The poetry crosses the barrier between Ireland and Scotland, between professional and amateur; does it cross one between men and women? An interesting poem in this connection is quoted by Professor Cathal Ó hÁinle: it is by Bríd O'Donnell (born a FitzGerald) in reply to one sent to her by Cuchonnacht Maguire. She tells her aristocratic suitor that the poem betrays by its professionalism that it was not really written by him but by the bard O'Hussey. The amateur tradition embraces both men and women. Perhaps it would be truer to say that one kind of barrier, connected with love poetry, had not yet arrived in Ireland: the notion of the woman as somebody unearthly, virtuous and static. The earlier idea that she was lustful and dangerous at least did not tie down the imaginative picture of her, especially if it combined with the magical powers suggested by much Celtic mythology. In the old stories, women (Gráinne, Deirdre) are often the aggressors in love. But in a poem by Laoiseach Mac an Bháird the lady pines for love just like a medieval *male* poet. The fact that it is all something of a joke doesn't stand in the way of a sympathetic picture of two people:

> A sad sight, lady,
> Your strange grief
> Under your kinsmen's eyes
> I'm shocked to see you
>   weep . . .
>
> Whoever it is you love,
> Tell me his name,
> Don't suffer in silence
> Even if it were me . . .

Because the action of these poems is mostly psychological, the external circumstances relating to that action often remain mysterious. In no other European literature can I imagine a poem which some scholars have taken as 'a picture of a woman swaying between two loves' (to quote Robin Flower) while others believe it is about the predicament of a poet between two patrons. One would think it meant a defect in the poem, that it is capable of two such different interpretations, but the poem, 'Féach féin an obair-se, a Aodh', is fine. It reminds the modern reader sharply both how far we are in reality from the seventeenth century, and also how near, at times, we seem to be. It is tantalizing, but it is an essential part of the discovery. We think of the love poem as rather a separate kind of literature – even the binding of books of love poems used to follow certain rules – a special genre with rules of its own like detective stories or science fiction; in short, genteel pornography. To the Gaelic poet, love and its vocabulary seem to overflow into all human relationships. What about the expressions the poet uses of his patron in O'Hussey's 'Ode to the Maguire', as Mangan translates it: 'his face, the strawberry-bright' – 'his majestic bearing, his fair, stately form'? The language of Tadhg Dall Ó hUiginn in his lament for Cathal O'Conor is full of such phrases: '*a rosg realtunntais, a ghruadh fhrithir, a rún ban*' – 'O star-soft eye and glowing cheek, O beloved of women'. This is a convention, but it's one in which everyone seems to be superhumanly beautiful, gentle, illuminated by a soft heroic light. The women to whom the *Dánta Grá* are addressed may be praised like goddesses, but they live in a world of men who were praised like gods and offered almost religious homage and loyalty.

The explanation in the end may be that both kinds of poem were written to people with power: sexual power or political power or maybe both; that all these people and their poets lived in an unstable and arbitrary world, partly at the mercy of one another's whims, but that they knew that in the end they would all sink or swim together, and that one symbol of their joint predicament was the culture, the poetic conventions and finesses, the private jokes that nobody but they would ever laugh at, the ancient stories which they responded to in a way nobody but they ever could.

The poetry of friendship comes I suppose half-way between the love poems and the poems to great men; friendship between equals who are important to each other as personal companions *and* as political allies. It's equally likely to use the vocabulary and conventions of erotic love, but there is a difference. We find, in the seventeenth century, that poets, not necessarily professionals, are still writing in old patterns on the old subjects of love and the deaths of great men. Piaras Feiritéar enumerates his beloved's physical perfections and begs her to hide them or the country will be depopulated as everyone dies of love. Pádraigín Haicéad, a Dominican who spent his life between Ireland and the Continent, laments his friend and patron Lord Dunboyne – comparing himself to Queen Gormfhlaith, Deirdre, Oisín and Andromache. The dead man was 'the husband of the River Suir, the lover of the Shannon and the Liffey'. In Feiritéar's lament for Maurice Fitzgerald banshees wail all over Munster. We seem to be in a world of ancient, obsessive grief and love. But the same poets can also write in a surprisingly relaxed way about friendship. Haicéad has occasional poems, congratulating a friend on his safe arrival in France, a bridegroom on his marriage on May Day. A poem on hearing of a woman's death has a surprising acuteness, concentrating on the shock of the news, rather than bursting into lamentation: '*Níor bhuaigh bás ar Mháire im mheabhairse fós*' – 'Death has not conquered Maire yet in my mind.' This concentration on the occasion gets rid of the mysteriousness of so much of the love poetry; the title becomes part of the poem, just as it does for such contemporaries as Donne and Herbert.

These poets were politicians too, in an era when party politics was just being invented. It may be that their relationship with their friends was altered by that fact. The cohesiveness of a party is different from that of a nation or even of a social class. It was still a matter of life or death (or death in exile, in Haicéad's case) but there was something perhaps fragile, contingent, about these precious relationships, which evoked in the poet a new informal intimacy. The opening quatrain of Feiritéar's poem to his friend Risteard Husae has the directness of the *Dánta Grá*, but there is also this newly relaxed tone:

Ní maith uaigneas don annsa,
Atá a heolas agamsa.
Do mhúin damhsa flaith re fios
Nach maith don annsa uaigneas.

It is the same with the affectionate, witty poem written in France by Pádraigín Haicéad, to his friend Éamonn Buitléar. Here the ancient metre has given way to the later long line, the mystery and discretion are gone – the poem's title and the ones that precede it in the manuscript explain the occasion of writing it. The poet's friend in Ireland broke his foot; Haicéad has now broken his own foot in France. But however far from the difficult highborn ladies, it is certainly a poem about love. The translation is by Pearse Hutchinson:

A chos bheag shiubhalach, fuiling i
  gclúid faoi chléith,
Ó's cor ag druidim nios goire dom
  mhuirnín é ;
Dob olc 'na choimhideacht mise, dá
  spiúntaoi mé,
'S a chos sin briste, mun mbrisfinn mo
  chrúibín féin.

My little wandering limb the
  splint must thole:
it brings me nearer my dear one
  to console.
How poor a friend I'd be,
  examined home,
if, his bone broken, I broke not
  my own.

Michael Hartnett
Wrestling with Ó Bruadair

It is not rare for a poet to be obsessed by the work and mind of another poet. The obsession can express itself in many ways – scorn (which is often public), awe before a massive superiority (which is always private), and love, which can become a bore to readers who do not share the obsession. I am obsessed by the work and mind of Daibhí Ó Bruadair and, though I certainly love it and him, my obsession usually expresses itself in frustration. And it has done so since 1954, when I was thirteen. Like many Irish children I was reared on a diet of folktale, Republicanism and mediocre ballads. I knew some Gaelic but it was merely another school subject, not a key to another culture. But in 1954 a friend, Seán Brouder, told me of Ó Bruadair. He recited some verses, which he translated for me. He claimed that the poet had been born in my own town and had lived most of his life in my own county. I was enthralled. I knew what poets looked like from their portraits in library books, so I invented my own picture of Ó Bruadair. The following year I wrote and published my first poem – in English.

A man in his sixties and a boy of thirteen discussing, in a decrepit country town, the life and work of a poet who had been dead for over two hundred and fifty years, a poet of an extinct society whose works were not published in his lifetime and which were now available only in distant city libraries; this event, I later saw, profoundly illustrated the obstinacy of the Irish mind, its constant connection with the past. Even though I did not read a word of Ó Bruadair's until the late fifties, he had become for me the symbol of what I wanted to be. But when I read him, in some secondary-school anthology of Gaelic verse, I was shocked. I could not understand his verse! It seemed a gnarled, concertina'd kind of Gaelic written for a distant and savage people. I went for consolation to the more accessible fields of Hopkins, Yeats and Eliot. I continued to read simpler Gaelic poetry, most of it written in the two centuries before Ó Bruadair's death. Why was my hero so unapproachable? How could an old man quote him with so much reverence and fluency? I determined in 1962 not to let him escape me, to unravel his language and to restore him as my idol. I still have not done so to my satisfaction.

The name Ó Bruadair (Brouder, Broderick) has been found in West Limerick since the ninth century; it is possibly of Danish origin. The poet Daibhí was born about 1625. As is the case with most Gaelic poets our information on him is scant, but a number of details can be gleaned from his poetry. One of my dreams vanished when I read that it was unlikely he was born in my own town (Newcastle West, County Limerick) but more probably in the barony of Barrymore in East Cork. My addiction to his work however did not vanish, and at least I found that he had lived most of his life in County Limerick, where his main patrons were the Fitz-geralds of Springfield near Dromcollogher, and the Burkes of Cahirmoyle. Patronage was still deemed essential to a poet's sur-vival: there were no publishers, no royalties, no grants; there were gifts, hospitality, cattle, horses, clothing and sometimes gold. But the Gaelic poet was no mere pensioner. Ó Bruadair was a recorder of his race's history, and because of his place of birth two great local Norman-Irish families, the Fitzgeralds and the Burkes, became the symbols of that race for him. Indeed he did not write just for the contemporary Burkes and Fitzgeralds, but for all of them who had ever existed and who ever would exist.

Living as he did throughout almost all of Ireland's most tragic century, he was also deeply immersed in the affairs of his time. Frank O'Connor said: 'The poetry of . . . David Ó Bruadair and a hun-dred other peasant poets is that of the sleep-walker; their thought is so much of the old dead world that it is as though a veil had fallen between them and reality.'[1] This is not entirely true: Ó Bruadair was no peasant, and if there was a harking-back in his poetry there was also a looking-forward: his overall attitude to history (and in Gaelic society history *was* poetry) was cyclical. In his lifetime, while an active poet, he witnessed in Ireland the Popish Plot, the coming of Cromwell, the battle of the Boyne, the Treaty of Limerick and its non-ratification, the dispersal of the Irish leaders and their armies, and the selling into slavery (mainly to the Barbados) of thousands of women and children; these were fatal blows to an already tottering structure.

But Ó Bruadair was no mere chauvinist. As his first translator,

1. *Kings, Lords and Commons,* 1959, Preface.

John Mac Erlean S.J., points out when speaking of the long poem 'An Longbhriseadh' ('The Shipwreck'): – 'he ascribes all the misfortunes of his native land to the dissensions that prevailed among the (Irish) leaders and the insubordination of the irregular troops.'[2] In that poem Ó Bruadair says (I translate literally): 'I do not wonder at the foreigners' success: their agreements and friendships are discreet and lasting – not like my people's: their so-called unity would fall apart if pulled by a hair.' Ó Bruadair also believed that the dishonouring and disregarding of old customs contributed to the downfall:

> All the same, it would make you
>   laugh –
> instead of the dances and games
>   of the past
> not a tittle is raised abroad in
>   this land –
> we ourselves have buried the
>   summer at last.
>
> Once all the girls of our world
>   would play
> mustered in companies on May
>   Day:
> now their cacophony tears my
>   brain
> as I witness their cunning,
>   pointless games.
>
> Our priests are scarred with
>   greed and pride,
> and all our poets are cut down
>   to size:
> but worst of all I realize
> that no one poor is considered
>   wise.

2. *The Poems of David Ó Bruadair*, Vol. I, Irish Text Society, 1910.

Blast you, world, you sneaky
   bitch
may your guts and liver in
   agony split!
What's it to you if *I* become
   rich?
What's it to you if your children
   slip?

The once-proud men of this land
   have swapped
giving for gaining, music for
   crap:
no tunes on the pipes, no music
   on harps –
We *ourselves* have buried the
   summer at last.

That poem reflects very accurately the minds of Irish country-people today who maintain that the summers are bad because there is no longer any 'respect' for the old ways!

After 1690 Ó Bruadair's life assumed a pattern that was to become sadly commonplace among poets in the next few years: the *file*, the professional poet, the dignified chronicler of his race, gave way to a ragged horny-handed itinerant, muttering under his breath. Although Ó Bruadair's predicament was not unique, he felt, like many poets of his time, that he was the sole survivor, the last receptacle of Gaelic culture, and that his death would be the end for all. He was right, in a way. His death, and the death of the culture he stood for, was not a total annihilation: the eighteenth century was perhaps the most active time ever known for the production of poetry; but it was the *people*, rather than the professional poets, who began to sing – the poetry came out of cabins rather than castles. Ó Bruadair would have hated it. He would have looked down his nose at the sometimes flaccid extravagances of the Munster poets of the 1740s. But there had been a change of priorities; their purpose was to save a language, not a culture. Culture, as Ó Bruadair understood it, was gone. The style of poetry had already changed in his time: he wrote no 'songs' (*amhráin*) but the poets of the eighteenth century seemed to write nothing else.

To see the art of poetry lost
with those who honoured it
    with thought –
its true form lowered to a silly
    chant,
sought after by the dilettante.

Those who write the Gaelic
    tongue
just mumble – when they should
    stay dumb –
the flaw's admired, the lack of
    passion,
now that doggerel is in fashion.

If one now writes to the proper
    rule,
in the way demanded by the
    schools,
then some smart-alec Paddy or
    such
will say that it is obscure as
    Dutch.

God of Heaven, preserve and
    keep
the one man who protects from
    need
the climbers who scale true
    poetry
and avoid the lovers of English
    and ease. Amen.

Ó Bruadair died, with his culture, in 1698 – as we know from a manuscript written in 1702 by the scribe Eoghan Ó Caoimh: '*Daibhí Ó Bruadair d'éag a mí January A. Domini 1698, et aduairt Eogan "as trua liom a éag gan amhras".*' ('Daibhí Ó Bruadair died in the month of January AD 1698, and Eoghan said "I really grieve for his death".') It was always customary for Irish poets to write laments for their fellows. Ó Bruadair was famous in his lifetime, but there is no lament in Gaelic extant that mentions his death; this fact reflects the breakdown, the chaos, of the 1690s.

Ó Bruadair, who wrote for his race, had a fierce and deep contempt for the lower-class Irish, the peasants, the little shopkeepers, the 'hucksters'. But this attitude was common among the the professional Gaelic poets and even persisted right up to the 1740s. When I came to discover him, this aristocratic *hauteur* was something I disliked. Almost all my illusions were vanishing – but I was making the mistake of judging him by mid-twentieth-century liberal standards – I had to reconsider his real position within his *own* society. He was 'anti-Irish', though writing in Gaelic; he was anti-clerical, though a Catholic; witness his satire on two priests:

> I call ye ruffians! Not to ye for
>   succour
> can we turn, I swear by law:
> ye lie befuddled in sops and
>   puddles
> suffering, fasting, pissing in
>   straw.
>
> Ye pair who huddle in meanness
>   doubled
> I ask, though troubled by such
>   speech:
> could the holy chapter do
>   nothing after
> but make priests of characters
>   the likes of ye?
>
> Ye barrel-begrudgers to poetry
>   authors,
> ye sleep unapparelled so your
>   pockets won't be pawed
>   with:
> though I have no wish to slight
>   *noble* fathers
> they were shifty bishops who
>   gave ye holy orders!

Ó Bruadair upheld and was upheld by what was left of the aristocracy of his time. He lived in an Ireland where for centuries the Holy Trinity was not so much Father, Son and Holy Ghost as

Prince, Prelate and Poet. The Prince, to Ó Bruadair, had to have an impeccable pedigree, had to be a cultured man and a generous one: he was the living symbol of Ireland; he did not own the land, he was married to it (more than once in the poems Ireland is referred to as a widow and as a deserted wife) and we must remember, a wife in Gaelic society was not the chattel she was under English law. So, to the end of his life, when he seemed just a beggar among beggars, Ó Bruadair was an unrepentant aristocrat. Almost all his insults are aimed at the *dubh-thuataigh* ('the black boors'), the peasant Irish who immediately took to learning English language and customs – *béarla binn* ('simpering English') and *códaibh galla-chléireach* ('foreign manners').

Mairg atá gan béarla binn	Pity the man who English lacks
ar dteacht an Iarla go hÉirinn:	now that turncoat Ormonde has
ar feadh mo shaoil ar chlár Chuinn	come back.
dán ar bhéarla do bhéaruinn.	As I have to live here, I now wish
	to swap all my poems for squeaky English.

And again:

Nach ait an nós so ag morchuid	How daft this mode of most of
d'fhearaibh Éireann,	the men of Éireann
d'at go nó le mórtus maingléiseach:	fattened newly with bold
gidh tais a dtreoir ar chódaibh	ostentation –
gallachléire,	though rapt they pore on the
ní chanaid glór acht gósta	*mores* of Gallic agents
garbh-bhéarla.	their cant's no more than a ghost of garbled aping.

But peasants in all ages are flexible – they have to be. Ó Bruadair took their action as a personal insult to himself, which it was not, and an insult to Ireland, which it was. His bitterness was made all the more deep by the reversal of situations: illiterate peasants, now beginning to prosper, were able to insult the destitute poet. *Daoiste dubh díobaighthe duairc gan dán* one of them called him: 'a dirty-faced dour dumb-bell'.

But the unpleasant side of the poet's personality was the least of my difficulties; I had to face his poetry. Many would say that I have created an unnecessary and insurmountable barrier between myself and Ó Bruadair in my insistence that a poet who is such a consummate craftsman should be translated with obsessive care, that his techniques should be brought across as faithfully as possible. 'Poetry is that which gets lost in translation' is a widely-held notion; I do not agree with it. A poet/translator, if he loves the original better than he loves himself, will get the poetry across; he may even get the whole poem across or, at second best, force his own version – within the strictures laid down by the original author – as close as possible to poetry.

In Ó Bruadair's verse the translator is faced with opaque compound words: they look Germanic in their length and seem uncrackable. But I did to his poems what should be done to all poems: I read them aloud – and slowly began to understand them. He uses archaic words; his compounds, though often a strange juxtapositioning of simple words, were sometimes inventions of his own (I must add, he invented no new *single* words, but his binding together of often disparate ones created images that were almost surreal). Also, Ó Bruadair had a medieval mind. Would that mind or the poetry that mirrored the mind be acceptable to a twentieth-century reader? The Gaelic poets' love for the art of poetry, for politics, religion, history and above all genealogy – these are his themes. Is it possible to make him attractive to our society with its fashionable and ever-changing ragbag of sex, psychology and philosophies? Any poetry of any age can be adapted to our way of thinking. Robert Lowell spread a wide net over times and languages and made them all twentieth-century American, and brilliantly so. But he was not translating, he was using poems as *themes*.

In 1647 Ó Bruadair wrote a lament for his patron Sir Edmund Fitzgerald. It contains four hundred and twenty lines, written in different metres, and enshrines the whole of the poet's attitude towards his world. But is it a poem in the sense we would accept today, whether we are Irish or not? Is it a poem in the sense that, say, 'The Deserted Village' is? It has music, stanzas, alliteration, rhyme – all the recognizable paraphernalia. But it is not a 'poem'. It is a ritual lament, a cry, given by the voice of a land for a husband of that land: the very rivers and trees cry, and their crying has nothing to do with pathetic fallacy. It goes beyond medievalism, back to a Celtic system where the whole world was alive.

And there is the problem of his metres. Gaelic metres and poem-structures are notoriously complicated. Gerald Murphy in his *Early Irish Metrics* mentions eighty-four 'professional' metres (and there were hundreds of variations capable of being played in the 'non-professional' metres). If the seventeenth century saw the end of Gaelic society, it also saw the end of the professional poets; their poem-structures went with them. Ó Bruadair witnessed this, but he adopted the new metres like the master he was. The 'new' metres were not new: they were the metres used by the lower ranks of versifiers and for peasant songs. *Sráid-éigse*, Ó Bruadair called their users – 'street poets'. The professional poets had always used what they called *Dán Díreach* – 'direct composition'. I call them 'poem-structures' to emphasize their uniqueness. They were not accentual metres; they were syllabic and had a very complex sound-structure based on strict rules – even the consonants had values relative to each other. The popular metres (*amhráin*) were looser; they were accentual, and were not bound by the rules of consonant-relation, but nevertheless they were, and are, very difficult to master. Even though Ó Bruadair despised the changing times, he did move with them, complicating the translator's task.

Because I want to find a way to make his poetry acceptable to our tastes, and to employ as much of his technique as I can master, I also want to find a 'voice' for him; and this task is most important of all. It is as difficult as trying to find a 'voice' for Milton in Chinese. I do not wish to afflict the poet with *my* voice: to do that, too much of what survives of the original in my versions would be distorted. I am fortunate, however, because no one has attempted Ó Bruadair on a large scale since his first translator, whose style of English is no longer current; this should keep me free of influences. For instance, another Gaelic poet, Aogán Ó Rathaille, has found a 'voice' in Frank O'Connor's translations. And O'Connor, though he did not translate all of Ó Rathaille, has so powerfully become the 'voice' of that poet for our generation that anyone else who attempted to translate those poems could not help but fall into his (O'Connor's) cadences. But sufficient unto the generation are the translators thereof.

O'Connor's versions of Ó Rathaille must soon be superseded, as will Mac Erlean's versions of Ó Bruadair.

The few poems I have given so far do little to illustrate the complexity and brilliance of Ó Bruadair's poetry. He is at his most powerful and inventive in his longer poems. Here are some verses from a lament for a schoolfriend; it's an early poem, showing at once his medievalism and also a certain compassion for the individual not often evident in his later work:

Scéal do scaoil fan mBanba
    mbraonaigh,
ní binn lem chluais bheith dá éisteacht,
do bheir mo chroidhe go cráidhte céasta
gan é a ndiu an té bhí a ndé againn.

I wish that I had died before him
before the stones had slanted
    over him
the pulse of his heart was my
    own heart breathing
my care, my cure, my herb of
    healing.

Death will be the theme of my
    writing
until I am stretched in the earth
    beside him:
because he, athletic, slim and
    playful
lies abandoned in a lonely
    graveyard.

The sun with grief was
    near-demented,
water and earth and air
    lamented,
world and wave and moon were
    weeping,
land and fish and bird were
    grieving.

He was my love, beautiful to
  look on
the glance of his eyes, his hair,
  his forehead:
white hands, white limbs and
  whiter shoulders –
a breast like froth of a
  strong-waved ocean.

Ní thug gean na searc do ghréithibh,
ní thug toil do thoice an tsaoghail,
níor chuir suim i séad ná i séadaibh,
i n-ór ná i n-earradh, i n-each na i
  n-éadach.

Farewell, my Norman-Irish
  sapling
cunning glensman, hawk of
  mountain
sorcerer, delightful otter,
brave as bear, lithe as lion.

Knowing craftsman, boldest
  chieftain
loyal soldier, support of clerics
vision seer, prince to poor men,
philosopher, poet, Fenians'
  huntsman.

Precious tree-trunk, friend of
  poets
golden apple, help of heroes
learning's mirror, assemblies'
  teacher
white-limbed man that courted
  women.

My friend alone in your far
  coffin,
I sadly cannot go to see you,
I am here and you're in
  bondage:
That is not our old condition.

Is beag nar chailleas leath mo chéille,
is béad go deo go brónach céasta,
anois cráidhte, mar táim id dhéidhse,
ní raibh Oisín d'éis na féinne.

Until we meet again together
doom's day on the crowded
    mountain
my blessing and God's blessing
    on you:
as you are now, so all men
    finish.

Until we meet again, myself and
    my companion,
I must stay behind here, tortured
    and abandoned.
You must lie beneath this earth,
    which I sadly stand on:
My blessing go to God with
    you, my shy companion.

Go gcastar le chéile mé féin is mo
    chompánach
madh fada mo ré béad céasta
    díoghbhálach,
ó theastaidh uaim féin an té seo i
    n-úir sáithte
mo bheannacht chum Dé leat, a
    chéile chaoin náirigh.

Some verses at least of a poem to which we referred earlier, 'An Longbhriseadh' ('The Shipwreck'), may be familiar as 'reincarnated' by James Stephens; here are the Gaelic and English together:

Níl tuisle ná taitneamh fá ar scamaladh
    sluagh an phuirt
re tuilleadh agus ceathrachadh
    sámhfhuin nár fuaigheasa

I will sing no more songs! The
    pride of my country I sang
Through forty long years of
    good rhyme, without any
    avail;

*is mithid damh scaradh re seanmaibh
  suaracha
is nach ionamhas eatha na eallaigh a
  luach dom thigh.*

*Cine mo charad dá measa gur gua mo
  ghuth
táid m'uilleanna is m'easna na
  dteastaibh le dua mo chruibh
tré thurrainn a ngradaim gé
  leathchiorruigh lua mo ruisc
ní shilfinn an dadamh dá rabhainn im
  chluanaire.*

*I gcuilithe a maise do mharthainn go
  buabhallach
gé chrithnigh mo mheanma tathamh a
  dtuarasca
culaith ná capall do rachmas an ruathair
  si
ná oiread an phaspuirt re breacadh ní
  fhuarasa.*

*Sirim an Ceard lear ceapadh an chuach
  's an chuil
'san bile do cheannuigh le peannaid mo
  bhuain a bruid
spioraid an tseaca do bhearbhadh i
  bhfuarchroidhthibh
go dtuillid fir Bhanbha malairt na
  duaine si.*

And no one cared even the half
  of the half of a hang
For the song or the singer – so,
  here is an end to the tale!

If you say, if you think, I
  complain, and have not got a
  cause,
Let you come to me here, let
  you look at the state of my
  hand!
Let you say if a goose-quill has
  calloused these horny old
  paws,
Or the spade that I grip on, and
  dig with, out there in the
  land?

When our nobles were safe and
  renowned and were rooted
  and tough,
Though my thought went to
  them and had joy in the
  fortune of those,
And pride that was proud of
  their pride – they gave little
  enough!
Not as much as two boots for
  my feet, or an old suit of
  clothes!

I ask of the Craftsman that
  fashioned the fly and the bird;
Of the Champion whose passion
  will lift me from death in a
  time;
Of the Spirit that melts icy
  hearts with the wind of a
  word,
That my people be worthy, and
  get, better singing than mine.

77

*Gé shaoileas dá saoirse bheith seascair
    sódhail*
*im stíobhard ag saoi acu nó im
    ghearraphróbhost*
*os críoch di mo stríocadh go
    seanabhrógaibh*
finis dom scríbhinn ar fhearaibh Fódla.

I had hoped to live decent, when
    Ireland was quit of her care,
As a poet or steward, perhaps,
    in a house of degree,
But my end of the tale is – old
    brogues and old breeches to
    wear!
So I'll sing no more songs for
    the men that care nothing for
    me.

Ó Bruadair could be funny, obscure and anguished. He had
immense dignity and immense bitterness. If he is anti-democratic it
is because he confused survival with betrayal. He was concerned
with culture.

He would not have liked the Ireland of the 1980s.

*D'aithle na bhfileadh n-uasal
trua-san timheal an t-saoghail
clann na n-ollamh go n-eagna
folamh gan freagra faobhair.*

Bereft of its great poets
our old world's in darkness.
The orphans of those masters
offer answers that lack
    sharpness.

*Truagh a leabhair ag liathadh –
tiacha na treabhair baoise:
ar ceal níor chóir a bhfoilcheas
toircheas bhfear n-óil na gaoise.*

Their books are sadly mildewed
– books that were not flippant –
their lore unjustly *passé*,
the lore of wisdom-drinkers.

*D'aithle na bhfileadh dar ionmhus éigsi
    's iúl
is mairg do chonnairc an chinneamhain
    d'éirigh dúinn,
a leabhair ag tuitim i leimhe 's i léithe i
    gcúil,
's ag macaibh na droinge gan siolla dá
    séadaibh rún.*

I pity the man who must witness
    the fate of himself
now that poets are gone, who
    valued both wisdom and
    verse:
while their sons retain not one
    scrap of that lore in their
    heads
old volumes disintegrate, dusty
    and mouldy, on shelves.

John Jordan
Aogán Ó Rathaille

In any approach to the literary culture of the extraordinarily diverse island of Ireland, it is sometimes illuminating to consider certain curious coincidences of dates. When an Irishman recalls that 1856 saw the birth of Bernard Shaw in Dublin, and of Tomas Ó Criomhthain on the Great Blasket Island off the coast of Kerry, he may, or should, experience a *frisson*, a minor thrill, in the realization that he can embrace in his heritage the antipodes of *John Bull's Other Island* and *An tOileánach*.[1]

For myself, I take pleasure in the fact that Jonathan Swift was born in Dublin in 1667, only about three years before the birth of Aogán Ó Rathaille, in the Sliabh Luachra region of County Kerry, more precisely at Screathán an Mhíl – Scrahanaveale – a mile north of Meentogues and ten miles east of Killarney. It is a sombre pleasure: the mighty Latin epitaph which Swift made for himself, and which may be read over his resting-place in St Patrick's Cathedral in Dublin, would not be inapposite on the grave of Ó Rathaille in Muckross Abbey near Killarney. I am not of course the first to link the *saeva indignatio* of Swift with Ó Rathaille's defiant ululation. Most recently, John Montague did so in the Introduction to his *Faber Book of Irish Verse*, linking both with Daibhí Ó Bruadair, still alive when both were growing up: 'three angry men' he calls them.[2]

But the worlds of Swift and Ó Rathaille were vastly different. Swift for large sections of his life could look across the water, aspire even to the real and glittering spoils that lay on the other side. Ó Rathaille never left Munster and when he looked across the water it was to envisage the illusory rewards coming in the wake of an illusory Saviour, the Old Pretender, son of that Catholic Stuart King, James II, whom other Irishmen called 'Séamus a' Chaca' – 'Messy James' with cloacal overtones – but who for Ó Rathaille had been the liege lord of the Brown family of Kenmare, who were his

---

1. Tomas Ó Crohan, *The Islandman*, trans. by Robin Flower, 1937.
2. *The Faber Book of Irish Verse*, ed. John Montague, 1974, p. 30.

liege lords, as the great, dispossessed, MacCarthy clan had been the acknowledged masters of his forefathers.[3]

To appreciate the poignancy, and sometimes the theatrically savage power of Ó Rathaille's verse, it is necessary to accept certain facts perhaps unpalatable in democratic, nation-conscious societies. Ó Rathaille had no notion of nationalism as such, not even as it may be seen emerging in, say, *The Faerie Queene* of Spenser, some seventy years before his birth. Nor had he any notion of what used to be called egalitarianism; less so, indeed than many of those, including Milton, who had thrown in their lot with the Cromwellian revolutionaries. By heritage and, I would say, by temperament, he was a monarchist, accepting in the order of things the principle of hierarchy; in cruder terms he believed, naturally and unquestioningly, in the caste system, in which he saw himself as occupying an honourable and honoured place. He was an *ollamh*, a bard.[4] Without that system, he could not fulfil his vocation. If he could not practise his craft, he could not make a livelihood. He became a displaced person. Appreciation of Ó Rathaille's high and lonely utterance depends, largely, on acceptance of these factors. His first and only editor in full, the great Patrick S. Dinneen, tends to gloss over Ó Rathaille's dependence on and acceptance of the medieval system into which he had been born: 'The energies which other poets devoted to the praise of wine or woman, he spent recounting the past glories and mourning over the present sorrows of his beloved land, whose history he had studied as few men have ever done . . .'[5] The comment of Fr Dinneen's sympathetic biographers, Prionnsias Ó Conluain and the late Donncha Ó Ceileachair, is apposite: 'Ó Rathaille is more of a poet and less of a patriot than Dinneen imputes to him.'[6] (My translation.) They instance a *marbhna* or elegy which Ó Rathaille wrote for John Blennerhasset of Ballyseedy, County Kerry. A decade or so before his death Blennerhasset had been one of the

3. See Seán Ó Tuama, *Filí faoi Sceimhle*, Dublin, 1978, pp. 87–124, for a full discussion of Ó Rathaille, the MacCarthys and the Browns.
4. On the Bardic Schools, see Douglas Hyde, *A Literary History of Ireland*, 1899, Chapter XIX; new edition, 1967.
5. *Dánta Aodhagáin Uí Rathaille*, ed. P. S. Dinneen and Tadhg O'Donoghue, 2nd edition, 1911, p. xxxii.
6. *An Duinníneach*, Dublin, 1958, p. 318.

prime movers in an attempt to plant Protestant settlers on the estates of Nicholas Brown, second Viscount of Kenmare, a Catholic attainted for his participation in the Williamite Wars. Ó Rathaille proclaimed allegiance to the Browns, but made no bones about later composing an elegy of 120 lines for Blennerhasset. And it should be remembered that he could mourn with equal intensity the MacCarthys, the Gaelic overlords of his forefathers, and the Anglo-Irish (or Hiberno-English) Browns who dispossessed them. Both families are associated with some of his most plangent verse.

Sometime between 1703 and 1708–9[7] he was compelled to move to Corcaguiny on the Dingle Peninsula, where the great wave of Tóim, Tonn Tóime, is said to be the tutelary spirit. One night, kept awake by the storm, he meditated on his present misery as against the putative comfort of life under the patronage of the MacCarthys. But he also laments Sir Nicholas Brown.[8] Seán Ó Tuama has noted the juxtaposition in this poem of the sea's rage and the poet's mental anguish:[9]

Is fada liom oíche fhír-fhliuch gan
    suan, gan srann
Gan ceathra, gan maoin caoire ná
    buaibh na mbeann.
Anfaithe ar toinn taoibh liom do
    bhuaidhir mo cheann.
Is nár chleactas im naoidhin fíogaigh ná
    ruacáin abhann.[10]

From the last line of that first stanza, 'and I was unused in my childhood to dogfish and periwinkles',[11] James Stephens took a hint for a proud little poem of his own in his *Reincarnations* (1918), called 'Egan Ó Rahilly'. Eavan Boland has made a fine free version of the whole poem, from which the following are the second, third, and final stanzas:

7. Ó Tuama, op. cit., p. 94.
8. ibid., p. 95.
9. ibid., p. 95.
10. *Dánta*, op. cit., p. 26.
11. ibid., p. 27.

O if he lived, the prince who
  sheltered me
And his company who gave me
  entry
On the river of the Laune,
Whose royalty stood sentry
Over intricate harbours, I and
  my own
Would not be desolate in
  Dermot's country.

Fierce McCarthy Mór whose
  friends were welcome,
McCarthy of the Lee a slave of
  late,
McCarthy of Kenturk whose
  blood
Has dried underfoot:
Of all my princes not a single
  word –
Irrevocable silence ails my heart.

Take warning, wave, take
  warning, crown of the sea
I, O'Rahilly – witless from your
  discords –
Were Spanish sails again afloat
And rescue on our tides,
Would force this outcry down
  your wild throat,
Would make you swallow these
  Atlantic words.[12]

But no translation can convey the outrageous splendour of Ó
Rathaille's last line, which might be absurd were it not for the occult
significance of Tonn Tóime, harbouring god or fairy: *Do ghlam nach
binn do dhingfinn féin it bhraghaid.*[13]

In that poem he refers to 'the prince who sheltered me', Sir
Nicholas Brown, but in a later poem he is at odds with Sir Nicholas's

12. *Faber Book of Irish Verse*, op. cit., p. 144.
13. *Dánta*, op. cit., p. 28.

son, Valentine Brown. Never more bitterly has 'patient merit spurned' reacted in circumstances of misery and decrepitude:

Do leathnaigh an ciach diachrach fám sheana – chroí dúr	That my old bitter heart was pierced in this black doom
Ar dtaisteal na ndiabhal iasachta i bhfearann Chuinn chughainn;	That foreign devils have made our land a tomb
Scamall ar ghrian iarthair dár cheartas ríoghacht Mumhan	That the sun that was Munster's glory has gone down
Fá deara dham triall riamh ort, a Bhailintín Brún.	Has made me a beggar before you, Valentine Brown.
Caiseal gan chliar, fiailteach na macraidhe ar dtúis	That royal Cashel is bare of house and guest.
Is beanna – bhruigh Bhriain ciar-thuilte 'mhadraibh úisc,	That Brian's turreted home is the otters' nest
Ealla gan triair triaithe de mhacaibh riogh Mumhan	That the kings of the land have neither land nor crown
Fá deara dham triall riamh ort, a Bhailintín Brún.[14]	Has made me a beggar before you Valentine Brown.[15]

While Frank O'Connor's translation of those first two stanzas from 'Bhailintín Brún' is in acceptable simple language, the language of the original is relatively baroque – 'and Brian's turreted mansions, black-flooded with otters'[16] – but Ó Rathaille, as we shall see, was capable of punitive starkness, and, while addicted in traditional mode to alliteration and imaginative compounds, was seldom an exemplar for the next major Munster poet, Eoghan Rua Ó Súilleabhain, who often expires in a morass of loveliness.

In so far as he was an *ollamh* or bard, Ó Rathaille – perforce almost – is a learned poet, presenting a peculiar difficulty as far as his allusions and nomenclatures are concerned. He draws on the mythology and history of Greece and Rome and from the Bible, but also, often to the bewilderment of even the Irish reader, from the more arcane Irish mythology and from the earliest Irish historical records. We must add to this load numerous references to town-

14. ibid., p. 30.
15. *Kings, Lords and Commons*, 1959, p. 102.
16. *Dánta*, op. cit., p. 31.

lands, villages, hills, dales, rivers and streams, not only in his native Kerry, but all over Ireland. He carried in his heart the outlines of a country most of which he had never seen.

Yet it is not, I believe, in his poems for patrons of whatever rank, in which he deploys the bardic armoury, that his personal genius is best articulated. This can find expression in what by the middle of the eighteenth century had become almost a folk-mode: I mean of course the *aisling* or vision-poem.

This form became widespread both in the North and South of Ireland in the eighteenth century as a mode of political allegory. In a vision, the poet meets a beautiful woman in distress – a *spéir-bhean*, or sky-woman – who is mourning a lost hero or lover. The poet either comforts the lady and promises redress, or is comforted by her. In the North of Ireland, the lost hero may be identified with one of the exiled O'Neills or O'Donnells, the great families who went into exile after the Battle of Kinsale (1603). In Munster, the lost hero and expected redeemer is identified with one or other of the Stuarts. In his lifetime Ó Rathaille saw two dynasties as usurpers of the House of Stuart: the House of Orange and the House of Hanover. But as did his patrons, Catholic and Protestant, he remained a Jacobite, and with one major exception his *aislingí* are geared to the Stuart cult. The exception (if in fact it be one) is 'Mac an Cheannaí' (or 'The Merchant's Son'), in which the poet meets a distressed maiden on the seashore awaiting the arrival of the merchant's son and the succour he will bring with him. The poet tells her that the saviour she is expecting has died in Spain. Here there is no evidence that any Stuart is in question: Seán Ó Tuama opines that the death in Spain may refer to the death of the young King, Luis I, in 1724 and the foundering of all hope of military aid from that source.[17] This *aisling* is slighter, certainly, than 'Gile na Gile' (or 'Brightness of Brightness') or 'Maidin sul a smaoin Titan . . .' (or 'One Morning Before Titan Thought . . .') but there is a special Virgilian pathos in the picture it sketches of the lady gazing over the waves for the lover-hero who will never come.

There is no doubt that Ó Rathaille has James II's son, the Old Pretender, in mind in 'Maidin sul a smaoin Titan . . .', an *aisling*

17. Ó Tuama, op. cit., p. 164.

which celebrates openly the restoration of 'the three kingdoms' through the splendid grouping of the hooded woman lighting three candles which blaze indescribably:

Lasaid-sin trí coinnle go solas nach
   luadhaim
Ar mhullach Chnuic aoird Fhírinne
   Conallach Ruaidh,
Leanastar linn scaoth na mban gcochall
   go Tuamhain,
Is fachtaim-se dhíobh díograis a n-oifige
   ar cuaird.[18]

Here is how the poet learns the significance of the three unearthly lights, as rendered by Edward, sixth Earl of Longford (1902–61):

> Then I caught pretty Aoibheall
>   and asked her to say
> Why they lit their three candles
>   o'er every bay.
> ''Tis a light,' she replied, 'for a
>   king that ere long
> Shall win back his Three
>   Kingdoms and save them
>   from wrong.'[19]

'Maidin sul a smaoin Titan . . .', until the poet's dream dissolves, is a fantasy of hope and joy. Austin Clarke, in an exquisite paraphrase, has captured something of the poem's gossamer lightness:

> One day before Titan had
>   lighted the way from his
>   doorstep,
> I climbed to a hilltop silled by
>   mist and, wherever I looked,
> were blue hooded women who
>   knew no envy:

18. *Dánta*, op. cit., p. 22.
19. *The Dove and the Castle*, Dublin, 1946, p. 174.

> They came from a mound
> without sound through the
> grey of heather.[20]

Ó Rathaille's other great *aisling*, the breathtaking 'Gile na Gile' (or 'Brightness of Brightness'), is one of the miracles of Irish literature – after its fashion as solitary and inexplicable as 'Kubla Khan'. Superficially, it is no more than a political allegory in a familiar mode. The poet in a dream meets a beautiful woman who symbolizes Ireland. She addresses him cryptically, flies, is followed by him to a fairy mansion, where both are imprisoned by a band of remotely demonic creatures. But the poet goes free, while she remains in the control of a sensual boor. While she is being disposed of to the boor, the poet upbraids her with unfaithfulness to her prince – the Old Pretender – and with a *slibire slímbhuartha* – 'an awkward, sorry churl'.[21] It would be absurd to interpret this poem solely in terms of modern psychology: thus we might see the lady's surrender to a masterful brute as an instance of the victory of sexual appetite over romantic love. But I do not think it absurd to take cognizance of the piteously human pattern coexisting with the patent political allegory. The poet has seen his 'brightness of brightness' befouled, and must live to record the grand disillusion. As for the 'Brightness of Brightness' it is scarcely possible to render in English the description Ó Rathaille gives of this, the premier sky-woman of the *aisling* literature; the translator is James Clarence Mangan:

Gile na gile do chonnarc ar sligh in uaigneas,	The Brightest of the Bright met me on my path so lonely;
Criostal an chriostail a goirm-roisc rinn-uaine,	The Crystal of all Crystals was her flashing dark-blue eye;
Binneas an bhinnis a friotal nár chríon-ghruamdha,	Melodious more than music was her spoken language only;
Deirge is finne do fionnadh 'na gríos-ghruadhnaib.[22]	And glorious were her cheeks, of a brilliant crimson dye.[23]

20. *Collected Poems*, 1974, p. 229.
21. *Dánta*, op. cit., p. 21.
22. ibid., p. 18.
23. *Faber Book of Irish Verse*, op. cit., p. 142.

88

Lord Longford has been more successful, I think, in his version of the second stanza, which in the original begins, '*Caise na caise i ngach ruibe dá buidhe-chuachaibh . . .*':[24]

> Curling of curling gold was in
>   every hair of the heap;
> Thro' a world turned dusty and
>   old would her locks in their
>   lustre sweep,
> With a gleam that glittered as
>   glass on the swell of her
>   bosom full –
> High Heaven had brought it to
>   pass that her bosom be
>   beautiful.[25]

The unfortunate 'heap' may be forgiven for the remarkable second line. Though the last line barely approximates to '*do geineadh ar ghineamhain dise san tír uachtraigh*',[26] which lends to Ó Rathaille's lady a supernatural dimension that has nothing to do with the otherworld of faery. It has something to do with 'I was set up from eternity, and of old, before the earth was made'.[27]

The *ceangal* or 'binding' of the poem speaks of the lovely lady being without respite '*go bhfillid na leoin thar toinn*' – 'until the lions return from over the wave'. Ironically, any lions that came across the wave came some seventy years after Ó Rathaille's death: soldiers of revolutionary France stained with the blood of a king whose forefathers Ó Rathaille regarded as the natural allies of the Stuarts. And Ó Rathaille himself seems to have gone on an increasingly desolate path: 'that Dante of Munster', Daniel Corkery called him.[28] And it might be said, without bathos, that his devotion to his Gaelic and Jacobite Beatrice, *la dolce guida* beckoning him ahead in Sliabh Luachra, was to bring him to the plight, where on the lip of

---

24. *Dánta*, op. cit., p. 18.
25. *The Dove and the Castle*, op. cit., p. 175.
26. *Dánta*, op. cit., p. 18.
27. Proverbs, 8, xxiii.
28. *The Hidden Ireland*, Dublin, 1924; 2nd edition, 1969, p. 156.

the grave, it seems, he made the incomparable confessional poem that begins: '*Cabhair ní ghoirfead go gcuirtear mé i gcruinn-chomhrainn*'[29] ('I will not cry for help before I'm put into a narrow coffin'; the usual translation 'until I'm put' is an absurdity). Of that line Corkery has exclaimed, 'It seems to me we are hearing a voice that outLears Lear!'[30] He is right up to a point. But there is *hysterica passio* in Ó Rathaille's blend of defiance and impassioned stoicism, in which one may hear the voice of an older tragic hero, the Philoctetes of Sophocles, or of another Shakespearean figure of archetypal doom – Timon of Athens:

> Then, Timon, presently prepare thy grave;
> Lie where the light foam of the sea may beat
> Thy grave-stone daily: make thine own epitaph,
> That death in me at others' lives may laugh.[31]

But it is also John Donne, I think, and sonnets such as 'Batter my heart, three person'd God' and 'Death be not proud', that provoke a tingling in the blood comparable to the effect produced by Ó Rathaille's poem. It continues on its high level of disconsolation until, as it were, reaching 'port after storm':

Stadfadsa feasta, is gar dom éag gan mhoill,
Ó treascradh dragain Leamhan, Léin is Laoi;
Rachadsa 'na bhfasc le searc na laoch don chill,
Na flatha fá raibh mo shean roimh éag do Chríost.[32]

I will stop now, a quick death is coming, since those fierce men of the Laune and the Léin and the Lee have been toppled. I will follow to the grave after the most beloved of heroes, princes under whom my forebears served before Christ's death.

Even a plain prose translation reverberates in the mind with the resonance of the highest verse. I am thinking of Phèdre: 'Soleil, je te

29. *Dánta*, op. cit., p. 114.
30. *The Hidden Ireland*, op. cit., p. 179.
31. IV. 3. 380–83.
32. *Dánta*, op. cit., p. 116.

viens voir pour la dernière fois'; of the final Chorus in *Oedipus Rex*: 'Call no man happy until he is dead'; of Shakespeare's song: 'Fear no more the heat of the sun'.

The last line of Ó Rathaille's poem found its way into Yeats's poem 'The Curse of Cromwell' which appeared in *Last Poems* (1939):

> And there is an old beggar wandering in his pride –
> His fathers served their fathers before Christ was crucified.[33]

Yeats came of course to Ó Rathaille through his working association with Frank O'Connor.[34] But the spirit of Ó Rathaille, not merely a paraphrase of his words, shines through that section of 'The Municipal Gallery Revisited' which begins 'My medieval knees lack health until they bend'.[35] Ó Rathaille was all too willing, perhaps, to bend the knee. But his verse also suggests that he was unwilling to bend it to upstarts, to the kind of louts he saw in possession of the MacCarthy and Brown estates. The twin summits of his art, 'Gile na Gile' and 'Cabhair ní Ghoirfead', are marvellous paradigms of the poet in ecstasy and *in extremis*. They are also the desperate euphemism, and the passing bell, of a dying civilization. Aogán Ó Rathaille is a poet of the deluge.

33. *Collected Poems*, 2nd edition, 1950, p. 350.
34. cf. *Kings, Lords and Commons*, op. cit., pp. v and 109.
35. *Collected Poems*, op. cit., p. 369.

Benedict Kiely
A Sense of Place

Oliver Goldsmith's Traveller, wandering remote, unfriended, melancholy, slow, or by the lazy Scheld or wandering Po, or onward where the rude Carinthian boor against the houseless stranger shuts the door, found that his heart remained untravelled and, over long distances, turned in affection to his brother and, at each further remove from home, he dragged a lengthening chain. That was a thought that seemed to be much in the mind of a writer, so French in his style and so Irish in his heart and who may in his boyhood have heard the songs and harp-music of Toirealach Ó Cearbhalláin called, inaccurately, the last of the Irish harpers. For in the wisest and most delightful series of essays ever put together in English he makes his imaginary citizen of the world, Lien Chi Altangi, a man from Honan, write from England and to his friend and mentor in the Orient and at the far end of two continents: 'The farther I travel I feel the pain of separation with stronger force: those ties that bind me to my native country and you are still unbroken. By every remove I only drag a greater length of chain.' For the Traveller the question all this sentiment posed was: but where to find that happiest spot below? In a splendid passage that is not, perhaps, without a certain absurdity, he imagined the 'shuddering tenant of the frigid zone' proclaiming – that is, we may pardonably think, if he could find anybody in the igloo to listen to him – that that happiest spot was his own. Goldsmith even imagined the shuddering fellow extolling the treasures, presumably the cod-fishing and the whaling, of his stormy seas, and his long nights of revelry and ease; and, by way of utter contrast, the naked negro, panting at the line, boasted, when he had the breath to spare, of his golden sands and palmy wine.

An idyllic picture of what we now, in euphemism, call the Third World. Yet the passage ends in a fine couplet and an impeccable sentiment and an almost unchallengeable statement: 'Such is the patriot's boast where'er we roam; His first best country ever is at home.' As impeccable and unchallengeable as: ''Mid pleasures and palaces though we may roam, be it ever so humble, there's no place like home.' But more nobly expressed; and more nobly expressed, again, in the case of the wanderer in Homer's epic who longed as he journeyed to see once more the smoke going up about his own homestead and after that to die.

This attachment to place, to the home places, even the mythologizing of place-names, is not confined, obviously, to ourselves the Irish, nor even to island people. But it is possible that it may be more emphasized in the case of island people, and made more poignant when their destiny takes them far from the island of their earliest associations and affections, Ithaca or Ireland. Remembering a city, James Joyce was also remembering an island. He had various good reasons for sending Leopold Bloom walking in the shadow of Ulysses and one of them may have been, although as far as I know or remember, he never said so, that Ulysses was, in our civilization, the most notable of all islandmen.

And among our neighbours of the larger island I think first of the heart-torn cry of Robert Louis Stevenson, a writer who, as in the novel *Catriona* and indeed in all the adventures of David Balfour, had his highland, Gaelic moments. Exiled by ill-health from his own grey city and the mountains to the north of it, he wrote:

> Home no more home to me, whither must I wander,
> Hunger my driver I go where I must.

Or of Hilaire Belloc exalting the places and people of the South Country over all the places and people on that island, and commencing his poem on Duncton Hill with a most significant statement relevant here to our purpose:

> He does not die that can bequeath
> Some influence to the land he knows,
> Or dares persistent, interwreath
> Love permanent with the wild hedgerows;
> He does not die, but still remains
> Substantiate with his darling plains.

That interweaving of love permanent with the hedgerows and the beech-trees is most important: for with all true love goes the living imagination, and the interweaving of love and imagination with locality is something that our ancestors were particularly good at,

96

back to the days of the earliest written records and beyond. For what the scribes wrote down in the topographical, etymological and mythological prose and poetry of the *dinnseanchas* in the ninth, tenth and eleventh centuries must have been alive for a long time in the imaginations and on the tongues of the people.

The island itself was the central myth or symbol. W. B. Yeats wrote: 'Have not all nations had their first unity from a mythology that marries them to rock and hill'. It would seem from the evidence of the earliest literature that our ancestors were irrevocably and mystically bound to the island; and it is idle to say that the idea of one island, united, bound in by the triumphant sea was merely a modern political notion. Whatever the trampling of later generations and invasions may have done the idea was there in the beginning as clear as blossom on a spring morning. The island was something much more than a refuge and a home or a port after stormy seas; it could be the goddess – more, perhaps, a mother-goddess than a tantalizing virgin rising from the foam – at any rate a living being that the magic of enchanters could seem to change to a black monster riding the billows, so as to prevent the chosen people coming to haven. Its remoteness and isolation defined it as exactly as a strong hedge or a wall latticed with fruit branches would define a man's own garden.

In the Christian Dawn of the sixth century, Bran sailed towards the island of delight, an idealized island, an idealized Ireland, a heaven upon earth, and heard across the waters, the song of Manannan, the son of Lir:

> The sea is clear
> So thinks Bran when sailing
>   here.
> I in a car, with purer powers
> know the happy plain of
>   flowers . . .
>
> Rivers run with honey clear
> In the fair land of Mac Lír.
> Bran the ocean's gleaming glint
> Sees, and billow's pallid tint:
> I the bounteous hand behold
> Decked with azure and with
>   gold.

97

Speckled salmon leap for him
From the water's bitter brim:
I can see o'er lovely lawns,
Lambkins play and frolic fawns.

Wide the plains the hosts are
  great,
Bright their colours high their
  state,
Streams of silver gleams of gold,
Welcome and abundance hold.

Branches rich with fruit and
  bloom
Breathing forth the vine's
  perfume . . .
We are here since time had birth
Aging not, nor called to
  earth . . .

The 'mysterious, runic poem' of Amergin hails, as it rises from the sea, what one might call the mortal as against the immortal island; but even that island, made up of rock and hill, fertile valley, spreading plain, lake and river – and thus inspiring a people to create a mythology – is as much a haven.

And for centuries onward from Colmcille, the first exile – a theme dealt with so well in Robert Farren's fine poem – to turn the back on that island was heartache and desolation. In Colmcille's Glen of Gartan, near Letterkenny, you can still see the Flagstone of Loneliness, Leac an Uaignis, on which, tradition held, the saint had slept penitentially on the night before he sailed from Ireland. Right into our time men and women going into exile would make the *turas*, or pilgrimage, to and around the Glen of Gartan, and lie on that stone and pray to the saint, who was also a poet, to be preserved against the pangs of homesickness. Attachments to place go no further than that; and in the ears and minds of some of them, as they lay on the cold stone, the saint's own words, in Irish or in borrowed English, could have their echoes:

Faoileanna Locha Feabhail
Romham agus im dheaghaidh,
Ní thigid liom im churach
Uch! Is dubhach ar ndeadhail.

Mo radharc tar sál sínim
Do chlár na ndarach ndíoghainn;
Mór déar mo ruisg ghlais ghléinboill,
Mar fhéaghain tar mh'ais Éirinn.

The seagulls of Loch Foyle
before me and after,
They come not with me in my
  currach.
Oh sad is our separation!

I stretch my gaze over the
  salt-water,
From the ship's deck of strong
  oak.
Many are the tears of my grey
  wet eye
As I look back to Ireland.

Derry, the grove of oaks, was Colmcille's first religious institution and, as Douglas Hyde wrote in his *Literary History of Ireland*: 'like every man's firstling it remained dear to him to the last'. Years afterwards, when the thought of Derry came back to him on the barren shores of Iona, he expressed himself in passionate poetry:

For oh! were the tributes of
  Alba mine
From shore unto centre, from
  centre to sea,
The site of one house to be
  marked by a line
In midst of fair Derry were
  dearer to me.

That spot is the dearest on
  Ireland's ground
For the treasures that peace and
  that purity lend,
For the hosts of bright angels
  that circle it round,
Protecting its borders from end
  to end.

The dearest of any on Ireland's
    ground,
For its peace and its beauty I
    gave it my love:
Each leaf of the oaks around
    Derry is found
To be crowded with angels from
    heaven above.

My Derry, my Derry, my little
    oak grove:
My dwelling, my home and my
    own little cell,
May God the Eternal in heaven
    above
Send death to thy foes and
    defend thee well.

It is a long time and a troubled history since the poet-saint wrote in
that fashion about the oak-grove above the spreading Foyle. But
neither time nor history can change our instincts, good or bad, and
the heart of any true son of Colmcille's Derry will still respond to
those fine lines. And Gerald Nugent, a contemporary of the poet
Edmund Spenser, and one of those Normans who became more
Irish than the Irish themselves (almost as if the seductiveness of the
place and the easy manners of the people had devoured them), wrote
in Irish about the sorrow that it was to part from Inisfail or to sail
away from the shores of Ireland: the land of the bee-glad mountains,
the island of the steeds and fountains.

Fód is truime toradh crann,   Shore of fine fruit-bended trees,
Fód is féar uaithne fearann,   Shore of green grass-covered leas;
Sean – chlár Ír braonach beartach,   Old plain of Ir, soft, showery,
An tír chraobhach chruithneachtach. Wheatful, fruitful, fair, flow'ry.

Tír na gcuradh as na gcliar,   Home of priest and gallant
Banhba na n-ainnear n-óir cliabh,   knight
Tír na sreabh ngoirm – ealtach nglan Isle of gold-haired maidens
's na bhfear n-oirbheartach n-óghmhear. bright
                                     Banba of the clear blue wave
                                     of bold hearts and heroes brave.

Seathrún Céitinn in the seventeenth century, as a student in Bordeaux, bestowed his blessing on his verses and sent them as ambassadors to the island and all the places in it; late in the eighteenth century, Donncha Rua Mac Conmara, far away, perhaps in Hamburg, perhaps Talamh an Éisc, or the land of the Fish which we now call Newfoundland, sent the blessing of his heart to the land of Ireland, to the hills of Ireland green and fair. For my own private delectation I prefer to think that Donncha wrote that most moving poem in the Land of the Fish, sending the beautiful melancholy words, from hoarse stormy shores and primeval forest to green hills and remembered fertile plains far away, making them into the first message that an Irish exile, the first of many thousands, was to send across the broad Atlantic.

Douglas Hyde, though, to whose authority we all must bow, holds that the poem was apparently written on the continent of Europe, and goes on to say about the poet: 'He led a ranting, roving wild life, changed his religion a couple of times with unparalleled effrontery, but becoming blind in his old age, he repented of his sins and his misspent life and died some time about the beginning of the nineteenth century.' That ranting, roving life and its long dark aftermath gave the late Francis MacManus the matter for his fine trilogy of novels, *Stand and Give Challenge*, *Candle for the Proud*, and *Men Withering*: perhaps the best study written of a Gaelic poet and his background.

It is significant that Donncha's longest poem 'Eachta Ghiolla an Amaráin' is a sort of mock Aeneid, a wandering poem, telling of his voyage to America and how his ship was chased by a French cruiser, of his voyage to the other world and how, quite aptly, he found there Conán the Bald, the mocker out of the Fiannaíocht, doing the job of Charon, the Ferryman. Yet his greatest poem and certainly the one by which he has been, is, and will be most remembered is 'Bánchnuic Éireann Ó!':

Beir beannacht óm chroí go tír na
  h-Éireann,
   Bán-chnuic Éireann Ó!
Chun a maireann de shíolra Ír is Éibhir
  Ar bhán-chnuic Éireann Ó!

Take a blessing from my heart
  to the land of my birth,
   And the fair hills of Éire O!
And to all that survive of
  Éibhear's tribe on earth
   On the fair hills of Éire O!

An áit úd 'n-ar bh'aoibhinn binn-ghuth éan *Mar shámh-chruit chaoin a' caoine Gaodhal;* *'Sé mo chás bheith míle míl' i gcéin* *Ó bhán-chnuic Éireann Ó!*	In that land so delightful the wild thrush's lay Seems to pour a lament forth for Éire's decay; Alas! alas! why pine I a thousand miles away From the fair hills of Éire O!

Bionn barr bog slím ar chaoin-chnuic Éireann, *Bán-chnuic Éireann Ó!* *'S is fearr ná'n tír seo díogha gach sléibh' ann,* *Bán-chnuic Éireann Ó!* *Dob árd a coillte 's ba dhíreach réidh,* *'S a mbláth mar aol ar mhaoilinn géag,* *Tá grá am chroí im inntinn féin* *Do bhán-chnuic Éireann Ó!*	The soil is rich and soft, the air is mild and bland Of the fair hills of Éire O! Her barest rock is greener to me than this rude land – O! the fair hills of Éire O! Her woods are tall and straight, grove rising over grove, Trees flourish in her glens below and on her heights above. O! in heart and in soul I shall ever, ever love The fair hills of Éire O!

Is osgailte fáilteach an áit sin Éire, *Bán-chnuic Éireann Ó!* *'Gus tora na sláinte i mbarr na déise* *I mbán-chnuic Éireann Ó!* *Ba bhinne ná méar' ar théadaibh ceóil* *Seinm is géimre a laogh 's a mbó* *Agus taithneamh na gréine orra, aosda 's óg,* *Ar bhán-chnuic Éireann Ó!*	A fruitful clime is Éire's, through valley, meadow, plain, And the fair hills of Éire O! The very bread of life is in the yellow grain On the fair hills of Éire O! Far dearer unto me than the tones music yields Is the lowing of the kine and the calves in her fields, And the sunlight that shone long ago on Gaelic shields On the fair hills of Éire O!

With all respect to the translator, James Clarence Mangan, his refrain 'On the fair hills of Éire O!' does not appeal to me; better 'the fair hills of Ireland'. Donncha has not been, of Gaelic poets, the best served by his translators or interpreters.

I want to go back now a century and a half before that song was made, to Seathrún Céitinn, saluting Ireland from Bordeaux. Aodh de Blacam in *Gaelic Literature Surveyed* links this masterpiece of syllabic verse with our early and medieval poetry, and writes of the magic of its vision.

Mo bheannacht leat a scríbhinn
Go hInis aoibhinn Ealga –
'S truagh nach léir damh a beanna,
Gidh gnáth a dteanna dearga.

My blessing with you, my
   writing
to pleasant Inis Ealga
I would I saw her mountains
though often red with beacons.

Slán dá huaisle as dá hoireacht
Slán go rói-bheacht dá cléirchibh:
Slán dá bantrachtaibh caoine,
Slán dá saoithibh re héigse.

Hail to her nobles, her councils:
hail all hail, to her clerics:
hail to her gentle women:
hail to her poets and scholars.

Mo shlán dá maghaibh míne
Slán fá mhíle dá chnocaibh,
Mochean dón tí tá innti
Slán d'á linntibh 's dá lochaibh.

Hail to her level places
and a thousand times to her
   hillsides:
oh, lucky he that dwells there,
hail to her lochs and waters.

Slán dá coilltibh fá thorthaibh,
Slán fós dá corthaibh iascaigh,
Slán dá móintibh 's dá bántaibh,
Slán dá ráthaibh 's dá ríoscaibh.

Hail to her heavy forests,
hail likewise to her fish-weirs:
hail to her moors and meadows:
hail to her raths and marshes.

Slán óm chroí dá cuantaibh
Slan fós dá tuarthaibh troma,
Soraidh dá tulchaibh aonaigh,
Slán uaim dá craobhaibh croma.

Hail from my heart to her
   harbours,
hail, too, to her fruitful
   drylands:
luck to her hilltop hostings:
hail to her bending branches.
O writing, my blessing.

Gidh gnáth a fóirne fraochda
In inis Inaofa neambocht,
Siar tar dromchladh na díleann
Beir, a scríbheann, mo bheannacht.

Though often strive the peoples
in that wealthy holy island –
westward over the surging flood
bear, O writing, my blessing.

Through that poem de Blacam found it possible to look back to an early nature poetry whose 'peculiar and magic virtue' was to concentrate within a lyric 'a vision of a spacious region. We are given an image of Alba or of Eire as the Creator (we think) might see it; or as some hunter who had ranged all its hills might imagine it in peaceful memory at life's end.'

In an Ossianic poem, for instance, describing the reveries on the life of the warrior running through the mind of Fionn, places are mentioned as far apart as Assaroe on the Erne, and Slieve Gua in the Decies, Slemish in Antrim and Erris in Mayo:

> It was a desire of the son of Cumhall to listen to the sound of the wind in the trees at Drumderg, to sleep to the sound of the current at Assaroe, and to hunt in Feeguile of the wolf-litters.

> The warbling of the blackbird of Letterlee, the wave of Rury beating on the strand, the belling of the stag from the plain of Maev, the crying of the fawn from Glendamale.

> The thunder of the chase in Slieve Crot, the sound of the deer on Slievegua, the whistle of the seagulls beyond in Erris, the rushing of the three streams by Slemish . . .

Places so loved, names so often repeated as if they were charms and words of power and invocations of the very spirit of place, gathered about them their own sanctities and mythological significance. That other Amergin, not he who might have been a demigod, but an Amergin Mac Amhalgaidh – who was, it seems, poet in the sixth century to a King, Diarmuid Mac Cearbhaill – was much affected by that mysticism and mythology of place. To him is attributed the completion, from earlier oral sources it is to be supposed, of the *dinnseanchas* or Lore of Famous Places already referred to. Each place-name had its root in a dim pagan past, and Douglas Hyde said of the work: 'The oldest copy is in the Book of Leinster and treats of nearly two hundred places and contains eighty-eight poems.' The copy of the Book of Ballymote contains one hundred and thirty-nine place-names – and that in the Book of Leccan even more. The total number of all the poems contained in the different copies is close on one hundred and seventy.

As one thinks of the assiduity of the bard fourteen centuries ago, and of the coloured imagination of the people whose legends he compiled, it is interesting also to look at a great work of scholarship of our own time: *The Festival of Lughnasa* by Máire Mac Néill, in which the learned author considers the lore and traditions connected with places all over Ireland, where for centuries the people of this island celebrated the Celtic festival of the first fruits of harvest, the rebirth of Lugh the god of light, the downfall of the dark evil god, Balor or the Evil Eye or Crom Dubh; and how survivals of such ancient customs lingered on in those places right into our own time. It is a book that leads one into a world of high imagination and symbol and, taking a wide view of her subject, Máire Mac Néill writes:

> To know that every year it had been the custom of our ancestors to assemble on these hills in festivity and high spirits, to look out over the plains and pick out the landmarks, is to understand better Irish history, our passion for the wide land, for the itinerary literature which was one of our predilections. Those gatherings, too, must have played a part in keeping place-mythology alive.
>
> Generation after generation, our country people met once a year at this festival on the hills, made the customary rounds (on what used to be called Garland Sunday) picked bilberries and wild flowers, danced, played, and fell in love, raced and wrestled, competed in tests of strength and agility, joined in the routine fights, met old friends and exchanged news, heard old stories from the elders and grew to know the landmarks. They upheld the custom until they became its recorders.

They grew also to know and to preserve the legends, and the poets among them wrote of the places, either of that first, best country that ever is at home or, by way of contrast, to boast – in what Máire Mac Néill so well describes as the 'itinerary literature which was one of our predilections' – of the places they had seen in their travels.

A field's distance from a man's own cabin wonders might begin, and Brian Merriman drinking in the wine of the air of County Clare could walk into the court of the faery queen, or the sky-woman appear to talk of love – love between men and women, or love of the land they walked on. And stepping by the faery fort of Bruff in the Maigue Valley more than two hundred years ago, Brian O'Flaherty thought the thoughts that he put into these Irish words and which

James Clarence Mangan translated:

Lá meidhreach dá ndeaghas-sa liom féin
Ar bhinnlisín aerach an Bhrogha,
Ag éisteacht le binnghuth na n-éan
Ag cantain ar ghéaga cois abhann.

The birds carolled songs of
delight
And the flowers bloomed bright
on my path
As I stood all alone on the
height
Where rises Bruff's old faery
rath.

An breac taibhseach san linn úd faoi
réim,
Ag rinnce san ngaortha le fonn,
Más tinn libhse radharc cluas ná béal,
Tá leigheas luath ón éag daoibh dul
ann.

Before me unstirred by the wind
The beautiful lake lay outspread
Whose waters give sight to the
blind
And would almost awaken the
dead.

Níor chian dúinn cois diantsrúill na
séad,
'Nar mhian le fir Éireann dul ann,
An tráth thriall chugainn an
ghrianmhilis-bhé,
Go dian 's í in éagchruth go lom.

As I gazed on the silvery stream
So loved by the heroes of old
There neared me as though in a
dream
A maiden with tresses of gold.

A ciabhfholt breá niamhrach go féar,
Ag fás léise roimpi 's na deaghaidh:
'A Bhriain dhil créad é an dianghol so
ghniír?'
Do chéas mé go haeibh os mo chionn.

I wept but she smilingly said:
'Whence Brian, my dearest,
these tears?'
And the words of the
gentle-souled maid
Seemed to pierce through my
bosom like spears.

To mention even one significant place-name could, and still can, invoke an entire civilization. Repeat, to this day, the name of Kilcash in Murphy's pub in Grangemockler and the reaction of the country people will show you that something special has happened – so great a glory does the song still confer. Climb up the lower slopes of Slievenamon, in itself a magic name, and the wind in drying autumn beeches still laments the passing of the glory of the Butlers:

Cad a dhéanfaimid feasta gan adhmad?	What shall we do without timber
Tá deireadh na gcoillte ar lár,	The last of the woods are down.
Níl trácht ar Chill Chais ná a teaghlach	Kilcash and all of its people
Is ní cluinfear a cling go bráth.	And the bell of the house are gone.
An áit úd 'na gcónaíodh an deighbhean	The spot where that lady waited
Fuair gradam is meidhir thar mná	Who shamed all women for grace
Bhíodh iarlaí ag tarraint thar toinn ann	When earls came sailing to greet her
Is an tAifreann doimhin á rá.	And Mass was said in the place.

In the West a hundred and fifty years ago the blind poet Anthony Raftery brought fame to many places but immortality to two: Ballylee in Galway for the rural Helen who lived there, and Killaden in Mayo his own birthplace:

Anois teacht an Earraigh beidh an lá dul 'un síneadh	Now, with the coming in of the spring, the days will stretch a bit;
Is tar éis na Féil' Bríde ardóidh mé mo sheol,	And after the Feast of Brigid I shall hoist my flag and go:
Ó chuir mé im cheann é ni stopfaidh mé choíche	For, since the thought got into my head, I can neither stand nor sit
Go seasfaidh mé síos i lár Chontae Mhuigheo.	Until I find myself in the middle of the County of Mayo.
I gClár Cloinne Muiris bheas me an chéad oíche,	In Claremorris I should stop a night to sleep with decent men;
Is i mBalla taobh thíos de thosós mé ag ól,	And then I'd go to Balla, just beyond, and drink galore;
Go Coillte Mach rachaidh mé go ndéana mé cuairt míosa ann	And next I'd stay in Kiltimagh for about a month; and then
I bhfoisceacht dhá mhíle do Bhéal an Átha Mhóir.	I should only be a couple of miles away from Ballymore!

Ó fágaim le huacht é go n-éiríonn mo
  chroíse
Mar éiríonn an ghaoth nó mar
  scaipeann an ceo
Ag smaoineamh ar Chearra is ar
  Ghaillean taobh thíos dhó
Ar Sceathach a'Mhíle is ar Phlandaí
  Mhuigheo.

Cill Aodáin an baile a bhfásann gach
  ní ann,
Ta an sméar 's an sú-chraobh ann is
  meas ar gach sórt,
Is dá mbeinnse im sheasamh i gceartlár
  mo dhaoine
D'imeodh an aois díom is bheinn arís
  óg.

I say and swear that my heart
  lifts up like the lifting of a
  tide;
Rising up like the rising wind till
  fog or mist must go,
When I remember Carra, and
  Gallen close beside,
And the Gap of the Two Bushes,
  and the wide plains of Mayo.

To Killaden then, to the place
  where everything grows that
  is best;
There are raspberries there, and
  strawberries there, and all
  that is good for men;
And were I only there, among
  my folk, my heart would
  rest,
For age itself would leave me
  there, and I'd be young again.

One of the most curious samples of that itinerary literature that was our predilection comes from my own county of Tyrone: the 'Seachrán Chairn tSiadhail' – the Carnteel Wanderer. Carnteel is a spot on the road between Aughnacloy and Benburb and the poet saw there his vision on a bright morning and set off for twenty-eight verses, in an almost intoxicated celebration of the place-names of Ireland.

It was a mode that passed on to popular balladry in English, to roam through Roosia and likewise Proosia and sweet Kilkenny and distant Spain, and to return in the end to that first, best country and to see the smoke rising above your own rooftree:

Bím go haerach ar mhalaidh sléibhe
Ag déanamh véarsaí 's ag ceartú ceoil,
Seal ag pléideáil le mná ar aontaí
'Gus seal ag bréagadh na gcailín óg;

Sometimes I'm strolling on a
  hillside lonely
Making poetry and melodious
  sound,
Or on a fair day with the pretty
  ladies
Making hay while the sun shines
  down:

Seal 'mo úcaire, seal 'mo mhéire,
'Mo bhuachaill spéiriúil i dtoigh an óil,
Seal mo' thunnadóir ag cartú léabthach
Eadar an Éirne 'gus an Mullach Mór.

Bhí me ar an Mhuine Mhór 's i
    gCaisleán Cába,
I mBaile Uí Dhálaigh is i Lios na
    Sgiath,
Bhí mé i Muineachán 'gus ar an
    Ghráinsigh
Is ag Droichead Chúil Áine le corradh
    is bliain.
'Réir a tharla i nDroichead Átha mé
Is anocht atá mé fá Charn tSiail:
Is anois más roghain leat ar fheara Fáil
    me
Seo mo lámh duit – bíom ag triall.

My trades are many to turn a
    penny
I'd drink with any when the
    bottles pour;
I'd tan a hide and spend the prize
From Erne's river down to
    Mullaghmore:

From Moneymore to Castlecabe
From Ballydaly to Lisnaskee –
From Monaghan town to
    Grange's boundaries
And Coolaney bridge, I've
    walked a year
Last night I happened to be in
    Drogheda
And now to-night I'm in
    Carnteel
So then my darling if it's me
    you'd rather
We'll seal the bargain and make
    all speed.

By way of footnote: About my own hometown there is, as far as I know, no song in Irish. But some unknown balladeer did the needful in English in a song that will serve very well as epilogue:

From sweet Dungannon to
    Ballyshannon,
From Cullyhanna to old Ardboe,
I've roamed and rambled,
    caroused and gambled,
Where songs did thunder and
    whiskey flow.
It's light and airy I've tramped
    through Derry
And to Portaferry in the County
    Down:
But with all my raking and
    undertaking
My heart was aching for sweet
    Omey town.

Cosslett Ó Cuinn
Merriman's Court

'Cúirt an Mheán Oíche' does not mean 'courting at midnight' as is said to have been assumed by whoever was responsible for refusing permission to erect a monument to Brian Merriman in Feakle graveyard in 1947. Just so, in 1957, the Archbishop refused to let the body of Nikos Kazantzakis lie in state in an Athenian Church. He, among a lot of other things, had written a sequel to Homer's *Odyssey* in a very countrified dialect of spoken Greek. There were so many words, collected from farmers and fishermen, and unintelligible to the urban lumpen-intelligentsia, that he had to provide a new dictionary. Again, the idylls of Theocritus were written not in Attic or Koine Greek but in a difficult Doric dialect. Peasant Literature? Yes, but with a very ancient and living tradition behind it, both written and oral. And in these respects those two great masterpieces, two thousand years apart, were very similar to the Midnight law-court, or rather judicial enquiry with royalty on the bench; the word 'Cúirt' can suggest that, and maybe also remind you of the proverb 'If you go to a court or a castle, have a woman on your side'.

The author, Brian Merriman, was born about the year 1749 at Ennistimon, County Clare, the son of a travelling mason, who moved to Feakle some miles away. There Brian grew up, and taught for about twenty years (c. 1765–85) in a 'hedge-school', one of the clandestine rural academies of the Hidden Ireland. He had a little land, which he farmed successfully enough to win two prizes for flax crops from the (Royal) Dublin Society in 1797. He married a woman from the parish (c. 1787), and had two daughters, and the family moved to Limerick. There, after two or three years, he died in 1805. He was described in the press notices as 'Teacher of mathematics, etc.', as could also have been said of Lewis Carroll . . .

Seven years before his marriage, in 1780, Merriman had written his brief epic of 1026 lines. It circulated orally, and in copious manuscripts, and achieved a wide popularity, but was not printed till 1850. In 1905 Stern's edition, with German translation, introduced it to scholars all over Europe. Since then, English translations have been published by Percy Arland Ussher, the late Lord (Edward) Longford, Frank O'Connor, David Marcus, Patrick Power, and (in part) Brendan Behan. I am venturing to use a translation of my own in this essay: quotations from the original are taken from the revised text prepared by the late David Greene which was, until very recently, the best available (it has now been superseded by a definitive edition, the work of Liam Ó Murchú).

I also rely heavily on the research and judgement of Seán Ó Tuama. He has a fine passage on Merriman's *líofacht dhochreidte*, that incredible speed and gusto, that rolls along like a tidal wave, and yet is kept in control by the rider as if a stallion. But why does he find fault with Merriman for not being like Rabelais or Aristophanes? Why ask *poitín* to be like absinthe or ouzo? Abstract things, like 'deep personal insights' and 'criticisms of life' are found in books *about* writers. Let me be shockingly concrete: I have struggled with the difficult old-fashioned French of Rabelais, chosen fifty years ago as a Christmas present from a maiden aunt, and I'd suggest that the Abbey of Theleme, that co-educational College for students of both sexes with its motto 'Do as you like', is akin to Merriman. As for Aristophanes, he was a conservative, hankering for the pre-war *status quo*. He never tried to understand progressives like Euripides and Socrates, and poured out a lot of jeering propaganda against them which probably contributed to Socrates' fate. His plays were part of a pagan fertility rite in which bawdiness was a religious duty, but they contain some good fun and exquisite poetry. The 'New learning' advocated by Rabelais meant the study of those ancient classics. To Calvin, whose French is much more clear and lucid, it meant the study of the Greek New Testament. Satirists and Bishops are often better at looking back, and telling us what is wrong with the world. That's their job – but they must *not* try to quench the spirit, or silence the prophets. T. S. Eliot has well said that poetry is great through the width and precision of its expression of emotion, not through its intellectual framework.

Seán Ó Tuama shows that there are hardly any ideas (including the abolition of celibacy and marriage!) that were not discussed in the Courts of Love and associated literature between the thirteenth and sixteenth centuries. Merriman takes up these abstract themes and puts life and passion into them, as well as a certain bawdy humour, altogether in a medieval sort of way, not unlike Ariosto. He could do so in the Irish-speaking world; itself, in good as well as bad ways, a mainly oral tradition from still earlier times. The prologue to his 'Court' will be not unfamiliar to those who have read Chaucer or Langland.

The poet sets off on his favourite walk on a July day – surely barefoot:

> *Ba ghnáth mé ag siúl le ciumhais na habhann*
> *Ar bháinseach úr is an drúcht go trom . . .*

> I choose the river path, where feet
> In dewy grasses cool their heat.
> Through a tree-fledged glen I edge my way
> Made by the daylight brisk and gay.
> Then my heart brightens into eyes
> That see to where Lough Gréine lies.
> Earth, land, and circumambient air
> Are mirrored in its waters fair.
> What a formidable beauty show
> The mountain ranges, row on row,
> Purple above, and green below!
> The dry heart would grow bright again,
> Long feelingless, or filled with pain,
> One pauperized and penniless
> Would cease to feel his bitterness
> If he took time to stop and stare
> Over the green treetops to where
> The awkward squads of ducks look queer
> Upon the mistless water clear,

As, slipping through their midst,
      a swan
Leads them majestically on.
Fish, full of fun, jump one perch
      high,
Their speckled bellies catch my
      eye.
Lake waters sport upon the
      shore,
Raising a great gay blue-waved
      roar.
On merry boughs the loud birds
      sing,
Near me the deer mid green
      shaws spring,
The huntsman's horn with
      merry sounds
Calls me to see the fox and
      hounds.
Yes, yestermorn did not betray
Dawn's promise of a cloudless
      day,
And Cancer topically let fly
One tropic day in late July;
Fresh from night's rest, the sun
      could play
At work, and burn all in its
      way,
But did not strike and had not
      found me
Where treeleaves wrapped the
      green flag round me.

Then he finds a shady ditch amid the green growths, and sinks to sleep and dream. Amid an electric storm a huge Brobdignagian policewoman arrests him as a vagabond bachelor. She talks of oppression and misgovernment and declining population (although it can be shown that the rural proletariat was rapidly increasing in numbers at the time). She hauls him off to the Fairy Palace of Magh Gréine, where Aoibheall of Craigléith, Queen of the Munster *Sídhe* (faery otherworld) is holding a Judicial Enquiry into the state of the country. The first witness is a *Cailín Domhnaigh* ('Sunday Girl') –

always well dressed to attract men, yet always outdistanced by fat, ugly or smelly girls with dowries:

> *Táim in achrann daingean na*
> *mblianta*
> *Ag tarraing go tréan ar na laethaibh*
> *liatha*

> The years have crept up, held,
> and caught me
> And gripped me fast: till day by
> day
> I wither and grow old and grey.
> I've not had one proposal: I
> Lose hope of more before I die.
> Let me to no dim spinster fade
> Nor be a meaningless old maid
> Without her man to give
> protection
> Or child or friend to lend
> affection
> Huddled beside the fire, now
> grown
> Unused to vistors, alone.

There is some real pathos there, over a subject usually a butt for raucous humour. But now the rebuttal: an old wheezy man staggers to his feet and rage fires him to a vigorous attack:

> *Is furas, dar liom, do chúl bheith*
> *taibhseach*
> *Chonac lem shúile an chúl 'na*
> *loigheann tú . . .*

> Your hair-dos do show easy
> grace
> And many make-ups give you
> face,
> But don't you air that high horse
> head

For I've seen where you make
    your bed;
No sheet, not even one coarse
    spun thread
Of blanket, quilt or coverlet,
Only a tattered mattress set
Upon the floor, full of your wet,
In a dark filthy cabin where
There is no stool, bench, seat or
    chair;
The water oozes from the
    ground
And trickles down the walls all
    round.
Though weeds grow thick in
    rotting thatch
Full of the paths that lean hens
    scratch,
Though couples sag and ridge
    holes slip
And rafters have begun to dip,
The roof's still up to drop and
    drip.
Or if a rainstorm comes, to
    drown
All in a torrent of dark brown.

Where, he asks, did the girl get her finery? And answers himself: she got it for love. *He* married a similar young lady, who too speedily presented him with a fine healthy boy. So why not abolish marriage? It would save money, and remedy the depopulation, and all children would be equally legitimate or illegitimate, as among the animals. And here, like Shakespeare in *King Lear*, he gives vent to praise of bastards (in the old sense of the word). But the girl counter-attacks:

Oh it's easy to talk for old lepers
    like you
Of the woman you've never yet
    gone into:

That subject needs somebody
    strong and firm
And you are an old limp
    boneless worm . . .
If that modest matron's
    desperate need
Led to escapades, then her case I
    plead:
Is there fox on the hill, is there
    fish by the shore,
Are there eagles that sweep on
    their prey and soar
Or hinds that are blithe when
    the stags get gay,
That would go for a year or a
    single day
Without snatching pasture or
    catching prey:
'Twould be unnaturally absurd
For any animal or bird . . .

In the Irish the words are really winged, shooting out in parabolas in
all directions like tracer bullets.

An bhfuil sionnach ar sliabh, ná iasc i
    dtrá,
Ná fiolar le fiach, ná fia le fán,
Chomh fada gan chiall le bliain ná lá
A chaitheamh gan bia, 's a bhfiach le
    fáil.

Notice the metre, with the double assonance *ia/ia* in the middle, and
the vowel rhyme in *á* at the end of the line; it's much easier in Irish
than in English to find the 'good bad rhyme' Yeats looked for. And
Merriman varies not only the rhythm, but the weight and texture of
his verses – 'making the sound echo the sense'. A vaguer, more
questioning rhythm leads on to another still relevant problem – not
yet fully solved:

*Is mithid dom chroí bheith líonta ' e
léithe
Is m'iongántas tríd gach smaointe
baotha
Cad do bheir scaoilte ó chuíbhreach
céile
In Eaglais sínsir suim na cléire . . .*

My head has hairs now turning
grey
Wondering through wandering
thoughts away,
The object of my fond research
Is in my old ancestral Church:
Why are its clergy woman-free
And given to celibacy? . . .
Some we'll do without, who'd
require
Castrati from the papal choir,
Insects whose business is to ail,
Colts who know only how to
stale!
But how can men whose
manliest part
Could drive its nail straight in
with art
Go idling off to dream and *Roam*
And shirk the work there is at
home . . .
Their praise I've often heard,
none mocks
But lauds such fathers of their
flocks . . .
We've seen good fruits too of
their games
In children bearing borrowed
names . . .

If Merriman was one of *these* – not just illegitimate as Seán Ó Tuama
has suggested, but if his father was in fact a Roman Catholic priest –
it explains the mixture of indulgence and indignation and passion
with which he dwells on these matters.

Aoibheall takes up the subject with a final prophecy of a Papal decision:

> Keep silent if you can't agree
> Don't contradict the Hierarchy
> Leave them since they're so
>   sensitive
> In that past age in which they
>   live
> Yet married men they still shall
>   be
> Whoever lives long enough to
>   see:
> Those red hot pokers go on duty
> To soothe the soft desires of
>   beauty.

As President of the Court, Aoibheall is a flop, a mere *chair-person* who sums up what others have already stated. But she enacts some Draconian legislation. Old bachelors to be liquidated – with torture:

> Let me see agonies and groans
> Before you kill the old spent
>   drones!

Young ones, beginning with Merriman, to be stripped and scourged (giving a chance of amendment of life) by the ladies present!

> That babe who hated
>   spinsterhood
> Clenched her two fists as there
>   she stood
> Like one who's on to something
>   good:
> And then she jumped her own
>   full height
> Crying in rapturous delight
> I've got the object of my lust.
> How long I've longed you stale
>   old crust

> To have that seat of yours to
>   dust . . .
> You lazy slob, make no pretence
> To try to put up a defence.
> What woman witness will
>   advance
> Due proof of work as a free
>   lance?
> What good have you done in
>   your life?
> Show you've consoled one
>   lonely wife!
> With your permission I present
> Him, Maiden Ma'am Right
>   Reverent
> For medical examination
> Strip quick . . . commence the
>   operation . . .

There follows a portrait of the poet himself – unflattering at first, but admitting certain social qualities. Is it a self-portrait – or a wry acknowledgement of what Merriman assumed to be the popular view of him? We can only speculate.

> He's palely puffy for a man
> I for my part prefer suntan
> He isn't married yet we see,
> Owing to some foul deformity
> He hides with much dexterity,
> – See how the cross slob scowls
>   at me –
> Which still, 't would seem has
>   left him free
> To enter high society
> A music maker and a sporter
> He's popular in every quarter
> Drinking, gambling without
>   cessation
> With cultured men of education
> And all his friends stand high in
>   station
> – But if I had him as a spouse

I'd tame and I'd house-train that
  louse –
And I can give full proof that he
Is of th'extremest villainy
Merriman is this scoundrel's
  name
Yet he's impressive all the same
And pleasant too when that's his
  aim
His solid qualities can claim
Profits for others from his fame
And merry witty airy game.

And now they set to execute the sentence –

Bind his hands, Máire, behind
  his back
Let Maeve and Muirinn join the
  pack,
Sheila and Saiv the rope's end
  crack:
Come carry out with many a
  whack
The penalty our Queen
  prescribes –
Let every cord cut separate
  kibes,
Let the big pink pig squeal
  afresh,
Each time they sink deep in his
  flesh,
Lavish all torments you can find
And don't spare Brian's big
  behind . . .
Cut deep, and pay him all we
  owe
Flay off his skin from top to toe
Round Ireland let the echoes go
Let all the bachelor hearts know
And tremble where they're lying
  low.

A believer in healthy sexual fertility, he very properly denounced mass-produced celibacy, but was a bit blind to the vocation and grace that can make virginity fruitful – the 'ideal of our Lady'.

But let him have the last word, and testify to the Faith that was in him, as in an extraordinary passage he calls on Aoibheall of the *Sídhe*, as an immortal who has been an eyewitness of the incarnation:

> Pearl, to whose perfect memory
> The Great Event's contemporary
> The Heavenly vision present
> sight
> The History a mystery of light:
> Set that eternal music free
> Let words declare that victory.
> O let the Lamb damn lies and
> say
> Out truths that cannot pass away
> It was no spinster made God
> human
> God's mother was a married
> woman,
> He through his prophets rules
> what's good
> And highly favours
> womanhood.
> *Dia nárbh áil leis Máthair aonta*
> *Is riail gach fáidhe i bhfábhar*
> *béithe . . .*

So while they thus gloat gleefully over this poor victim, the secretary inscribes the date of the decree – 1780 –

> Slow she wrote the slow date,
> the Guard
> Sat and watched me, their eyes
> were hard:
> Then torment ends, the storm
> clouds break.
> I jump up, rub my eyes and
> wake!

And so it ends. Seven years later, as we have noted, Merriman married, and I'm sure was a good husband and father. That one wild prophetic outburst preserved, and also expressed, the sanity of an orthodox yet liberal traditionalist.

He could not claim the 'intellectual power of light-giving imagination' of major poets like Shakespeare or Aeschylus or Dante; but Dante shows some of Merriman's type of humour when Virgil and he are 'protected' by a bodyguard of ten devils marching along to music furnished by their leader's behind (so like some of our self-approved protectors today!), and again Beatrice in Paradise talks to him as a mother does to a cracked child. Dante, according to Boccaccio, suffered from *lussuria* in his maturer as well as his younger years, and played with fire in the form of a romantic passion for another man's wife, so as to produce the most sublime of all jokes – the Divine Comedy. Merriman played with a more fleshly fire of *drúis* (which is the Irish brand of *lussuria*) by socializing rather than sublimating it. It taught both of them humility, and a power to poke fun at themselves, that is rare among poets. So I would suggest that the 'Midnight Court' is such a *kathartic* – smelly as it ought to be: not porn, but anti-porn – a sort of karate in which the attacker is allowed full momentum so that he may knock himself out.

An chuid acu tá go táir 'na smaointe
Foireann nach foláir leo a gcáil
bheith sínte . . .

Some think, whose minds are
    cruel and base,
They'll find distinction in
    disgrace,
Drop names of ladies whom
    they woo,
The public get a private view
Of everything they say they do.
They find it pleasant to act thus,
They even term it chivalrous.
Even she who has denied a
    favour
Will find denials cannot save her.
They've thus corrupted and
    betrayed

Many a chaste matron and
   young maid.
Yet it was not concupiscence
That was the cause of their
   offence,
Or heat of blood, or lust intense,
Or pleasure in the joys of sense,
Or a priapism too immense –
They want a noisy audience
That roars and gloats and licks
   its chaps,
They well deserve to get the
   claps.
At some no women set their
   caps,
Hundreds have never felt at all
The pleasure of their sex's call
Their manliness is just a loud
And empty boast before a
   crowd,
Incapable of any action
Which is to women's
   satisfaction,
Destructive female rage must
   follow,
Abolishing deceits so hollow.

Seán Ó Tuama
Seán Ó Ríordáin

The generation of poets writing in Irish after the war (1939–45) was possibly the first since the seventeenth century to be in touch quite naturally with contemporary work in other countries. Seán Ó Ríordáin, more than any other of these poets, was in the classic European tradition. In his work, he stamped a unique Irish personality on a West-European mood and metaphysic which had been making themselves felt since the time of Baudelaire. While the influence of Eliot and Hopkins is to be discerned in his early verse, one cannot say that any one modern poet left a lasting impact on him – least of all Yeats and the Anglo-Irish school. His great achievement is the manner in which he has married a modern sensibility to the rich Gaelic literary tradition.

About the year 1945, the poetry of Seán Ó Ríordáin began to be noticed. In that year, at the age of twenty-eight, he published his poem 'Adhlacadh mo Mháthar' ('My Mother's Burial'). The verse he wrote before this was interesting – but undistinguished. His mother's death is crucial then to his poetic development: it seems to have helped him to overcome the linguistic and psychological difficulties which had previously hindered his writing. The rich talent now released combined Irish and European features in a new and surprising way.

'Adhlacadh mo Mháthar' did in fact surprise, and even astonish, those whose reading had hitherto been confined to traditional literature in Irish. They were straight away in a territory of the imagination which poetry in Irish had not previously entered. The effect was sometimes akin to reading modern English poetry in an Irish translation:

Grian an Mheithimh in úllghort,
Is siosarnach i síoda an tráthnóna,
Beach mhallaithe ag portaireacht
mar screadstracadh ar an nóinbhrat.

A June sun in an orchard,
A rustle in the silk of afternoon,
The droning of an ill-natured
    bee
Loudly ripping the film of
    evening.

Despite a certain lack of mastery apparent now and then in the poem, and despite an over-obvious intrusion of English influences, 'Adhlacadh mo Mháthar' still stands as a unique poetic achievement: it is the first work in Irish where modern imagistic techniques are used – and fused – with a traditional storytelling or dramatic voice. The fusion is especially successful in those verses where the poet thinks back on his relationship with his mother in tones of unabashed tenderness. The English translation is by Valentin Iremonger.

Do chuimhníos ar an láimh a dhein an
    scríbhinn,
Lámh a bhí inaitheanta mar aghaidh,
Lámh a thál riamh cneastacht
    seana-Bhíobla,
Lámh a bhí mar bhalsam is tú tinn.

I remember the hand that did the
    writing
A hand as familiar as a face,
A hand that dispensed kindness
    like an old Bible,
A hand that was like the balsam
    and you ill.

Agus thit an Meitheamh siar insteach
    sa Sheimhreadh,
Den úllghort deineadh reilig bhán cois
    abhann,
Is i lár na balbh-bháine i mo thimpeall
Do liúigh os ard sa tsneachta an
    dúpholl.

And June toppled backwards
    into Winter,
The orchard became a white
    graveyard by a river,
In the midst of the dumb
    whiteness all around me,
The dark hole screamed loudly
    in the snow.

Gile gearrachaile lá a céad chomaoine,
Gile abhlainne Dé Domhnaigh ar
    altóir,
Gile bainne ag sreangtheitheadh as na
    cíochaibh,
Nuair a chuireadar mo mháthair, gile
    an fhóid.

The white of a young girl the
    day of her First Communion,
The white of the holy wafer
    Sunday on the altar
The white of milk slowly issuing
    from the breasts:
When they buried my mother –
    the white of the sward.

Bhí m'aigne á sciúirseadh féin ag
    iarraidh
An t-adhlacadh a bhlaiseadh go
    hiomlán,
Nuair a d'eitil tríd an gciúnas bán go
    míonla
Spideog a bhí gan mhearbhall gan
    scáth:

My mind was screwing itself
    endeavouring,
To comprehend the interment to
    the full
When through the white
    tranquillity gently flew
A robin, unconfused and
    unafraid.

Agus d'fhan os cionn na huaighe fé mar go mb'eol di	It waited over the grave as though it knew
Go raibh an toisc a thug í ceilte ar chách	That the reason why it came was unknown to all
Ach an té.a bhí ag feitheamh ins an gcomhrainn,	Save the person who was waiting in the coffin
Is do rinneas éad fén gcaidreamh neamhghnách.	And I was jealous of the unusual affinity.

Towards the end of the poem the lines occur which gave the title to his first book: '*Ranna beaga bacacha á scríobh agam*, Ba mhaith liom breith ar eireaball spideoige' ('I would like to catch a robin's tail') – here we surely sense he is looking for what is unattainable: the live presence, the affinity, the *stability* of his mother.

The struggle for stability – for some belief (or person) to give meaning to his life – is the focus of all his major work from this time on. Born in the bilingual community of Ballyvourney he had grown up in an unstable cultural environment: the struggle between two languages, two cultures, as experienced in his youth, left an indelible mark on his work. Later, when he moved to near Cork city and worked as a clerk in the local municipality, he encountered (as he himself remarked) Eliot's typical 'hollow men, stuffed men', circulating with the necessary forms and documents in their possession. Their life and thinking was entirely through English, as was most city life. Ó Ríordáin often feels now that Irish is not completely satisfying the needs of his personality. In one poem he speaks of the Irish language he 'carries', being suckled by the foreign 'whore' English.

The foreign 'whore' did, of course, perform a necessary service for him as for all modern writers in Irish: she brought in with her a great slice of the contemporary life – and of the contemporary confusion – which literature in Irish had missed out on in the previous two or three centuries. Post-Christian Europe with its doubts, moods, and attitudes, began to really affect the traditional Irish mind from the mid-forties on. Ó Ríordáin's poetry – no matter how esoteric some of it may appear – is for me the artistic achievement which best represents this turmoil as felt by the 'plain people' of Ireland.

Doubts about religion and morality – as well as chronic bouts of sickness – had begun at an early stage to aggravate Ó Ríordáin's basic feelings of instability. In his long poem 'Cnoc Mellerí' ('Mount Melleray') he struggles with his doubts about Catholic dogma, and its effects on the human personality. Here he begins to shed the awkwardnesses which are noticeable in 'Adhlacadh mo Mháthar'. His exuberant and inventive imagery remains his principal poetic characteristic, but he manages to give everything a more Irish, more homely shape. In this section of 'Cnoc Mellerí' – the positive, sunny section of the poem – the cartoonist side of his imagination is to the fore. The English translation is by Peter Denman.

Sranntarnach na stoirme i Mellerí aréir
Is laethanta an pheaca bhoig mar
    bhreoiteacht ar mo chuimhne,
Laethanta ba leapacha de shonaschlúmh
    an tsaoil
Is dreancaidí na drúise iontu ag
    preabarnaigh ina mílte.

Last night over Melleray the
    storm clouds came snarling
And sin's easy past had my
    memory tumoured: –
Those soft days when life
    bedded down in fine linen
Though the itchings of lust were
    like fleas going through me.

D'éirigh san oíche sidhe gaoithe
    coisceim
Manaigh ag triall ar an Aifreann,
Meidhir, casadh timpeall is rince san
    aer,
Bróga na manach ag cantaireacht.

A windgust of footsteps swept
    up through the dark,
At midnight the monks were
    making for chapel,
Giddiness, twirlings and heels in
    the air,
Oh their sandals were singing
    out happily.

Bráthair sa phroinnteach ag riaradh
    suipéir,
Tost bog ba bhalsam don intinn,
Ainnise naofa in oscailt a bhéil,
Iompar mothaolach Críostaé mhaith.

In the dining-hall supper is
    served by a brother
(Silence applied on the mind like
    a poultice)
And he mouthing phrases holy
    and hollow –
Naïve carry-on of a natural-born
    Christian.

Do doirteadh steall anchruthach gréine
    go mall
Trí mhúnla cruiceogach fuinneoige,

A dollop of sunlight infiltrated
    itself
By means of a humpy-arched
    casement:

Do ghaibh sí cruth manaigh ó bhaitheas go bonn
Is do thosnaigh an ghrian ag léitheoireacht.

Then this same sun, assuming the guise of a monk,
Studiously started perusing some pages.

Leabhar ag an manach bán namhdach á léamh,
Go hobann casachtach an chloig,
Do múchadh an manach bhí déanta de ghréin
Is do scoilteadh an focal 'na phloic.

A book had engrossed this pale alien cleric,
Of a sudden the clock gave a cough,
The monk made of sun was snuffed out in a second,
In mid-sentence his reading cut off.

Ó Ríordáin spent quite a deal of his early manhood in sanatoriums, and, possibly, at that period, once or twice on the point of death. In one early poem 'Oíche Nollaig na mBan' ('Little Christmas Night'), he imagines death as a melodramatic stormy event:

Bhí fuinneamh sa stoirm a éalaigh aréir,
Aréir oíche Nollaig na mBan,
As gealt-teach iargúlta tá laistiar den ré,
Is do scréach tríd an spéir chughainn 'na gealt,
Gur ghíosc geataí comharsan mar ghogallaigh gé,
Gur bhúir abhainn shlaghdánach mar tharbh,
Gur múchadh mo choinneal mar bhuille ar mo bhéal
A las 'na splanc obann an fhearg.

Last night – the Woman's Christmas Night –
From the madhouse behind the moon
There escaped a storm that had Samson's might
As it screamed through the sky like a loon.
The grating gates were gaggling geese,
The river a bronchial bull,
My candle was doused with a splutter of grease
By wind that hit it full.

Ba mhaith liom go dtiocfadh an stoirm sin féin
An oíche go mbeadsa go lag
Ag filleadh abhaile ó rince an tsaoil
Is solas an pheaca ag dul as,

I hope that selfsame storm will come
The night that I am weak,
From the dance of Life returning home
As the light of sin grows bleak,

Go líonfaí gach neomat le liúirigh ón
  spéir,
Go ndéanfaí den domhan scuaine
  scread,
Is ná cloisfinn an ciúnas ag gluaiseacht
  fám dhéin,
Ná inneall an ghluaisteáin ag stad.

That the chilling screams will
  lash like whips
And the crazy cries will drown
Both the sound of the silence as
  through me it slips
And the battery running down.

When he did have a real encounter with death, however, he found
it a matter of no great terror or melodrama: in fact, a rather over-
rated event. He tells us of this experience in his poem 'An Bás'
(which is very reminiscent of some of the work of Emily Dickinson,
the American poet). The English translation is my own.

Bhí an bás lem ais,
D'aontaíos dul
Gan mhoill gan ghol,
Bhíos am fhéinmheas
Le hionadh:
Adúrtsa
'Agus b'shin mise
Go hiomlán,
Mhuise slán
Leat, a dhuine.'

Death stood beside me
I agreed to go
No tears, no cry,
Just analysed
Myself in wonder.
I said
'So that was me,
Whole and entire,
Goodbye brother.'

Ag féachaint siar dom anois
Ar an dtráth
Go dtáinig an bás
Chugham fé dheithneas,
Is go mb'éigean
Domsa géilleadh,
Measaim go dtuigim
Lúcháir béithe
Ag súil le céile,
Cé ná fuilim baineann.

As I look back now
At that time
When death came panting
To take me
And I was forced to yield,
I think I recognize
The ecstasy of a woman
Expecting her lover
– Tho' I'm far from female.

Anyone reading this poem in its entirety would not be in the least
surprised that Ó Ríordáin – having wrestled with his doubts for a
long time – formally reverted to Rome. (He tells us more explicitly
of this in another poem, 'Teitheadh'.) But a poet's deepest feelings

do not always coincide with his philosophy; and some of his later poetry continues to tell us of a poet who cannot find rest or assurance in the institutions, ideas or conventions he has been persuading himself to accept.

His second book – *Brosna* – one of the most distinguished collections of verse ever published in Ireland, is most revealing in this regard. Here on one hand we have a series of poems which tell in philosophic terms of the poet's schizophrenic quest for his real stable immortal self. One of the most graceful of these is 'Fill Arís' where he argues – rather improbably – that his real self can only be realized in the Kerry *Gaeltacht* when he has shaken off the crippling effect of English civility, of Shelley, Keats and Shakespeare:

Fág Gleann na nGealt thoir,
Is a bhfuil d'aois seo ár dTiarna i
    d'fhuil,
Dún d'intinn ar ar tharla
Ó buaileadh Cath Chionn tSáile,
Is ón uair go bhfuil an t-ualach trom
Is an bóthar fada, bain ded mheabhair
Srathar shibhialtacht an Bhéarla,
Shelley, Keats is Shakespeare:
Fill arís ar do chuid,
Nigh d'intinn is nigh
Do theanga a chuaigh ceangailte i
    gcomhréiribh
'Bhí bunoscionn le d'éirim:
Dein d'fhaoistin is dein
Síocháin led ghiniúin féinig
Is led thigh-se féin is na tréig iad,
Ní dual do neach a thigh ná a threabh
    a thréigean.
Téir faobhar na faille siar tráthnona
    gréine go Corca Dhuibhne,
Is chífir thiar ag bun na spéire ag
    ráthaíocht ann
An Uimhir Dhé, is an Modh
    Foshuiteach,
Is an tuiseal gairmeach ar bhéalaibh
    daoine:
Sin é do dhoras,

Dún Chaoin fé sholas an tráthnóna,
Buail is osclófar
D'intinn féin is do chló ceart.

The conversational style here – in particular the resigned quirky tone of 'Goodbye brother' – certainly punctures the authority of death. His acceptance of Death as his lover for eternity similarly punctures the authority of Christ. The sudden darts of nonchalant humour which often appear in Ó Ríordáin's verse at critical moments are usually evidence of his struggle to master the unknown or the authoritarian. It is his puckish defence against chaos.

In his first book – *Eireaball Spideoige* – Ó Ríordáin, exploring his need for stability and at the same time his need for personal freedom, finds both finally only within very set limits, indeed within the bonds of tradition and authority. In his well-known poem 'Saoirse', translated here by Cosslett Ó Cuinn, he tells us how he discovered that freedom was to be found only within servitude; within the bonds of religion, of traditional thought and behaviour:

Rachaidh mé síos i measc na ndaoine
De shiúl mo chos,
Is rachaidh mé síos anocht.

I'll descend mid other men,
Becoming pedestrian again,
Starting tonight.
Give me slavery I beseech,
Free from freedom's frantic
    screech
And my plight.
Let a chain and kennel bound
The packed thoughts that snarl
    around
My solitude.
Organized religion rather,
Temples where the people gather
At set hours.

So I've fallen in love with limits,
With all things with temperance
    in them,
With the derived.
With rule and discipline and
    crowded churches,

With common nouns and well
    worn words and
With stated hours.
With all abbots, bells and
    servants,
With the simile unassertive,
With all shyness,
With mice and the measured, the
    flea and the diminutive,
With chapter and verse, and
    things as simple as
The A B C,
With the drudgery of
    exchanging greetings,
And the penance of card-playing
    evenings,
And exits and entries.
With the farmer guessing at
    what wind
Will blow in harvest with his
    mind
On his field of barley.
With common sense and old
    tradition,
And tact with tiresome
    fellow-Christians,
With the second-hand.
And I declare war now and ever
On freedom's fruits and all
    unfettered
Independence.

On the other hand we also find in *Brosna* a handful of terror-stricken poems – poems of claustrophobia, fever, death, insanity – which are amongst the most memorable achievements of modern Irish literature. In these, as in the best of his poetry generally, one feels storms blowing, lights being quenched, life being strangled – in short, an overwhelming sense of the abyss to which Ó Ríordáin obviously fears he may finally be consigned. Here is 'Claustrophobia', for instance, which shows Ó Ríordáin's constant terror of being suffocated by the malignant forces of darkness:

In aice an fhíona
Tá coinneal is sceon,
Tá dealbh mo Thiarna
D'réir dealraimh gan chomhacht,
Tá a dtiocfaidh den oíche
Mar shluaite sa chlós,
Tá rialtas na hoíche
Lasmuigh den bhfuinneog;
Má mhúchann mo choinneal
Ar ball de m'ainneoin
Léimfidh an oíche
Isteach im scámhóig,
Sárófar m'intinn
Is ceapfar dom sceon,
Déanfar díom oíche,
Bead im dhoircheacht bheo:
Ach má mhaireann mo choinneal
Ach oíche amháin
Bead im phoblacht solais
Go dtiocfaidh an lá.

Two other poems in *Brosna*, for which I have translations, are 'Fiabhras' ('Fever') and 'Reo' ('Frozen'). 'Fiabhras' – printed here with a free English version by Richard Ryan – brings us most perceptively through all the steps of a debilitating fever. The fever is represented as distorting all normal geography, all normal dimensions:

Tá sléibhte na leapa mós ard,
Tá breoiteacht 'na brothall 'na lár,
Is fada an t-aistear urlár,
Is na mílte is na mílte i gcéin
Tá suí agus seasamh sa saol.

The slow climb out of the bed
From the wet heat of its valley
To where its mountains step off
    into nothing . . .
So far to the floor now
Though perhaps, there is,
    somewhere
A long way off, a world that
    still works.

Atáimid i gceantar bráillín,	We are in a region of sheets here –
Ar éigean más cuimhin linn cathaoir,	The thought of a chair in this
Ach bhi tráth sar ba mhachaire sinn,	place!
In aimsir choisíochta fadó,	So hard now to believe
Go mbímis chomh hard le fuinneog.	Sunlight back in the other world
	Where we stood once high as a
	window.
Tá pictiúir ar an bhfalla ag at,	The frame has dissolved and
Tá an fráma imithe ina lacht,	His image is rising out of the
Ceal creidimh ni féidir é bhac,	wall –
Tá nithe ag druidim fém dhéin,	No quarter there any more:
Is braithim ag titim an saol.	Wraiths ring me now,
	I think the world is melting . . .
Tá ceantar ag taisteal on spéir,	A region is growing out of the
Tá comharsanacht suite ar mo mhéar,	sky,
Dob fhuirist dom breith ar shéipéal,	There's a neighbourhood resting
Tá ba ar an mbóthar o thuaidh,	on my fingertip –
Is níl ba na síoraíochta chomh ciúin.	So easy to pick off a steeple!
	There are cows on the road to
	the north,
	But the cows of eternity are still
	making noise.

In the second last line of the poem, we encounter the first normally-focused thought in the poem: 'There are cows on the road to the north'. The poet is again in a world he recognizes, and this is possibly a sign of recuperation. However he is not quite sure that eternity or chaos is not still threatening: 'But the cows of eternity are still making noise'.

'Reo' is a poem of ten lines, where Ó Ríordáin perhaps unconsciously reverses one of the oldest European love-formulas, that of the poet walking out one summer morning and meeting a fair lady. Here it is a winter's morning, with frost in the air, the boughs bare – and finally he encounters not love but death. This may in fact be another lament for his mother; beautiful, unique, and absolutely in the Irish tradition. The English translation is by Valentin Iremonger.

Maidin sheaca ghabhas amach	On a frosty morning I went out
Is bhí seál póca romham ar sceach,	And a handkerchief faced me on
Rugas air le cur im phóca	a bush.
Ach sciorr sé uaim mar bhi sé reoite:	I reached to put it in my pocket
Ní héadach beo a léim óm ghlaic	But it slid from me for it was
Ach rud fuair bás aréir ar sceach:	frozen.
Is siúd ag taighde mé fé m'intinn	No living cloth jumped from
Go bhfuaireas macasamhail an ní seo –	my grasp
Lá dar phógas bean dem mhuintir	But a thing that died last night
Is í ina cónra reoite, sínte.	on a bush,
	And I went searching in my
	mind
	Till I found its real equivalent:
	The day I kissed a woman of my
	kindred
	And she in the coffin, frozen,
	stretched.

Ó Ríordáin, in this and in many other poems, is writing in an idiom and a tone that an eighteenth-century poet such as Ó Rathaille would have recognized; and yet he is absolutely modern. He and Ó Direáin amongst our poets, and Máirtín Ó Cadhain amongst our fiction-writers, have revitalized the Irish language; fitted it out for the contemporary mind, using most of its inherent resources.

Seán Ó Ríordáin, in his three volumes of original poetry, functions on what seems to be two contradictory levels. First of all he has a basic corpus of poems (including 'Oíche Nollaig na mBan', 'An Bás', 'Claustrophobia', 'Fiabhras', 'Reo', 'Adhlacadh mo Mháthar', etc.) in which he manages to recreate in the starkest forms the essence of his terror, his loneliness, his isolation. I doubt if we have had any poet since Yeats who has composed so many lyrics bearing, as these do, the marks of high creative genius. (And one should add to these a few lyrics of sheer happiness such as the well-known 'Cúl an Tí', 'Seachtain', 'Siollabadh', etc.) After this we have to reckon with a long series of philosophic or semi-philosophic poems (such as 'Saoirse', 'Fill Arís', 'Oileán agus Oileán eile', etc.) where the poet tries, in rational terms, to understand or explain (or explain away) his abysmal feeling of insecurity. While a few of these poems are marvellous, even Herculean, efforts to construct a system or an answer in which he can believe, I doubt if they will finally be estimated amongst his best work. They depend too much on an intellectual theory, which many people will find difficult to accept or be moved by – a common difficulty with poems which argue a philosophy or supply definitive answers to the meaning of life. Many of his minor philosophic poems, in fact, end up as game-playing with cold abstract concepts.

But taking his work as a whole, the level and magnitude of Ó Ríordáin's achievement is astonishing – especially when one considers that the language he is using might have been given up for dead fifty years before he began his work. He, and Aogán Ó Rathaille, are perhaps the finest poets to have written in Irish in the last three centuries.

Micheál Ó hUanacháin
Máirtín Ó Direáin

Máirtín Ó Direáin was born in the year 1910 in Árainn, the largest of the Aran Islands, in Galway Bay. The island, bleak and stormy, but inhabited since the dawn of history, was his home for seventeen years. In 1928 he went to work as a postal clerk in Galway city, and in 1937 moved to Dublin where he married and made his home. He was sometime Registrar of the National College of Art, and has recently been poet-in-residence at University College Galway. He is the author of eight volumes of verse and a book of prose essays. Such is the simple *curriculum vitae* of the distinguished but unpretentious doyen of contemporary writers in Irish.

Many years after he left the West, he wrote:

Aistriú ón gcarraig don chathair	A move from stones to towns
Ní indéanta gan a dheachú íoc . . .	Has its price, and you must
	pay . . .

Ó Direáin's payment of that price is evident in his work, and it is what lends the poetry its particular poignancy. His concern, especially in the early work, is continually for the decay of the tradition. Later he comes to an awareness of his own loss of roots – and, finally, to a concern about the rootlessness of all of our society.

The realities of island life contain little of novelty; nor does Ó Direáin's verse in reflecting that life. What is new is the way of saying things. Eliot wrote about that, especially in the 'Four Quartets':

. . . one has only learnt to get the better of words
For the thing one no longer has to say . . .

And again – and still talking about the same struggle with ideas and forms imposed on him by a long and firmly rooted tradition – he speaks of

. . . the intolerable wrestle
With words and meaning. The poetry does not matter.

Very much later in his life, Ó Direáin would come to grips with this
dichotomy; but, for the time being at least, it was not necessary to
have radically new devices, or techniques, or gimmicks. In fact, they
are distractions. There is no such problem with the early Ó Direáin.
His poetry was wrung from him, a poetry of simplicity, of directness. His first concerns were of the most central – the home, the
cultural roots, the leaving of them, and above all the remembrance
of hardship. It was in this last that the vatic and the historical voices
first appeared.

Cur in agaidh na hanacra
Ab éigean dom dhaoine a dhéanamh,
An chloch a chloí, is an chré
Chrosanta thabhairt chun míne,
Is rinne mo dhaoine cruachan
Is rinne clann chun cúnaimh.

What they must do, my people,
was to oppose the difficult,
tame rocks, make unruly
earth amenable.
And my people strained,
and made young ones to help
them.

Dúshlán na ndúl a spreag a ndúshlán,
Borradh na fola is súil le clann ar
ghualainn
A thug ar fhear áit dorais a bhriseadh
Ar bhalla theach a dhúchais,
Ag cur pot' ar leith ar theallach an
dóchais.

Their wants challenged, the
blood rush and to have a tribe
broke new door in the cottage
wall, and set
a new place at hope's table

Slíodóireacht níor chabhair i gcoinne na
toinne.
Ná seifteanna caola i gcoinne na gcloch
úd,
Ionas nárbh' fhearr duine ná duine eile,
Ag cur ithir an doichill faoi chuing an
bhisigh.
Gan neart na ngéag ba díol ómóis
Fuinneamh na sláinte is líon an
chúnaimh.

No sly scheme would best the
wave,
no clever plan those rocks
and, no man better than other,
increase yoked, ploughed
unwilling clay.
Weak hands hail
their firm héalth, the many sons.

The year was 1938. Forty-five years earlier the Gaelic League had
been formed; forty-five years before that, the Great Famine had all
but destroyed the Gaelic way of life in Ireland – or what was then left

of it. Writing in 1929, in *Gaelic Literature Surveyed*, Aodh de Blacam had remarked:

> For the lifetime of three generations, Ireland has been a nation drifting towards extinction. It is small wonder, therefore, if we find original literature ceasing when Humphrey O'Sullivan laid down his pen. After the Famine there were rhymers in the countryside, it is true – folk poets, or ballad-makers, whose names chance to survive.

Against that however, one must set the enormous stock of oral tradition which survived particularly in *Gaeltacht* areas such as the islands. This was not the stuff of the folk poets, or at least not exclusively: a body of pre-medieval stories, medieval poems and Renaissance songs formed the core of it. It is not surprising, then, that Ó Direáin began his first and only 'manifesto', in the preface to 'Ó Morna agus Dánta Eile', with a declaration that

> Poetry surrounded me as I grew. Not all of poetry can be invented. It's no slight to say she is like electricity in that poems are made only of a little of her, that much of her escapes.

Not unnaturally, Ó Direáin drew on the styles and mannerisms of what he had absorbed:

Aréir im' aonar 'sea bhíos,   Last night as I was alone
Ag siúl dom tré ghleann ciúin   Walking through a lone silent
uaigneach . . .   glen . . .

These lines from 'An Nidh a Bhí Áluinn' could as easily have been the opening lines of an eighteenth-century dream-poem. And, as Seán Ó Tuama remarked in the preface to his selection *Nuabhear-saíocht* (1950):

> On examining these poems, one finds that they are all based on traditional forms, if loosely . . . And whether deliberate or no, this is the case with his best poems – a personal and natural extension of settled form, the form of traditional poetry.

Indeed, in a later period, when Ó Direáin turns more obviously to *vers libre*, there remains a strong influence which increasingly reminds one of the very earliest extant Irish poetry, the lines attributed to Amergin (who may have lived c. 500 BC if folk-history be believed!); bearing out the point made by Aodh de Blacam in *Gaelic Literature Surveyed*:

> Gaelic literature intellectually is a literature of rest, not of change: of intensive cultivation, not of experiment. It is, moreover, the image of a civilization, half heroic, half pastoral, that continues down to the present day; that never has accepted industrialism and the city.

The texture of life on the island is a central concern to Ó Direáin in his early poetry – and even his later poems rely heavily on island images for city poems. But while the remembrance of his native place remained – and remains – a major part of his poetic preoccupation, he certainly did not remain aloof from the life of his new place, and a close reading of his poetry will show the young man growing old in the service of the state, and of poetry.

Nine years as a clerk in Galway gave way to a permanent exile in Dublin, working in the Civil Service. Galway at that time still retained a little of the culture of the western seaboard. Some Irish was spoken, particularly in the port area, the Claddagh, and even an Aranman could almost feel at home. Dublin, on the other hand, was already losing its British provincial character, and had long since been de-Gaelicized. It was a modern urban setting, inviting anonymity and nourishing alienation. Coming from a rural background, Ó Direáin absorbed the culture of the city rapidly, even though he felt at times cut off from it, as well as from his Gaelic background. And this is expressed, not in any antagonism towards the English language, but in a frustrated fury at the inflexibility of this instrument which he was now expected to use so often in daily life. These lines are from 'Béarla is Béarlagar':

Nuair d'aimsigh an duine téarma	When man discovered terms,
Neamhdhuinigh é féin den léim sin,	he unmanned himself in that leap
Tháinig béarlagar ar áit an Bhéarla,	jargon came in place of English!
Mairg nár choill an feic sular	woe it was not castrated at birth.
fhréamhaigh.	

Ó Direáin himself glosses this passage in 'An File Gaeilge is Saol na Cathrach' (from *Feamainn Bhealtaine*, his only prose collection and a key source for students of his work):

> . . . many words already in common use in English are still terms in Irish. . . . 'Words' are live things. They are on people's lips. They have souls. 'Terms' are things you must look for in a dictionary or even invent yourself if no one has done it yet. But in either case they are without souls, without shadows. There is poetry sometimes even in a single word, because of its shadows, but terms rarely have shadows.

Perhaps it is for this reason that city concerns are slow to dominate his work – although as early as 1939 he had based an elegiac piece on an entirely non-island image, the stage:

I dtigh do mhuintire,	In your people's house
Ag fleá nó féasta ;	At feast or party
Fial flaithiúil 'bhís :	The heart of generosity you
Teacht an bháis chugat :	were
Ró-dhoiligh a chreidiúint.	The coming of death to you
	Is too hard to believe.
B'fhearr linn a chreidiúint,	It's preferable to believe
Gur thuirsigh do pháirt thú,	You were tired of your part
I ndráma an tsaoil seo,	In the play that is life,
Ar stáitse na beatha seo,	On the stage of the world,
'S go ndeachais ar saoire uainn,	And took a holiday,
Seal an-fhada uainn.	A far, long holiday.

These were times of great change and ferment, in Ireland, and the world – the Great Depression, the rise of Hitler, the Spanish Civil War. Little of this was reflected, at first at least, in the poetry of Máirtín Ó Direáin. He had not published before he left the West, and I suppose it was only natural that he was primarily concerned with what he had left behind. The early poetry, in collections such as *Coinnle Geala* and *Dánta Aniar*, is romantic, even nostalgic:

Fóill a ghaineamh, fóill!	Stay, sand, stay!
Fearann tearmainn, seachain!	Do not break sanctuary!

Cosc do ghnó mall,	Hold back your slow advance
Do ghnó foighdeach fág,	Your patient slow advance
Is téadh Cill Mhic Chonaill slán . . .	And spare the holy place of Mac Conaill . . .
In oileán beag i gcéin san iarthar	On a small island, far to the west,
Beidh coinnle ar lasadh anocht . . .	Candles will be lighting this night . . .

This was a sentimentality about which the critics of the time were divided. To some it was entirely appropriate that an islandman, a native speaker of the language, would immerse himself in this reminiscence, this rather tired backward look. To Ó Direáin himself it seems to have become something of a millstone. His first process was to fine down the island-image: it became spare, lean, described by hint rather than *in extenso*. Within all of this there was a core of harshness reflecting the vicissitudes of island life, the symbolic nature of which was later to dominate his imagery.

Always the traditions, the life-style of the island – or, more generally, the rural culture – is set against the cruder, harsher personality of the city. Again and again the word 'crann' (tree) is used as a synonym for strength – and no one who has noticed the few proud if stunted trees on his native island can fail to appreciate the centrality of the tree-image in Ó Direáin's poems. This is from 'Bí i do Chrann':

Coigil do bhrí	Save your strength
A fhir an dáin,	Man of song
Coigil faci thrí,	Save, and thrice:
Bí i do chrann.	Be a tree.
. . .	. . .
Tá do leath baineann,	One half woman,
A fhir an dáin,	Man of song,
Bí fireann, bí sián	Be masculine and whole:
Bí i do chrann	Be a tree.

Gradually, there entered into Ó Direáin's poetry something of the hardness of the city. It tempered him, and the voice that was heard was bit by bit coming to be one of considerable stature. He had never, in fact, been particularly a traditional poet. When he took an old-established form or metre for a poem, he made it his own, but now he was breaking new ground – and it was ground not much favoured by the traditionalists. Their horizon was limited: in the one direction, they could see little beyond the folk-balladeer, in the other there was nothing to surpass imitation of the eighteenth century, the last period in which an intellectual, written poetry flourished in Irish. For their purposes only an adherence to one or other of these styles would suffice – anything else was 'alien' and therefore repugnant.

It is a measure of the power and confidence that now ruled in Ó Direáin's poetry that he could ignore that demand, and yet celebrate the dying *Gaeltacht*, in his own way. He began to write of the new life he was leading, as well as the old he had left. The two came together, at times, particularly when war came – and he was too much a realist to adopt the coy official term 'The Emergency'. By now he had sufficiently cast off the inward-looking island attitude to take more than a passing interest in social and political change as well as the burgeoning change in his own ideas and feelings. *Ó Morna agus Dánta Eile* (1957), his first truly post-war collection, has, apart from the title piece to which we will return, two interesting poems; one on a dockers' strike:

Druim le balla ag caoineadh an tuillimh	A group by the wall bewails its earnings
Ag agairt na hainnis' ar an sotal,	Calls down misery of the arrogant,
Scilling an focal, scilling an t-éileamh,	A shilling's the word, and the demand,
Bia, deoch, cíos is éadach.	Food, drink, rent, clothing . . .

There is also his reflection on the social change which affected all of Ireland as a result of the war – the poem 'Blianta an Chogaidh':

Ní sinne na daoine céanna	We are not the men we were
A dhiúgadh na cáirt,	Drinking our pints
Is a chuireadh fál cainte	And building a wall of talk
Idir sinn is ár gcrá.	To keep fear at bay.

Thuig fear amháin na mná
Is é a thuig a gcluain tharr barr,
An bhantracht go léir a thuig
I gcrot aon-mhná nach raibh dílis,
Is sinn ar thaobh an dídin
Den phéin is den pháis.

One man claimed to 'know'
    women:
He had the measure of their
    ways
Every treacherous one of them
In the shape of one who
    betrayed:
And the rest of us sat on the
    sheltered side
Of passion and pain.

D'fhaigmis an seic, an giota páir,
An t-ara malairteach fáin,
Ar an saothar aimrid gan aird
Is théimis chun an ósta ghnáith.

We'd get the cheque, the bit of
    paper,
In miserable exchange
For our little eunuch-jobs –
And then to the pub!

Níor chuireamar is níor bhaineamar
Is níor thógamar fál go hard,
Ach fál filíochta is argóna,
Idir sinn is an smaoineamh;
Go rabhamar silte gan sinsear
Go rabhamar stoite gan mhuintir
Go rabhamar gan gaisce gan ghrá
Gan aisce don fháistin
Ach scríbhinn i gcomhad.

We neither served nor reaped
Nor did we build a wall
But a wall of verse and
    argument
To keep at bay the thought:
That we were fatherless,
    motherless
Neighbourless, kinless
Courageless, loveless
With no stake in the future
Save a note on a file.

Is réab gach éinne againn
Cuing is aithne ina aigne;
Aicme a bhí gan fréamha i dtalamh,
Dream narbh fhiú orthu cuing a
    cheangal,
Drong nár rod leo a n-athardha.

And, in our minds, every one of
    us
Broke precept and yoke:
Rootless, rootless,
Not worth yoking
Careless of heritage.

Here is the new citizen, the city man, that was growing through the islander – but always the imagery was rooted in the island, and the things that were important there.

Coinneod féin an t-oileán
seal eile im dhán

I will keep the island
a while more in my song

toisc a ionraice atá	because of the honesty
cloch, carraig is trá.	of shore, rock and stone.

Even though by this time the island had ceased, for him, to be a myth of the perfect retreat, the realization that in part at least the island of his poetry was an illusion was not one that came easily to Ó Direáin. Indeed, we see hints of it in the poetry before he articulates it in prose.

It must be that I believed at one time in my life that there was no other place in the world apart from that beautiful western island in the bosom of the sea where I was born and raised. If so, then that belief didn't survive for long, because the world was encroaching on me, bit by bit.

From the early nostalgia, he develops the idea of the island as a retreat from this hostile community in which he now lives:

Dream iad siúd nach díobh mé	They are a crowd I don't belong
'S dearbhaímmse ós árd	to,
Gur duine den tsean-tsaol Ghaelach mé	And I declare aloud
'S gur díbhse mé o cheart.	That I am of the old Gaelic
	world
	And truly belong to you.

And, at the same time, a yearning for the clearer values of the old life:

Faoiseamh a gheobhadsa,	I'll find release
Seal beag goirid	a short while
I measg mo dhaoine . . .	among my people . . .
Ó chaint ghontach,	from bitter words
Thiar ag baile.	back at home.

It is not simply the 'better words' that distress him, but the complete lack of interest in his culture; as here, in 'Mó thaibhse':

Ní foláir nó is taibhse mé	I must be a ghost
I meabhair an tsóirt sin cheana . . .	in the minds of such, already.

153

But while he begins to take a more realistic view of the island and its ways, it is not yet dispassionate – as seen in the poem 'Iascairí an Chladaigh':

Ná bíodh bhur dtnúth le muir feasta
Ach tugaíg cúl léi go luath,
Tugaíg aghaidh ar chill is ar thír,
Ní fada uaibh anois an uaigh.

Hope no more for the sea,
but reject her, and soon:
face the church and its land –
not far from you, now the grave.

And, at the same time, his rather cynical view of the final disposition of the old order has something in it of the universal – it partakes of the city man's feeling of impotence:

Beidh cuimhne orainn go fóill:
Beidh carnán trodán
Faoi ualach deannaigh
Inár ndiaidh in Oifig Stáit.

We'll be remembered yet:
a pile of files
dust-laden
behind us in some Public Office.

This is a central piece. Eoghan Ó hAnluain, who updated de Blacam's *Gaelic Literature Surveyed* in 1973, sees in it

a theme which Ó Direáin has pursued relentlessly ever since: uprooted rural man astray in the complexities of the city and cut loose from the moral sanctions of traditional life. This theme receives its most exhaustive treatment in 'Ár Ré Dhearóil' (1963) where he explores the moral crisis inherent in *an chathair fhallsa* the city of deceit.

It would be improper, however, to examine *Ár Ré Dhearóil* without first scrutinizing an aspect of Ó Direáin's work which has not yet been mentioned: his love of poetry and his treatment of women. One critic groups these together as *leannáin* (usually translated as 'lovers', but having a wider overtone), including poems to his mother and to friends – and proceeds to seek for evidence of sensuality and sexuality in all ('An Ceathrar Leannán', Pádraig Ó hÉalaithe, *Irisleabhar Mhá Nuad*, 1970, pp. 77 ff.) – a somewhat dubious process, I fear. He does however reach one firm conclusion: by the later poems (in, for example, *Crainn is Cairde*) 'tá slán fágtha aige leis an *bpaisiún agus is go fuarchúiseach a labhrann sé anois ar mhná*' ('he has bade farewell to passion and now speaks clinically of women'). I would prefer '*réichúiseach*' ('calmly').

'Ár Ré Dhearóil' is perhaps Ó Direáin's first sustained city poem. Insofar as the island makes an appearance in it, it is not now central, but serves more as a theoretical ideal against which the exile may measure his new place. For he had made his peace with the island in the other long poem 'Ó Morna', a celebration of the island through the history of one man and his family. The island, thus concretized, no longer insists on dominating his poetry. What does, in terms of contemporary thought, distance some of Ó Direáin's work from a younger generation of readers is a recrudescence of a certain 'primitivism'. 'Ár Ré Dhearóil' is critical – almost without relief – of city ways and mid-century morality, in particular since the poet sees (rightly) that the vast majority of the city folk are but one step removed from a rural ancestry:

Crot a athar thalmhaí
Do shúil ghrinn is léir,
Ag teacht ar gach fear
Atá i meán a laethe,
A chneadaíonn a shlí chun suíocháin
I mbus tar éis a dhinnéir.

The sharp eye sees
his farming father showing
in each one, at man's
mid day of life,
wheezing after dinner
to his bus seat.

Ní luaifear ar ball leo
Teach ná áras sinsir,
Is cré a muintire
Ní dháilfear síos leo,
Ach sna céadta comhad
Beidh lorg pinn leo.

No family house or mansion
will be theirs, no
ancestral earth
to shroud them –
merely in a hundred files
a scratch from their pens.

Is a liacht fear acu
A chuaigh ag roinnt na gaoise
Ar fud páir is meamraim,
Ag lua an fhasaigh,
An ailt, an achta.

So many among them
disbursed their wisdom
on minute, on memo,
citing act, paragraph
and clause.

Is a liacht fear fós
A thug comhad leis abhaile,
Is cúram an chomhaid
In áit chéile chun leapa

And so many others
each brought briefcase home
and cared so for the files
his work his bedmate.

155

He contrasts the loveless sensuality that he sees around him (with what must be a slightly rose-tinted pseudo-memory, in many respects), not merely with the loving unions at the centre of country family life, but even with the beasts:

Nuair a fhaighid a gcuid dá chéile,
Ní gach ceann is luaithe chucu
A ghlacaid in aonchor.

When they couple with each
   other
not the first one that passes
will they choose at all.

Here too, the English is too coy to indicate the natural phrase 'faighid a gcuid dá chéile' – and even that is a little coy, for Irish! The new freedom, according to Ó Direáin later in the poem, has merely enslaved us, leading us into the Waste Land, the barren land:

Seal le teanga iasachta
Seal leis an ealaín,
Seal ag taisteal
Críocha aineola,
Ag cur cártaí abhaile
As Ostend is Paris . . .

A while at foreign languages
A while for the arts
A while travelling
In unknown parts,
Sending postcards home
From Ostend and Paris . . .

Tá cime romham
Tá cime i mo dhiaidh,
Is mé féin ina lár
I mo chime mar chách,
Is a Dhia mhóir
Fóir ar na céadta againn,
Ó d'fhágamar slán
Ag talamh ag trá,
Tóg de láimh sinn
Idir fheara is mhná
Sa chathair fhallsa,
Óir is sinn atá ciontach
I bhásta na beatha,
Is é cnámh ár seisce
An cnámh gealaí,
Atá ar crochadh thuas
I dtrá ár bhfuaire
Mar bhagairt.

A prisoner before
And a prisoner behind
And between the two
I am prisoner like all,
And great God
Save the hundreds of us
Since we bade farewell
To land, to shore,
Take us in hand,
Men and women
In this indolent city
For we are the guilty
Of waste of life
Our bone of sterility
Is the lunar one
Hanging above
In our cold time
As a threat.

Eliot's waste land is not very different, in a way, to this. He too sees the barrenness:

> Where are the roots that clutch, what branches grow
> Out of this stony rubbish?

he asks, and he describes the dwellers of that land:

> . . . red sullen faces sneer and snarl
> From doors of mudcracked houses.

If there is a difference between the two, it lies not in 'Ár Ré Dhearóil' itself, but in later work – a mellower tone, a revised cynicism turning somewhat to the sardonic and the wry, as in 'Dom Féin':

Tar ar do chéill feasta	Come to your senses, man!
Tá an leathchéad go tréan	The half-century is hot
Ar na sála agat,	on your heels,
Níl ribe ar do bhlaosc	your dome all hairless
Ná meigeall ar do smig	no goatee on your chin.
Is bean aosta féin	A dowager, even,
Ní ghlacfadh dán uait.	wouldn't accept your song.

The interesting thing here is that Ó Direáin is rather more obviously aware of himself, his concerns and his craft than many poets. He often talks about his poetry and writes poems about it. He does get very angry at the insensitivity of some city people, and can be scathing about their inhumanity. When he does that, as in 'Achasán', it's another area where the rural image, the pristine image of truth – and presumably beauty – is contrasted with the actions of urban louts:

Achasán éigin i ngarbhghlór	A rough shout mocked me
A chaith dailtín i mo threo	from an upstart
De dhroim ghluaisrothair:	on a motorbike.
D'imigh na focail le gaoth,	Wind whipped the words away –
Is an bhail chéanna a ghuím	a like fate I wish on
Ar a dtiocfaidh eile uaidh.	all the rest he'll say.

Mhionnóin go raibh aige féin	Sure he has a certificate
Teastas an léinn ó scoil éigin,	of learning from some school.
Ach geallaimse dósan gan bhréag	Truly I'd boast to him
Gur chaitheas-sa seal de mo laetha	I was apprenticed
I dteannta daoine uaisle gan 'léann'.	to good people without
Gan focal dá theanga ina mbéal.	'learning'
	– or his sort of talk.

Teastas ní raibh acu ná a dhath	No certificate, nor degree:
Ach lámh ar an bpeann is a marc,	a hand to guide the pen at 'X'.
Ach cheapas a gcaint i mo líon	*Their* talk I netted, caught
Mar ba thrua í ligean le gaoth:	before the wind could take.
Trua eile nár cheapas tuilleadh di.	Too little I harvested.

He would nearly go so far as to warn others off, because the craft is so demanding and unrewarding; but it has its advantages, even if the traditional garret, in some respects, is the price one pays.

Mair a mhic ar bhia cladaigh	Shore and shellfish feed you,
Ar chrústa aráin, ar fhata;	A crust of bread, a spud:
Ach ar a bhfacais, a dhalta,	These, but be sure, son,
Ceangal ná fulaing ná bagairt.	No chain for you, no threat.

Níor mhór liom duit, a chara,	I would wish for you, friend,
Malairt bail ort seach ar chreanas;	A different way than mine was:
Fear an mhisnigh ní chailleann	Courage will not lose the day
Is cá bhfios nach dtabharfá do cheann leat.	And who knows, you may survive.

But time and again he comes back to the poetry, and the making of poetry. Eliot, again, talks about 'fragments I have shored against my ruin'. There seems to be little of that in Ó Direáin's approach. He is by turns tortured by the poetry which is in him somewhere and won't come out, and then fascinated by the process of dragging it out. He speaks about chasing it out of the warren of his mind. He speaks of carrying it, as a woman carries a child. Indeed, one poem starting as a love-lyric ends as a verse about writing poetry! And, in a recent poem, he talks about critics, very scathingly indeed. In 'Cúirt ar Dhán', a man, grey-suited and umbrella-carrying, asks 'How's the writing going?' and on being invited to look over a new piece examines its prosody and metre. His cold comment is 'Namhaid an choird gan a fhoghlaim' ('a trade not learnt is an enemy', or, more idiomatically, 'a little knowledge is dangerous'). Ó Direáin's comment is wry:

Cara den namhaid tréan	Of that strong enemy, I
Ní dhearna mé fhéin fós	Have failed to make a friend
Tar éis tuilleadh is tríocha bliain,	In more than thirty years
Ó cuireadh cúirt ar mo dhán.	Since my poem went to court.

And again, berating himself for what he regards as failings in his work, he can be sharper still; here is 'Bailbhe':

Séard a deirim go bhfuil	What I say is, my
Mo thrumpa as gléas,	Trumpet's out of tune,
Ionas go molfainn dom féin	And I'd advise myself
Éirí as an ngnó go léir:	To give up the whole thing:
Níl mo theanga na comharsan agam:	Now I have neither my own nor
Sin é an bualadh cabblach	my neighbours' speech:
Ar deireadh, is bailbhe.	That's the sour note,
	Finally – silence.

A turning in on himself of his sardonic vision of others is notable particularly in his most recent collection, Ceacht an Éin. All joy, all youth, even the happier moments of the present, here find only a contrapuntal voice, contrasting themselves to the darker images of age, silence, winter '. . . is gnó leamh na huaire' ('and the moment's dull task'). There is no life in the egg, women lose their beauty – and yet Ó Direáin creates a curious grace and delicacy in all of this. The bitterness is self-directed: it is as if he has found hedonism, but too late.

The publication of Ó Direáin's Collected Poems in 1980 (complete except for the poems from Coinnle Ceala and Dánta Aniar which the poet had already discarded in the 1949 Selected Poems) was a major recognition of his stature. 'Is dualgas don fhile focla a chur ag rince ós ár gcomhair', he told himself (and us) in the preface to Ó Mórna . . .: it is a poet's duty to make words dance before us. The unmistakable echo of Pound reminds us that Ó Direáin had before him the examples of Eliot, Pound and (later) Thomas, any of which could have served as a headline for the new poetry of the Irish language. The harder task was to refuse to copy, to seek to forge his own language of vision, born on the Island and nurtured in the inhospitable City.

Máirtín Ó Direáin's poetry can be seen as taking a different direction to the long tradition of folk poetry and song in Irish, much of which he absorbed and refined; and a direction different too to the more formal written poetry of the seventeenth and eighteenth centuries particularly. He borrows and remoulds elements of both, but it is in the Irish poets of the early Middle Ages that we see his most direct ancestors. He and they share a quality, at the same time robust and delicate, of love for life.

John Montague
A Northern Vision

I would like to write of the Gaelic poet for whom I feel most sympathy, for reasons that will soon emerge – political and geographical as well as literary. For he is not an Irish, but a Scottish poet, and he writes in a Gaelic which resembles Ulster Irish, in both sound and idiom. His name is Sorley MacLean, a name I know well from my native Ulster, though my neighbours there would never call themselves Mac Gill-Eain, or speak in Gaelic. One of the most savagely ironic aspects of the present tragedy of Ulster is that some of the planters, at least, must have been Gaelic speakers, with whom we share a heritage.

So wandering through Antrim one hears an accent very close to Scots, and at night, the lights of Scotland glint across the sea, a narrow channel separating kindred peoples. The ancient kingdom of Dál Riada, Sweeney's Kingdom, stretched across the sea, and over it St Colmcille sailed into exile, to Christianize Scotland. In return we received Roaring Hugh Hanna, and Ian Paisley; but what I would like to stress here is not the bitterness of sectarianism which separates us, but how much we share, since the days when the word *Scotus* was the common name for both our peoples.

For the heritage persists. I am looking at a book with a green cover, *Nua-Bhàrdachd Ghàidhlig* (*New Gaelic Poetry*) – an Irish anthology you might think, but it consists of Sorley, his friends and disciples, younger poets who were stirred by his example – *Modern Scottish Gaelic Poems* is the subtitle. I was sitting with one, who is also his translator, Iain Crichton Smith or Iain Mac A'Ghobhainn, in a hotel bar in Oban, discussing the problems of poetry in general. Suddenly, hunching over his whisky, he demands: 'John, what are your obsessions? Do you know the Hag?' I point out that the Cailleach originally came from the Beara peninsula in West Cork and is one of the enduring muses of Gaelic literature and history; we have both borne witness to her power.

But the muse that inspired Sorley's early poetry, the poems that released Scottish Gaelic poetry from its long sleep, was the face of a young girl with golden hair, like *Niamh Chinn-óir*, or the young queen of a thousand *aislingí*, or vision poems.

In 1943, 'Dàin do Eimhir', an extraordinary sequence of love poems, appeared as part of a larger volume from William MacLellan of Glasgow. Even the 'Poems to Emer' are incomplete, forty-eight out of a potential sixty. The only place where we can find something approaching the full sequence now is in the translations by Iain Crichton Smith, issued as a Northern House pamphlet; they are separated in Sorley's *Selected Poems*, appearing mainly in the section 'The Haunted Ebb'. But one gets flashes of its first fire, the lightning of passion illuminating a traditional Highland landscape of mountain and water in 'Am Mùr Gorm'; the translation is Sorley's own:

> But for you the Cuillin would
>   be
> an exact and serrated blue
>   rampart
> girdling with its march-wall
> all that is in my fierce heart.
>
> But for you the sand
> that is in Talisker compact and
>   white
> would be a measureless plain to
>   my expectations
> and on it the spear desire would
>   not turn back.
>
> But for you the oceans
> in their unrest and their repose
> would raise the wave-crests of
>   my mind
> and settle them on a high
>   serenity.
>
> And the brown brindled
>   moorland
> and my reason would co-extend –
> but you imposed on them an
>   edict
> above my own pain.

And on distant luxuriant
      Summit
there blossomed the Tree of
      Strings,
among its leafy branches your
      face,
my reason and the likeness of a
      star.

Iain Crichton Smith translates that third last line as 'the harp of blossomed fire', perhaps echoing Coleridge's 'Aeolian Harp', one of the great Romantic symbols; but whatever the interpretation one can sense the excitement of what is happening. Like his master Yeats, to whom he dedicated a poem, Sorley MacLean is grafting the tradition of courtly love onto his native inheritance. In another poem to his beloved he lists her literary and historical equals; the title is 'A' Bhuaile Ghréine' and the English version is again made by the poet:

Do m' shùilean-sa bu tu Deirdre
's i bòidheach 's a' bhuaile ghréine:
bu tu bean Mhic Ghille Bhrìghde
ann an àilleachd a lìthe.
Bu tu nighean bhuidhe Chòrnaig
is Mairearad an Amadain Bhòidhich,
an Una aig Tómas Làidir,
Eimhir Chù Chulainn agus Gràinne,
bu tu té nam mìle long,
ùidh nam bàrd is bàs nan sonn,
's bu tu an té a thug an fhois
's an t-sìth bho chridhe Uilleim Rois,
an Audiart a bhuair De Born
agus Maoibhe nan còrn.

To my eyes you were Deirdre
beautiful in the sunny
      cattle-fold:
you were MacBride's wife
in her shining beauty.
You were the yellow-haired girl
      of Cornaig
And the Handsome Fool's
      Margaret,
Strong Thomas's Una,
Cuchulainn's Eimhir, and
      Grainne.
You were the one of the
      thousand ships,
desire of poets and death of
      heroes,
you were she who took the rest
and the peace from the heart of
      William Ross,
the Audiart who plagued De
      Born,
And Maeve of the drinking
      horns.

A tall order for any girl to follow, and Sorley later confesses that he was not the hero to win her; like Yeats, he has only 'poor words to offer', *na ranna pianta*. But as well as weaving these strands of Greek, Provençal and Celtic romanticism, the poems take place against a definite background, the period of the Spanish Civil War. In poems like 'Gaoir na h-Eòrpa' ('The Cry of Europe') – here translated by Iain Crichton Smith – the agonies are twined:

*Dé bhiodh pòg do bheòil uaibhrich
mar ris gach braon de 'n fhuil
   luachmhoir
a thuit air raointean reòta fuara
nam beann Spàinnteach bho fhòirne
   cruadhach?*

What is your kiss, electrical and
   proud,
when valued by each drop of
   precious blood
that fell on the frozen
   mountain-sides of Spain
when men were dying in their
   bitter pain?

*Dé gach cuach dhe d' chuail òr-bhuidh
ris gach bochdainn, àmhghar 's dórainn
a thig 's a thàinig air sluagh na
   h-Eòrpa
bho Long nan Daoine gu daors' a'
   mhór-sluaigh?*

What is each ringlet of your
   golden hair
when weighed against that
   poverty and fear
which Europe's people bear and
   still must bear
from the first slave-ship to
   slavery entire.

In another long, mournful poem 'Urnuigh' ('Prayer') he confesses his public guilt: how a private obsession obscured his public commitment. Again I use Sorley's own translation:

*Tha mi a' tuigsinn an dràsda
gun tàinig lìonsgaradh 's a' chàs seo,
gleachd a' chinne-daonna
   neo-bhàsmhor:
an neach mu choinneamh roghainn
   sàr-chruaidh,
bàs 's a' bheatha bhiothbhuan no beatha
   bhàsail.*

Just now I understand
that a fragmentation has come in
   this case,
the struggle of deathless
   humankind:
the being before the hardest
   choice,
death is immortal life or a
   death-like life.

Mo bheatha-sa a' bheatha bhàsail
a chionn nach d' fhal mi cridhe mo
    shàth-ghaoil,
a chionn gun tug mi gaol àraidh,
a chionn nach sgarainn do ghràdh-sa
's gum b' fheàrr liom boirionnach na 'n
    Eachdraidh fhàsmhor.

My life the death-like life
because I have not flayed the
    heart of my fullness of love
because I have given a particular
    love,
because I would not cut away
    the love of you,
and that I preferred a woman to
    crescent History.

Chunnaic mi 'n fhuil chraobhach ag
    éirigh,
tein-aighir an spioraid air na sléibhtean,
an saoghal truagh ag call a chreuchdan:
thuig is thur mi fàth an langain
ged nach robh mo chridhe air fhaileadh.

I saw the branching blood rising,
the bonfire of the spirit on the
    mountains,
the poor world losing its
    wounds:
I sensed and understood the
    meaning of the cry
though my heart had not been
    flayed.

Esan dh' am bheil an cridhe air
    ionnlaid
théid e troimh theine gun tionndadh,
dìridh e 'bheinn mhór gun ionndrainn;
cha d' fhuair mise leithid de dh' anam
's mo chridhe ach air leth-fhaileadh.

He whose heart has been washed
will go through fire without
    turning;
he will ascend the great
    mountain without
    homesickness;
I did not get such a spirit
since my heart is only half
    flayed.

'S e 'n ùrnuigh seo guidhe na duilghe,
an guidhe toibheumach neo-iomlan,
guidhe cam coirbte an tionndaidh,
an guidhe gun dèan mi guidhe,
gun ghuidhe 'n t-susbaint a ruigheachd.

This prayer is the hard and sorry
    prayer,
the blasphemous imperfect
    prayer,
the crooked perverted prayer
    that turns back,
the prayer that I may pray
without praying to reach the
    substance.

Chuala mi mu bhàs neo-aoibhneach	I have heard of unhappy death
agus mu acras gorta oillteil	and about the hunger of
a' tighinn an tòrachd na foille.	loathsome famine
Ciamar a sheasas mi ri 'm	coming in pursuit of treachery.
marc-shluagh	How will I stand up against their
's gun mo chridhe ach leth-fhailte?	cavalry
	since my heart is but half flayed?

An uair tha 'n spiorad air fhaileadh	When the spirit has been flayed,
caillidh e gach uile fhaileas,	it will lose every shadow,
caillidh e gach uile fhannachd.	it will lose every faintness.
Ach có a ghabhas air mo gheal ghaol	But who will call my white love
aomadh, fannachd no faileas?	surrender, faintness or shadow?

In these poems MacLean has an impossible leap to make, from what he himself calls 'a dying tongue' into contemporary history and literature. He makes it triumphantly, and the irony of the 1930s may be that this obscure poet, in a neglected language, produced verse of greater intensity than Auden, joining 'private grief and (public) agony into a universal cross'. He did not, of course, hurry into print, and he had the example of MacDiarmid at home. But the primary secret of his strength is his study of the Metaphysicals; as a First Honours student in English at Edinburgh he studied Grierson's great edition of Donne and his anthology of metaphysical poetry – works that were greeted by Yeats and Eliot. In 'An Sgian' ('The Knife') intellect is at war with instinct; the primary dilemma. In this remarkable poem – here translated by Iain Crichton Smith – his mind hears his love until it becomes as adamant as a star:

Bha a' chlach a fhuair a gearradh	The stone my intellect had cut
á m' aigne chumhang fhìn	in its cold hard inspecting course
air a bearradh gus a' mhórachd	gathered to the arrogant light
a thoilleadh domhain-thìr.	and majesty of a universe.

Pioct' as mo chom, bha a miadachd	Struck from my breast, its
os cionn mo thomhais chéin	greatness
's mar bhruan chrùb a creag-màthar	was measureless to my eye,
am Betelgeuse nan reul.	It crouched in its giant
	brightness
	like Betelgeuse in the sky.

And he concludes:

A luaidh, mur biodh gaol mo chridhe
ort mar chruas na léig
tha fhios gun gabhadh e gearradh
le eanchainn chruaidh gheur.

Dearest, if my heart's love
were not as strong as the
   jewelled stone
surely the intellectual knife
would have cut it from my flesh
   and bone.

The face of his love – *aodann* – is the recurring image of his single, most powerful love poem, 'The Haunting' or 'An Tathaich'. The English translation of this, and all that follow, is his own:

Tha aodann 'ga mo thathaich,
'ga mo leantuinn dh'oidhche 's latha:
tha aodann buadhmhor nìghne
's e sìor agairt.

A face haunts me
following me day and night,
the triumphant face of a girl
is pleading all the time.

Tha e labhairt ri mo chridhe
nach fhaodar sgaradh a shireadh
eadar miann agus susbaint
a' chuspair dho-ruighinn . . .

It is saying to my heart
that a division may not be
   sought
between desire and the substance
of its unattainable object . . .

I spoke of Donne, as the majority of writers on Sorley MacLean have, but for Donne love transcends time, whereas in 'The Haunting' there seems to be no consolation for the erosion of beauty, the dimming of the beloved face:

O aodainn a tha 'gam thathaich,
a mhìorbhail a tha labhar,
am bheil aon phort an tìm dhuit
no balla-crìch ach talamh?

O face that is haunting me,
O eloquent marvel,
is there any port in time for you
or march-wall but earth?

O luathghair dhaonda chuimir,
am bheil seòl-tomhais 's a' chruinne
a bheir dhut barrachd slànachd
na ceòl no clàr no luinneag?

O shapely human paean,
is there a dimension in the
   universe
that will give you a greater
   wholeness
than music, board or lyric?

169

One is reminded of Shakespeare's great plea against process in Sonnet 65, more stately but no less humanly anguished:

> Since brass, nor stone, nor earth, nor boundless sea / But sad mortality o'ersways their power, / How with this rage shall beauty hold a plea, / Whose action is no stronger than a flower?

The alert listener or reader will have already noticed something: Emer may have been a particular girl but she is also an *aisling*. Nearly two hundred years after Duncan Bán McIntyre, and the love poet Uilliam Ross, the Celtic Muse reappeared in Scots Gaelic poetry – as it did in our own country – during the last war. This phenomenon is almost an exact parallel to what happened in Scots, with the appearance of MacDiarmid two centuries after Burns; and the great Lowlander saluted 'Dáin do Eimhir' with lines that echoed O'Rahilly's vision poems. Although they shared the same intense political beliefs, and Sorley would certainly have read MacDiarmid's Marxist poetry of the early thirties, it is the central Muse figure that MacDiarmid greets:

> At last, at last, I see her again
> In our long-lifeless glen,
> Eidolon of our fallen race,
> Shining in full renascent grace,
>
> She whose hair is plaited
> Like the generations of men,
> And for whom my heart has
>   waited
> Time out of ken.

I have emphasized the love poems, but there are other aspects to MacLean's work. Raasay, his island home, is celebrated in a long poem, 'The Woods of Raasay', like an extended Fenian lay. The sense of place is central to Gaelic poetry but in 'Hallaig' it is a haunting as well as a homage; the dead have been seen alive, or have become part of the woods.

And the historical wrong of his country is evoked in poems like the 'Two MacDonalds' – the Highland Clearances, and Jacobite and

Bonaparte dreams, which we share. It is clear that Ireland means a great deal to MacLean, and it meant even more to his brother Calum, whom he celebrates in a traditional but splendid elegy; Gaelic rhetoric at its best, the rise and fall of the *caoin*:

Tha sgeul ort an Cois-Fhairge
Ann an Eirinn thall:
Eadar an Ceathramh Ruadh is Spideal
Dh' fhàg thu iomadh snaim.
Bha thu aig Gaidheil Eirinn
Mar fhear dhiubh fhéin 's de'n dream.
Dh' aithnich iad annad-sa an fhéile
Nach do reub an cuan,
Nach do mhill mìle bliadhna:
Buaidh a' Ghàidheil buan.

You are talked of in Cois
    Fhairge
Over in Ireland.
Between Cararoe and Spideal
You left many a knot.
You were to the Gaels of Ireland
As one of themselves and of
    their people.
They knew in you the humanity
That the sea does not tear,
That a thousand years did not
    spoil:
The quality of the Gael
    permanent.

There is also a Yeatsian poem, 'The Heron', where the intent dabbling of the bird resembles that of the poet, though his purpose is distracted:

My dream exercised with
    sorrow,
    broken, awry, with the glitter
    of temptation,
    wounded, with but one
    sparkle;
brain, heart and love troubled.

I have mentioned none of the war poems, when the tanks and artillery of the North African campaign enter Gaelic verse: for George Campbell they fought there as well. My impression is that Sorley planned a long poem on his favourite mountain range – the Cuillins – as a symbol of courage and sorrow, a *Macchu Picchu* of Scotland the Brave:

heroic, the Cuillin is seen
rising on the other side of
sorrow

But this grand enterprise was interrupted, like MacDiarmid's
'Clann Albann', and I would like to end instead with one of his most
passionate poems, although it is among his earliest. Here the anguish
is not introspective as in his confession poem, 'Remorse', but it is no
less intense: attacking God on the behalf of humble motherhood:

Am faca Tu i, Iùdhaich mhóir,
ri 'n abrar Aon Mhac Dhé?
Am fac' thu a coltas air Do thriall
ri strì an fhìon-lios chéin?

Hast Thou seen her, great Jew,
who art called the One Son of
God?
Hast Thou seen on Thy way the
like of her
labouring in the distant
vineyard?

An cuallach mheasan air a druim,
fallus searbh air mala is gruaidh;
's a' mhios chreadha trom air cùl
a cinn chrùibte, bhochd, thruaigh.

The load of fruits on her back,
a bitter sweet on brow and
cheek,
and the clay basin heavy on the
back
of her bent poor wretched head.

Chan fhaca Tu i, Mhic an t-saoir,
ri 'n abrar rìgh na Glòir,
a miosg nan cladach carrach, siar,
fo fhallus cliabh a lòin.

Thou hast not seen her, Son of
the carpenter,
who art called the King of
Glory,
among the rugged western
shores
in the sweat of her food's creel.

An t-earrach so agus so chaidh
's gach fichead earrach bho 'n tùs
tharruing ise 'n fheamainn fhuar
chum biadh a cloinn 's duais an tùir.

This Spring and last Spring
and every twenty Springs from
the beginning,
she has carried the cold seaweed
for her children's food and the
castle's reward.

Almost end, that is, because in the best tradition of Celtic art, I should waver back to my beginning: Sorley MacLean's concern for our common hurt, and heritage. 'Ard-Mhusaeum na h-Eireann' ('The National Museum of Ireland') is not his most complex poem, but its noble rhetoric is an outcry against, and an attempt to share, the pain of what is happening in the North of Ireland today:

Anns na laithean dona seo	In these evil days,
is seann leòn Uladh 'na ghaoid	when the old wound of Ulster is
lionnrachaidh 'n cridhe na h-Eòrpa	a disease
agus an cridhe gach Gàidheil	suppurating in the heart of
dh' an aithne gur h-e th' ann an	Europe
Gàidheal . . .	and in the heart of every Gael
	who knows that he is a Gael . . .

Typically, it is Connolly he remembers among the heroes of Easter week; the great socialist who had done his stint in Scotland as well. The way the poem moves from the problem of Ulster to the National Museum of Ireland, then pans in on the rusty red spot of blood on the shirt Connolly wore when he was executed, to finish with the harsh sarcasm of:

> The great hero is still
> sitting in the chair
> fighting the battle in the Post
> Office
> or cleaning streets in Edinburgh.

is also typical of the non-linear associative process of his imagination. As Donal MacAulay puts it:

> Love and politics, history and love of country are so inextricably interwoven that sometimes we are not entirely sure which one is being referred to. The point, in fact, is that they are all being referred to simultaneously.

This process now extends from particular poems to the whole corpus of his work, and it would be fascinating to analyse the way Sorley deploys his major symbols in *Spring Tide and Neap Tide;*

Selected Poems 1932–72 (1977). But I will have to leave you with that last glimpse of the heir to the eighteenth-century poets of the North, both Scotland and Ulster, still speaking powerfully across the dividing straits.

Thomas Kinsella
Another Country . . .

It was late in my literary career, when things were firmly committed, that I looked seriously for the first time at Gaelic literature and at the tradition and culture that produced it. It seems in retrospect a long dereliction or blindness, yet I was shaken from it only by a series of accidents.

In 1969, for example, I published a translation of the *Táin Bó Cuailnge*, an old Irish prose epic dated by scholars to the eighth century. There are numerous verse interpolations in the story, and some of these are possibly two centuries older still, making *The Táin* the oldest vernacular epic in Western Europe. The task had been self-contained and antiquarian enough not to have aroused, by itself, broad questions about its relevance to my own poetry or about a possible relationship between that poetry and the existence (or non-existence) of a supporting tradition. But when the English distributors, in their publicity for the season's publications, listed *The Táin* under 'Old English', a *personal* nerve twitched . . .

Some years ago I was asked by the curriculum committee of the university in the United States where I teach if I would like to give a course on 'The Irish Renaissance'. I agreed to this and received, in due time, official confirmation that I was scheduled to take a class in 'British Literature: 1880 to 1920'. I recognized that this was probably the nearest convenient category in the established curriculum, but argued nonetheless for restoration of the original title (debatable as that might be on other grounds). This was not from mere patriotic emotion but from a wish for accuracy: not to mislead our students.

Above all, there was the accident, in 1966, of my being invited to join a discussion at the annual meeting of the Modern Languages Association in New York on the topic of Ireland's divided tradition, and my taking of that first serious look at the Gaelic element in the modern Irish inheritance. I have been occupied with it ever since, in one way or another, making up for my former neglect. I have even developed a missionary zeal, leading me to work on two anthologies, one of them bilingual, and the setting-up of an annual four-month programme of study of the Irish tradition – the history, literature and much else – from its origin to the present day, and taking account of both languages; the programme is run in Dublin by my American university and is now in its seventh year.

I feel certain that the need for these things is great and I hope that their effects will grow. But apart from that I found much pleasure in the work. On the personal level, as one whose natural language is not Irish, and never will be, it is a relief to sense the effective and enlarging sympathy between some whose natural language *is* Irish, and whose 'business' is Gaelic literature, and some who are merely very interested, like myself. It is not so long since a total commitment was asked as the price of fellowship, a commitment that involved abjuring the English element in the Irish inheritance. This was a relic of the Gaelic League mentality at its narrowest and most unattractive. What is worse, its exclusiveness was quite as falsifying as that of the related narrowness that sees nothing beyond 'Anglo-Irish'. We are in a generation where these limitations are being lifted – less effectively, for the time being, on the Anglo-Irish side, where doing it properly requires learning something of the Irish language; but whichever side one may find oneself on there is a sense that it is up to us together to overcome the old dividing idiocies and employ our energies directly, as best we can, on the actual material of the vital inheritance that unites and divides us.

There has also been the pleasure arising directly from the poetry of the Irish tradition itself: the discovery of poems (and whole genres of poems) I knew nothing of before; the rediscovery of poetry that I had misunderstood and dismissed; the discovery of cohesion and change inside an organic wholeness – as well as rupture and destruction in the organism; all of this where I had been shown nothing before, during my ordinary schooling, but a handful of ill-assorted samples.

It is partly for these reasons that I can offer no summary or synthesis, but present myself mainly as an exhibit – a late-awakened convert bent on greater understanding – and so perhaps accurately representing the two-tongued Irish tradition in its late-twentieth-century manifestation, turning confidently toward an act of self-scrutiny and re-definition. For the same reasons I prefer to offer merely one tentative finding about the course of Irish poetry, and a few poems chosen in what for me is a new light.

Literatures are complex and living things; they have personalities.

It may take an expert to analyse and define a personality, yet we can all recognize the thing easily enough, and name a few distinguishing marks. And there are some easily distinguishable elements, I believe, in the make-up of Irish poetry. Isolation, on the whole, is one, from the earliest surviving pieces until the early nineteenth century. There is an obvious isolation in the Old Irish hermitage and monastic poems; but the poets were men of faith and were on friendly and intimate terms with everything around them, so there is no loneliness. The entire bardic tradition functions in a kind of group isolation and so do the 'new' poets of the seventeenth and eighteenth centuries, or most of them at any rate.

Such a situation is the outcome of Ireland's cultural isolation from a Romanized Europe, an isolation that remained predominant despite frequent and important contacts with the Continent. Gaelic culture was untouched by the Romans; it made its own of Christianity; it absorbed the Vikings, and the Normans; it absorbed even the Cistercians and the Augustinians and the Franciscans. Whatever poetic influences may have come with these invaders were absorbed also; the course of Irish poetry continued and developed in its unique way with minimum adjustments to the 'outside' world. There is no deprivation involved in this; at all times the world of Irish literature is lively and busy, self-sufficient and varied.

To my newly interested eye, one of the most striking things about the poetry of the Irish tradition is that the poems are so often what we are accustomed to call 'occasional'. To call an English poem occasional is to suggest that the poet has taken time off from his principal work to react to some local stimulus, to honour some specific literal occasion. He may well write a very fine poem for the occasion but there is the feeling that his full seriousness is not engaged. Time and again in Irish poetry it is precisely the occasional poems that set the tone and are the masterpieces. This is not because the poets lacked serious concerns that might have given them great themes and great careers. On the contrary, it is that poetry played a much more direct part in the spending of people's lives than we are accustomed to in the English or any other Western tradition. Poetry was a significant part of living, of how Gaelic culture responded to its experiences, great and small, national, parochial and domestic. What need for a great theme when one's entire life is engaged?

This is, of course, a feature of medieval poetry generally, and of the cultural cohesion of the Middle Ages – to go no further back. But Gaelic Ireland retained a kind of medieval wholeness much longer than any other part of the Western world; call it a reward for its isolation, for not undergoing the Renaissance, the Enlightenment or the Romantic Revolution.

A few examples of these poems: firstly, by Pádraigín Haicéad. Haicéad was born in Cashel about 1600, and educated as a priest in Louvain. He was a Dominican friar and a supporter of Cardinal Rinuccini during the troubles of the 1640s, and left Ireland in the general flight after Cromwell; he died in Nantes, in France, in 1654. For all the considerable time he spent on the Continent he remained firmly attached to his Irish apron-strings, emotional and ecclesiastical. He was a volatile and intelligent man, with great linguistic gifts. In the following quatrain, dedicated to the harper Roiberd Óg Carrún, Haicéad employs his gifts to the full in an act of thanks for his music. (The translation is my own – as with all these poems except the last. The aim is to transmit the paraphraseable contents as accurately as possible, with something of the basic rhythm. Rhyme, alliteration, assonance and other effects are catch-as-catch-can.)

Bruthgháir beannacht id bhathas
anuas do ghnáth,
a chuid ghráidh ghlacas an
chrann-chruit chuardach cháidh;
le sruthán seanma snasta go.
suadhach sámh
an dubhán alla do bhainis a
cluasaibh cháich.

Blessings on your head in a glowing heap for ever, beloved, as you grip the great wooden travelling-harp. With a stream of polished playing, profound and sweet, you have banished the spiders' webs out of all our ears.

Exiled and ailing in France, he adopts the usual stratagem of the exile: he returns in dream to the nourishing isolation of the home country. In the following short poem, a graceful conceit with the common touch, he gives life to what is otherwise a dull, if painful, commonplace:

Isan bhFrainc im dhúscadh dhamh
in Éirinn Chuinn im chodladh;
  beag ár ngrádh uaidh don fhaire –
  do thál suain ar síorfhaire.

Awake, I am here in France.
When I sleep I am in the Ireland
  of Conn.
Who would choose to watch and
  wake?
I am watchful – to suckle sleep.

But Haicéad's large body of work is inadequately represented by these fragments. The following more substantial poem was written 'On hearing it has been ordered by the Chapterhouses of Ireland that the Friars must not make up Verses or Songs':

Do chuala inné ag maothlach
  muinteardha
mar nuadhacht scéil ó chéile Chuinn is
  Chuirc
gur duairc le cléir an Ghaedhealg
  ghrinnshlitheach,
suairceas séimh na saorfhear sinseardha.

I heard from a neighbourly
  person yesterday
a piece of news from 'the spouse
  of Conn and Corc':
that the Church condemns our
  Gaelic's subtle paths,
the polished pleasure of our
  noble fathers.

Ní bhuaileabh féin i gcléith a gcointinne
ó chuaidh an ré 'narbh fhéidir linn
  friotal
gach smuaineadh d'éirgheadh d'éirim
  m'intinne,
uair fár bhaoghal faobhar m'intleachta;

I will not spring at the flank of
  their argument
now that the time is past when I
  could utter
each thought erupting from the
  scope of my mind
– when the edge of my intellect
  was a thing to fear

go suaithfeadh sé gan saobhadh
  slimfhuinnimh
fá thuairim thaobh na gcléireach
  gcinsealach
nó anuas fá a mblaoscaibh maola
  millteacha
crua-ghlac ghéar do ghaethibh innlithe.

showering with no loss of pliant
  force
into the general flank of these
  arrogant priests
or down on top of their bald
  malignant skulls
a hard sharp fistful of
  accomplished darts.

Fuaifidh mé mo bhéal le sring fhite
's ní luaifead réad dá bpléid bhig
    sprionlaithe,
ach fuagraim tréad an chaolraigh
    chuimsithe
's a bhfuath, a Dhé, tar éis mo
    mhuintire.

I will stitch my mouth up with a
    twisted string
and say no word about their
    mean complaining,
merely condemn the herd of
    narrow censors
and the hate they bear my
    people, O my God.

All over the tradition there are scores of famous, and treasured, occasional poems. Many of them are lamentations: Blind Raftery's 'Eanach Dhúin', written after a drowning disaster on the Corrib river in Galway; Seamus Dall Mac Cuarta's poems 'An Londubh Báite' and 'Tithe Chorra an Chait', the first humorously tender over a young girl's drowned pet blackbird, the second as close to a curse – on a townland of ungenerous people – as a gentle poet can make it; Cathal Buí Mac Giolla Ghunna's mock lament for a yellow bittern; or the great anonymous folk songs 'Dónall Óg' or 'Liam Ó Raghallaigh'.

The following is a fine poem, less well known and older than these. It is an anonymous seventeenth-century greeting for the seasonal return of the herring. It is in one of the old syllabic forms, every line of seven syllables, with the usual device of assonance, both in alternate line-endings and internally. For all these apparent restrictions it has a wonderful comic ease, not to mention a finely cannibalistic ending:

Mo-chean do theacht, a scadáin;
druid liom, a dhaltáin uasail;
do chéad beatha 's do shláinte,
do thuillis fáilte uaimse.

Hail, herring! You've come!
My fine son, come close.
Your health! A hundred
    greetings!
You well deserve our welcome!

Dar láimh m'athar, a scadáin,
gé maith bradáin na Bóinne,
duit do dhealbhas an duainse
ós tú is uaisle 's is óige.

By my father's hand, herring,
though Boyne salmon are fine
I made this poem for you,
most noble and most fresh.

A fhir is comhghlan colann
nach déanann comann bréige
cara mar thú ní bhfuaras;
ná bíom suarach fá chéile.

Sir, whose wholesome body
gives no lying promise,
I have found no friend like you;
let nothing mean divide us.

Dá bhféachdaois uaisle Banbha
cia is mó tarbha den triúrsa:
is rí ar gach iasc an scadán
idir bhradán is liúsa.

Let Banba's best consider
the worthiest of these three:
over salmon, over pike,
herring is king of fish.

Is é ar bhféachain gach cósta
go crích bhóchna na Gréige,
iasc is uaisle ná an scadán
ní bhfuair Canán Chinn tSléibhe.

When he studied every coast
to the Greek land's ocean-edge
Canán Cinn tSléibhe could not
    find
a nobler fish than the herring.

A scadáin shéimhe shúgaigh,
a chinn chumhdaigh an Charghais,
a mhic ghrádhaigh mo charad,
liom is fada go dtángais.

Herring, gentle and jovial,
our mainstay in time of Lent,
my friends' favourite son,
it was long until you came.

Gé mór do thuit a-nuraidh
ded ghaol bhunaidh fán méis-se,
ná cuimhnigh fíoch ná fala,
ós tú cara na cléire.

Though many of your close kin
fell last year across this plate,
brood not in anger or spite,
you, that are friend to poets.

A scadáin shailltigh shoilbhir
nach bíonn go doilbhir dúinte,
liomsa do theacht ní hanait,
súil ar charaid an tsúilse.

Herring, salty, serene,
not shut in self or sour,
your coming causes no pang!
My eye rests on a friend.

I dtús an Charghais chéasta,
a fhir lé ndéantar comhól,
ortsa, go teacht na Cásca,
is mór mo ghrása 's is romhór.

As tormented Lent begins,
Sir (with whom we drink),
for you – till Easter comes –
my love is great and growing!

Another little-known poem is the 'Exodus to Connacht'; it gathers up in its simple way great masses of emotion centred on one of the greatest single occasions in Ireland's history, the expulsion to Connacht in the seventeenth century. The poet is Fear Dorcha Ó Mealláin, of whom we know nothing except that he was from Eastern Ulster and that he made this poem to give heart to his people in their time of hardship. Poetry can provide a fit medium for any mood and if there is a more perfect vehicle for simple and practical piety than this poem I am not aware of it:

In ainm an Athar go mbuaidh,
in ainm an Mhic fuair an phian,
in ainm an Spioraid Naoimh le neart,
Muire 's a Mac linn ag triall.

In the name of the Father full of virtue,
in the name of the Son Who suffered pain,
in the name of the Holy Ghost in power,
Mary and her Son be with us.

Mícheál feartach ár gcuid stóir,
Mhuire Ógh 's an dá aspal déag,
Brighid, Pádraig agus Eoin –
is maith an lón creideamh Dé.

Our sole possessions: Michael of miracles,
the virgin Mary, the twelve apostles,
Brigid, Patrick and Saint John
– and fine rations: faith in God.

Colam Cille feartach caomh,
's Colmán mhac Aoidh, ceann na gcliar,
beid linn uile ar aon tslí
's ná bígí ag caoi fá dhul siar.

Sweet Colm Cille of miracles too,
and Colmán Mac Aoidh, poets' patron,
will all be with us on our way.
Do not bewail our journey West.

Nach dtuigeann sibh, a bhráithre gaoil
cúrsaí an tsaoil le fada buan? –
gé mór atá 'nár seilbh,
beag bheas linn ag dul san uaigh.

Brothers mine, do you not see
the ways of the world a while now?
However much we may possess
we'll go with little into the grave.

Uirscéal as sin tuigthear libh:
clann Israel a bhean le Dia,
san Éigipt cé bhí i mbroid,
furtacht go grod a fuair siad.

Consider a parable of this:
Israel's people, God's own,
although they were in bonds in Egypt,
found in time a prompt release.

Do-chuadar trid an mhuir mhóir,
go ndearnadh dhóibh ród nár ghann,
gur éirigh an fhairrge ghlas
mar charraig 'mach os a gceann.

Through the mighty sea they
    passed,
an ample road was made for
    them,
then the grey-green ocean rose
out there above them like a
    rock.

Iar ndul dhóibhsin fó thír
fuair siad cóir ó Rí na rann,
furtacht, cabhair agus biadh
ón Dia bhí riamh is tá ann.

When they came to dry land
the King of Heaven minded
    them
– relief, succour and
    nourishment
from the God Who ever was and
    is.

Fuaradar ó neamh mar lón
cruithneachta mhór – stor nár bheag –
mil dá chur mar cheo,
uisce go leor ag teacht as creig.

Food from Heaven they
    received:
great wheat, in no small
    measure,
honey settling like a mist,
abundant water out of rock.

Amhlaidh sin do-ghéanfar libh:
do-ghéabhaidh sibh gach maith ar dtús;
atá bhur ndúithche ar neamh,
's ná bígí leamh in bhur gcúis.

Likewise it shall be done to you:
all good things shall first be
    yours.
Heaven is your inheritance.
Be not faint-hearted in your
    faith.

A chlann chroí, déanaidh seasamh,
's ná bígí ag ceasnamh le hanró;
Maoise a fuair ar agaill –
cead a chreidimh ó Pharó.

People of my heart, stand
    steady,
don't complain of your distress.
Moses got what he requested,
religious freedom – and from
    Pharaoh.

Ionann Dia dhúinn agus dhóibh,
aon Dia fós do bhí 'gus tá;
ionann Dia abhus agus thiar,
aon Dia riamh is bheas go bráth.

Identical their God and ours.
One God there was and still
    remains.
Here or Westward God is one,
one God ever and shall be.

185

Má ghoirthear dhaoibhse Páipis,
cuíridh fáilte re bhur ngairm;
tugaidh foighead don Ardrí –
Deo gratias, maith an t-ainm.

A Dhia atá fial, a thriath na
　　mbeannachta,
féach na Gaeil go léir gan bharanta;
má táimid ag triall siar go Connachta,
fágmaid' nár ndiaidh fó chian ar
　　seanchairde.

If they call you 'Papishes'
accept it gladly for a title.
Patience, for the High King's
　　sake.
Deo Gratias, good the name!

God Who art generous, O
　　Prince of Blessings,
behold the Gael, stripped of
　　authority.
Now as we journey Westward
　　into Connacht
old friends we'll leave behind us
　　in their grief.

The greatest occasional poem in Irish literature is probably 'Caoineadh Airt Uí Laoghaire', the lament by Eibhlín Dubh Ní Chonaill for her murdered husband. To emphasize that it gives expression to a private need by leaning on a strong supporting tradition is, I hope, merely to labour a point already made. To call such a poem occasional demonstrates the real limitations of the term when applied to Irish poetry. It is no turning aside. It is a turning *toward* – in desperation, for support, toward the traditional resources of a living culture. But the 'Caoineadh' is a classic – one of the world's great poems – and is on its way to proper recognition as such. I should like to urge on the reader's attention a lesser-known poem of the same kind, in token of the countless fine Gaelic poems that are waiting to take their place in the modern Irish consciousness. It is altogether a lesser poem than 'Caoineadh Airt Uí Laoghaire', but still a very good one, and important and moving for its own reasons. It was written by a father to mourn his drowned son; again, it is a turning toward the established traditional mode as a support in personal grief. But it has a further special quality in that its writer is one of the very last to have done this unselfconsciously. He was Pádraig Ó hÉigeartaigh, and he wrote his poem in Boston less than eighty years ago. Reading it, we are hearing the closing-down of a part of the long history of Irish poetry. The translation in this case is not my own; it was made by the editor to whom the writer sent his work, a man with diverse claims on our gratitude, among them that he is by far the most reliable of the twentieth-century translators of Irish poetry – the most respectful of his originals and the least interfering – Patrick Pearse:

Ochón! a Dhonncha, mo mhíle
    cogarnach, fén bhfód so sínte;
Fód an doichill 'na luí ar do cholainn
    bhig, mo loma-sceimhle!
Dá mbeadh an codladh so i gCill na
    Dromad ort nó in uaigh san Iarthar
Mo bhrón do bhogfadh, cé gur mhór mo
    dhochar, is ní bheinn id' dhiaidh air.

Ochón, O Donough! my
    thousand whispers stretched
    under this sod,
The sod of sorrow on your little
    body, my utter anguish!
If this sleep were on you in Cill
    na Dromad, or some grave in
    the West,
'Twould soften my suffering,
    though great my hurt, and I
    would not repine for you!

Is feoite caite 'tá na blátha a scaipeadh
    ar do leabaidh chaoilse;
Ba bhreá iad tamall ach thréig a
    dtaitneamh, níl snas ná bri iontu;
'S tá an bláth ba ghile liom dár fhás ar
    ithir riamh ná a fhásfaidh choíche
Ag dreo sa talamh is go deo ní
    thacfaidh ag cur éirí croí orm.

Withered and wasted are the
    flowers they scattered on
    your narrow bed,
They were lovely for a little
    time, but their radiance is
    gone, they have no
    comeliness or life;
And the flower I held brightest
    of all that grew in soil or
    shall ever grow
Is rotting in the ground, and will
    spring no more to lift up my
    heart.

Och, a chumannaigh! nár mhór an
    scrupall é an t-uisce dod' luascadh
Gan neart id' chuisleannaibh ná éinne i
    ngoire duit a thabharfadh fuarthan.
Scéal níor tugadh chugham ar bhaol mo
    linbh ná ar dhéine a chrunatain –
Ó! 's go raghainn go fonnmhar ar
    dhoimhin-lic Ifrinn chun tú a
    fhuascailt.

Alas, beloved! was it not a great
    pity, the water rocking you,
With no strength in your pulses
    nor anyone near you that
    might save:
No news was brought to me of
    the peril of my child or the
    extremity of his need –
Ah, though I'd gladly go to
    Hell's deep flag to rescue
    you!

Tá an ré go dorcha, ní fhéadaim
  codladh, do shéan gach só mé:
Garbh doilbh liom an Ghaeilge oscailte
  – is olc an comhartha é;
Fuath liom sealad i gcomhluadar carad,
  bíonn a ngreann dom' chiapadh;
Ón lá go bhfacasa go tláith ar an
  ngaineamh thú níor gheal an ghrian
  dom.

The moon is dark, I cannot
  sleep, all joy has left me:
Rough and rude to me the open
  Gaelic ('tis an ill sign);
I hate a while in the company of
  friends, their merriment
  tortures me;
From the day I saw you dead on
  the sand, the sun has not
  shone for me.

Och, mo mhairg cad a dhéanfad feasta
  's an saol dom shuathadh,
Gan do láimhín chailce mar leoithne i
  gcrannaibh ar mo mhalainn
  ghruama.
Do bhéilín meala mar cheol na
  n-aingeal go binn im' chluasaibh,
Á rá go cneasta liom: 'Mo ghraidhn,
  m'athair bocht, ná bíodh buairt ort.'

Alas, my grief! what shall I do
  henceforth, the world
  wearying me,
Without your chalk-white little
  hand like a breath through
  trees on my sombre brow,
Your little mouth of honey like
  angels' music sweet in my
  ears
Saying to me gently, 'dear heart,
  poor father, be not troubled!'

Ó, mo chaithis é! is beag do cheapas-sa
  i dtráth mo dhóchais
Ná beadh an leanbh so 'na laoch mhear
  chalma i lár na foirne,
A ghníomhartha gaisce 's a smaointe
  meanman ar son na Fódla –
Ach an Té do dhealbhaigh de chré ar
  an dtalamh sinn, ní mar sin
  d'ordaigh.

Ah, desolate! I little thought in
  the time of my hope
That this child would not be a
  swift valiant hero in the midst
  of the band,
Doing deeds of daring and
  planning wisely for the sake
  of Fódla,
But He who fashioned us of clay
  on earth not so has ordered!

An Appendix
More Poems for Pleasure

Early Nature Poems

Is Mo Chen In Maiten Bán

Is mo chen in maiten bán,
do-thét ar lár m'airiuclán,
is mo chen don tí rus-foí,
in maiten buadach bithnaí.

A ingen Aidche úaille,
a siúr na Gréine glúaire,
is mo chen, a maiten bán,
foillsiges orm mo lebrán.

Dawn

Come into my dark oratory,
    be welcome the bright morn,
and blessed He who sent you,
    victorious, self-renewing
    dawn.

Maiden of good family,
    Sun's sister, daughter of
    proud Night,
ever-welcome the fair morn
    that brings my mass-book
    light.

The Hermitage

Dúthraçar, a Maic Dé bí,
  a Rí suthain sen,
bothán deirrit díthraba
  commad sí mo threb.

Uisce treglas tanaide
  do buith ina taíb,
linn glan do nigi pectha
  tría rath Spirta Naíb.

Fidbaid álainn immocus
  impe do cech leith
fri altram n-én n-ilgothach
  fri clithar dia cleith.

Deisebar fri tesugud,
  sruthán dar a lainn,
talam togu co méit raith
  bad maith do cach clainn.

Úathad óclach n-innide –
  in-fessam a llín –
it é umlai urluithi
  d'urguidi ind Ríg.

Ceithri triir, trí cethrair,
  cuibdi fri cach les;
dá seiser i n-eclais
  eter túaid is tes.

The Hermitage

Grant me sweet Christ the grace
  to find –
  Son of the living God! –
A small hut in a lonesome spot
  To make it my abode.

A little pool but very clear
  To stand beside the place
Where all men's sins are washed
  away
  By sanctifying grace.

A pleasant woodland all about
  To shield it from the wind,
And make a home for singing
  birds
  Before it and behind.

A southern aspect for the heat,
  A stream along its foot,
A smooth green lawn with rich
  top soil
  Propitious to all fruit.

My choice of men to live with
  me
  And pray to God as well;
Quiet men of humble mind –
  Their number I shall tell.

Four files of three or three of
  four
  To give the psalter forth;
Six to pray by the south church
  wall
  And six along the north.

Sé desa do imfhorcraid
  immumsa fa-déin
co guidi tre bithu sír
  ind Ríg ruithnes gréin.

Two by two my dozen friends –
  To tell the number right –
Praying with me to move the King
  Who gives the sun its light.

Eclais aíbinn anartach,
  aitreb Dé do nim,
suṭrulla soillsi íar sain
  úas Scriptúir glain gil.

A lovely church, a home for God,
  Bedecked with linen fine,
Where over the white Gospel page
  The Gospel candles shine.

Óentegdais do aithigid
  fri deithidin cuirp,
cen drúis, cen intládud,
  cen imrádud n-uilc.

A little house where all may dwell
  And body's care be sought,
Where none shows lust or arrogance,
  None thinks an evil thought.

Is é trebad no gébainn,
  do-gégainn cen chleith:
fírchainnenn chumra, cerca,
  bratáin breca, beich.

And all I ask for housekeeping
  I get and pay no fees,
Leeks from the garden, poultry, game,
  Salmon and trout and bees.

Mo lórtu brait ocus bíd
  ónd Ríg as chaín clú,
mo buithsi im shuidiu fri ré
  oc guidi Dé i nach dú.

My share of clothing and of food
  From the King of fairest face,
And I to sit at times alone
  And pray in every place.

Winter

Fuit, fuit!
Fuar a-nocht Magh leathan Luirg;
  airde an sneachta ionás an sliabh,
  nocha roicheann fiadh a gcuid.

Fuit go bráth!
Ro dháil an doineann ar chách;
  abhann gach eitrighe a bhfán
  agus is linn lán gach áth.

Is muir mór gach loch bhíos lán
  agus is loch lán gach linn;
ní roichid eich tar Áth Rois,
  ní mó roichid dí chois inn.

Siubhladh ar iasc Inse Fáil;
  ní fhuil tráigh nach tiobrann tonn;
a mbroghaibh nocha tá broc,
  ní léir cloch, ní labhair corr.

Ní fhaghbhaid coin Choille Cuan
  sámh ná suan i n-adhbhaidh chon;
ni fhaghbhann an dre-eoán beag
  díon dá nead i Leitir Lon.

Is maith do mheanbhaigh na n-éan
  an ghaoth ghéar is an t-oighreadh
  fuar;
ní fhaghbhann lon Droma Daoil
  díon a thaoibh i gCoilltibh Cuan.

Sádhail ar gcoire dá dhrol,
  aistreach lon ar Leitir Cró;
do mhínigh sneachta Coill Ché,
  deacair dréim ré beanna bó.

Chill, chill!
All Moylurg is cold and still,
Where can deer a-hungered go
When the snow lies like a hill?

Cold till doom!
All the world obeys its rule,
Every track become a stream,
Every ford become a pool.

Every pool become a lake,
Every lake become a sea,
Even horses cannot cross
The ford at Ross so how can
    we?

All the fish in Ireland stray
When the cold winds smite the
    bay,
In the towns no voice is heard,
Bell and bird have had their say.

Even the wolves in Cuan Wood
Cannot find a place to rest
When the small wren of Lon
    Hill
Is not still within her nest.

The small quire of birds has
    passed
In cold snow and icy blast,
And the blackbird of Cuan
    Wood
Finds no shelter that holds fast.

Nothing's easy but our pot,
Our old shack on the hill is not,
For in woodlands crushed with
    snow
On Ben Bo the trail's forgot.

Cubhar Glinne Ridhe an fhraoigh
ón ngaoith aichir do-gheibh léan;
mór a thruaighe agus a phian,
an t-oighreadh do shiad 'na bhéal.

Éirghe do cholcaidh is do chlúimh –
tug dot úidh! – nochan ciall duit;
iomad n-oighridh ar gach n-áth
is é fáth fá n-abraim 'Fuit!'

The old eagle of Glen Rye,
Even he forgets to fly,
With ice crusted on his beak,
He is now too weak to cry.

Best lie still
In wool and feathers, take your
  fill,
Ice is thick on every ford
And the word I chose is 'chill'.

Ach, A Luin

Ach, a luin, is buide duit
  cáit 'sa muine i fuil do net,
a díthrebaig nád clinn cloc,
  is binn boc síthamail t'fet.

The Blackbird

Blackbird, it is well for you
wherever in the thicket be your
  nest,
hermit that sounds no bell,
sweet, soft, fairylike is your
  note.

Dom-farcai Fidbaidae Fál

Dom-farcai fidbaidae fál,
  fom-chain loíd luin – lúad nad cél;
húas mo lebrán, ind línech,
  fom-chain trírech inna n-én.

Fomm-chain coí menn – medair mass –
  hi mbrot glass de dindgnaib doss.
Débrad! nom-Choimmdiu coíma,
  caín-scríbaimm fo roída ross.

Writing Out Of Doors

A wall of forest looms above
  and sweetly the blackbird
  sings;
all the birds make melody
  over me and my books and
  things.

There sings to me the cuckoo
  from bush-citadels in grey
  hood.
God's doom! May the Lord
  protect me
  writing well, under the great
  wood.

Classical Bardic Poetry

Beatha an Scoláire

Aoibhinn beatha an scoláire
*   bhíos ag déanamh a léighinn;*
is follas díbh, a dhaoine,
*   gurab dó is aoibhne in Éirinn.*

Gan smacht ríogh ná rófhlatha
*   ná tighearna dá threise*
gan chuid chíosa ag caibidil,
*   gan moichéirghe, gan meirse.*

Moichéirghe ná aodhaireacht
*   ní thabhair uadha choidhche,*
's ní mó do-bheir dá aire
*   fear na faire san oidhche.*

Do-bheir sé greas ar tháiplis,
*   is ar chláirsigh go mbinne,*
nó fós greas eile ar shuirghe
*   is ar chumann mná finne.*

Maith biseach a sheisrighe
*   ag teacht tosaigh an earraigh;*
is é is crannghail dá sheisrigh
*   lán a ghlaice de pheannaibh.*

The Scholar's Life

Sweet is the scholar's life,
    busy about his studies,
the sweetest lot in Ireland
    as all of you know well.

No king or prince to rule him
    nor lord however mighty,
no rent to the chapterhouse,
    no drudging, no dawn-rising.

Dawn-rising or shepherding
    never required of him,
no need to take his turn
    as watchman in the night.

He spends a while at chess,
    and a while with the pleasant
    harp
and a further while wooing
    and winning lovely women.

His horse-team hale and hearty
    at the first coming of Spring;
the harrow for his team
    is a fistful of pens.

'This poem is apparently meant as a reproach to someone who had adopted the dress and manners of a Tudor courtier. He is contrasted with another, perhaps his brother, who had chosen the harder but more adventurous life of a rebel. As regards the language, it may be noted that the classical poets had no scruple about using the foreign word to denote the foreign thing, so that in this short piece we find several English loan-words. A couple of lines are obscure and perhaps corrupt.' (Osborn Bergin)

A fhir ghlacas a ghalldacht,
bhearras an barr bachalldocht,
seang-ghlac atú do thogha,
ní tú deagh-mhac Donnchadha.

Man who follow English ways,
who cut short your curling hair,
O slender hand of my choice,
you are unlike the good son of
Donnchadh!

Ni thréicfea, da madh tú soin,
do ghruag ar ghalldacht thacair –
maisi as fhearr fá fhíadh bhFódla –
'sní bhíadh do cheann corónda.

If you were he, you would not
give up your long hair (the best
adornment in all the land of
Ireland) for an affected English
fashion, and your head would
not be tonsured.

Ní modh leatsa an barr buidhe;
fuath leision na locuidhe,
is bheith maol ar ghrés na nGall –
bhar mbés ar-aon ní hionann.

You think a shock of yellow hair
unfashionable; *he* hates both the
wearing of love-locks and being
shaven-headed in the English
manner – how unlike are your
ways!

Fear nár ghrádhaigh an ghalldacht
Eóghan Bán, searc saor-bhanntracht,
don ghalldacht ní thug a thoil,
an alltacht rug do roghain.

Eóghan *Bán*, the darling of noble
women, is a man who never
loved English customs; he has
not set his heart on English
ways, he has chosen the wild life
rather.

Ní bhean th'aigneadh d'Eóghan Bhán,
do-bhéradh brísdi ar bhegán,
fear nár iarr do chlóca acht ceirt,
lé nár mian cóta is coisbeirt.

Your ideas are nothing to
Eóghan *Bán*; he would give
breeches away for a trifle, a man
who asked no cloak but a rag,
who had no desire for doublet
and hose.

Fuath leis ar chaol a choisi
mionn sbuir ar bhróig bhuataisi,
nó sdocaidhe ar sdair na nGall;
locaidhe air ní fhágbhann.

Ráipér maol nach muirfeadh cuil,
ní maisi lé mac Donnchaidh
meadh meanaidh thiar ar a thóin,
ag triall go tealaigh thionóil.

Beg a brígh a mbrat órdha,
ná a mbanna ard sholónda
nó a bhfail óir far ghabhtha ghoimh,
nó a sgarfa sróill go sálaibh.

Dúil a leaba chlúimh ní chuir,
annsa leis luighi ar luachair;
teach garbh-shlat ná táille tuir,
sáimhe lé dagh-mhac Donnchaidh.

Bró mharc-shluagh ar bhrú mbeirne,
troid gharbh, comhlann ceitheirne,
cuid do mhianuibh meic Donnchaidh,
's gleic d'iarraidh ar allmhurchaibh.

Ní hionann is Eóghan Bán
gáirit 'mad chois ar chlochán
truagh nach bhacas libh bhar locht,
a fhir ghlacas an ghalldacht.

He would hate to have at his
ankle a jewelled spur on a boot,
or stockings in the English
manner; he will allow no
love-locks on him.

A blunt rapier which could not
kill a fly, the son of Donnchadh
does not think it handsome; nor
the weight of an awl sticking out
behind his rear as he goes to the
hill of the assembly.

Little he cares for
gold-embroidered cloaks, or for
a high well-furnished ruff, or for
a gold ring which would only be
vexatious, or for a satin scarf
down to his heels.

·He does not set his heart on a
feather bed, he would prefer to
lie upon rushes; to the good son
of Donnchadh a house of rough
wattles is more comfortable than
the battlements of a castle.

A troop of horse at the mouth of
a pass, a wild fight, a ding-dong
fray of footsoldiers, these are
some of the delights of
Donnchadh's son – and seeking
contest with the foreigners.

You are unlike Eóghan Bán; men
laugh at you as you put your
foot on the mounting-block; it is
a pity that you yourself don't see
your errors, O man who follow
English ways.

The Child Born in Prison
Gofraidh Fionn Ó Dálaigh,
d. 1387

Under Sorrow's Sign

Bean torrach, fa tuar broide,
do bhí i bpríosún pheannaide,
bearar dho chead Dé na ndúl,
lé leanabh beag sa bhríosún.

A pregnant girl, under sorrow's
    sign,
Condemned to a cell of pain,
Bore, by leave of Creation's
    Lord,
Her small child in prison.

Ar n-a bhreith do bhí an macámh
ag fás mar gach bhfochlocán,
dá fhiadhnaibh mar budh eadh dhún,
seal do bhliadhnaibh sa bhríosún.

Swiftly the young lad flourished,
Eager as a bardic novice,
For those first years in prison,
Clear as if we were looking on.

An inghean d'fhagháil bhroide –
meanma an leinbh níor lughaide,
sí dhá réir gé dho bhaoi i mbroid,
mar mhnaoi gan phéin gan pheannaid.

Who would not be moved, alas,
As he darts playful little runs
Within the limit of his walls
While his mother falls into
    sadness!

Do shoillse an laoi níor léir dhóibh
acht a bhfaicdís – fáth dobróin! –
do dhruim iodhan an achaidh
tré ionadh thuill tarathair.

For all daylight brought to
    them –
O sharp plight – was the
    glimpse
A single augurhole might yield
Of the bright backbone of a
    field.

Mun n-orchra níorbh ionann dál
dá mháthair is don mhacámh ;
do aithrigh dealbh dá dreich gil
is an leanbh ag breith bhisigh.

Seeing one day on her pale face
A shining tear, the child cried:
'Unfold to me your sorrow
Since I follow its trace.

An leanbh dá oileamhain ann
dob fheirrde aige a fhulang,
níor léir don bharrthais óg úr
nárbh fhód Parrthais an príosún.

Does there exist another world
Brighter than where we are:
A home lovelier than this
Source of your heavy
    weariness?'

Seisean ag breith ruag reabhraidh,
sise ag dul i ndoimheanmain;
mairg, thrá, nach tiobhradh dá aoidh
ionnramh na mná 'sa macaoimh.

Ar bhfaicsin déar ré dreich ngil,
ráidhis an leanbh lá éigin:
ó tharla a fhuidheall ar mh'óidh,
cluineam damhna do dhobróin.

Neimhiongnadh gé dho-neinn maoith,
ar sise, a leinibh lánbhaoith;
is rian cumhang nár dhleacht dún,
teacht d'fhulang pian i bpríosún.

An bhfuil, ar sé, sódh eile,
is aoibhne ná ar n-innmhine,
nó an bhfuil ní as soillse ná so,
ó dho-ní an toirse tromsa?

Dar linn, ar an leanabh óg,
gé taoi brónach, a bheanód,
is léir dhúin ar ndíol soillse,
ná bíodh ar th'úidh attuirse.

A n-abrae ní hiongnadh dheit,
ar an inghean, a óigmheic;
dáigh treibhe an teagh do thoghais –
treabh eile ní fhacadhais.

'Seeing the narrow track we
    tread
Between the living and the dead
It would be small wonder if I
Were not sad, heedless boy.

But had you shared my life
Before joining this dark tribe
Then on the tender hobbyhorse
Of your soul, sorrow would
    ride.

The flame of the wide world
Warmed my days at first;
To be closed in a dark cell
Afterwards: that's the curse.'

Realising this life's distress
Beyond all balm or sweetness,
The boy's brow did not darken
Before his cold and lonely
    prison.

This image – this poem's
    dungeon:
Of those closed in a stern prison
These two stand for the host of
    living,
Their sentence, life
    imprisonment.

Against the gaiety of God's son,
Whose kingdom holds eternal
    sway
Sad every dungeon where earth's
    hosts
Lie hidden from the light of day.

                                John Montague

Dá bhfaictheá a bhfacaidh meise,
ré dteacht don treibh dhoircheisi,
do bhiadh doimheanma ort ann,
do phort oileamhna, a anam.

Os agadsa is fhearr a dhearbh,
a inghean, ar an t-óigleanbh,
ná ceil foirn fionnachtain de,
do mhoirn d'iomarcaidh oirne.

Loise an tsaoghail mhóir amuigh,
is eadh tháirreas ó thosaigh;
mé i dtigh dhorcha 'na dheaghaidh,
a fhir chomtha, is cinneamhain.

Le cleachtadh deacrachta dhe,
'snach fuair sé sódh is aoibhne,
níor cheis a ghruadh ghríosúr ghlan
ar an bpríosún bhfuar bhfolamh.

Baramhail do-bearthar dún –
an dream do bhí sa bhríosún:
lucht an bheatha cé an cúpla,
a ré is beatha bhríosúnta.

Ag féachain meadhrach Mheic Dé,
flaitheas aga bhfuil buainré,
cúis bhróin beatha gach dúnaidh,
slóigh an bheatha is bríosúnaigh.

N.B. John Montague's version,
which reflects admirably the
tone and spirit of this poem,
does not however follow the
precise stanza sequence of the
original.

Ar maidin, a mhacaoimh óig
iarr teagasc ar an dTríonóid ;
ionnail go cáidh, gabh go glan
gan sal id láimh do leabhar.

Every morning, my young lad,
pray guidance from the Trinity.
  Wash well, and take your
  book
  in clean hands without a
  mark.

Féach gach líne go glinn glic,
déan meabhrughadh go minic ;
ceacht bheag is meabhair ghéar
ghlan,
a leanaibh, féagh gach focal.

Study each line clearly, wisely,
get things often off by heart
  – a short lesson, a sharp
  mind.
  Study every word, my child.

Bheith ag féachain cháich ná cleacht,
tabhair t'aire dot éincheacht ;
taisigh í ó chúl do chinn,
bí léi, gé cruaidh an choimhling.

Don't stare around at everyone.
Attend to your assigned work.
  Root it deeply in your head.
  Stay at it, though the fight is
  hard.

Ar mhuir mhóir an léighinn láin
bí id loingseoir mhaith, a mhacáimh ;
bí, madh áil, it fháidh eagna
i ndáil cháigh do choimhfhreagra.

On ample learning's mighty
  ocean
be, my boy, a good sailor.
  Be a wise sage if you can
  answering out in front of all.

Ibhidh gach laoi láindigh dhi,
tobar na heagna uaisle ;
ní badh searbh id bheol a blas ;
badh sealbh aoibhneasa an t-eolas.

Take a copious draught each day
from wisdom's noble spring.
  It won't taste sour in your
  mouth.
  Knowledge is a hold on bliss.

Love Poems

Undying Love!

Ní bhfuighe mise bás duit,
a bhean úd an chuirp mar ghéis;
daoine leamha ar mharbhais riamh,
ní hionann iad is mé féin.

Créad umá rachainn-se d'éag
don bhéal dearg, don déad mar
bhláth?
an crobh miolla, an t-ucht mar aol,
an dáibh do-gheabhainn féin bás?

Do mhéin aobhdha, th'aigneadh saor,
a bhas thana, a thaobh mar chuip,
a rosg gorm, a bhrágha bhán,–
ní bhfuighe mise bás duit.

Do chíocha corra, a chneas úr,
do ghruaidh chorcra, do chúl fiar,–
go deimhin ní bhfuighead bás
dóibh sin go madh háil le Dia.

Do mhala chaol, t'fholt mar ór,
do rún geanmnaidh, do ghlór leasc,
do shál chruinn, do cholpa réidh –
ní mhuirbhfeadh siad acht duine
leamh.

A bhean úd an chuirp mar ghéis,
do hoileadh mé ag duine glic;
aithne dhamh mar bhíd na mná –
ní bhfuighe mise bás duit!

I Shall Not Die for Thee

For thee I shall not die,
Woman high of fame and name;
Foolish men thou mayest slay,
I and they are not the same.

Why should I expire
For the fire of any eye,
Slender waist or swan-like limb,
Is't for them that I should die?

Thy sharp wit, thy perfect calm,
Thy thin palm like foam of the
sea;
Thy white neck, thy blue eye,
I shall not die for thee.

The round breasts, the fresh
skin,
Cheeks crimson, hair like silk to
touch,
Indeed, indeed, I shall not die,
Please God, not I for any such!

The golden locks, the forehead
thin,
The quiet mien, the gracious
ease,
The rounded heel, the languid
tone,
Fools alone find death from
these.

Woman, graceful as the swan,
A wise man did rear me too,
Little palm, white neck, bright
eye,
I shall not die for you.

An Phóg

Taisigh agad féin do phóg,
  a inghean óg is geal déad;
ar do phóig ní bhfaghaim blas,
  congaibh uaim a-mach do bhéal!

Póg is romhillse ná mil
  fuaras ó mhnaoi fhir tré ghrádh;
blas ar phóig eile dá héis
  ní bhfagha mé go dtí an brách.

Go bhfaicear an bhean-soin féin
  do thoil ÉinMhic Dé na ngrás,
ní charabh bean tsean ná óg,
  ós í a póg atá mar tá.

The Kiss

Oh, keep your kisses, young
    provoking girl!
  I find no taste in any
    maiden's kiss.
Altho' your teeth be whiter than
    the pearl,
  I will not drink at fountains
    such as this.

I know a man whose wife did
    kiss my mouth
  With kiss more honeyed than
    the honeycomb.
And never another's kiss can
    slake my drought
  After that kiss, till judgement
    hour shall come.

Till I do gaze on her for whom I
    long,
  If ever God afford such grace
    to men,
I would not love a woman old
    or young,
  Till she do kiss me as she
    kissed me then.

Fainic   *Trust No Man*

Cumann fallsa grádh na bhfear!
  is mairg bean do-ní a réir;
gidh milis a gcomhrádh ceart,
  is fada is-teach bhíos a méin.

A false love is the love of men –
woe to the woman who does
their will! Though their fine talk
is sweet, their hearts are hidden
deep within.

Ná creid a gcogar 's a rún,
  ná creid glacadh dlúth a lámh,
ná creid a bpóg ar a mbia blas,–
  ó n-a searc ní bhfuilim slán.

Do not believe their secret
whisper, do not believe the close
squeeze of their hands, do not
believe their sweet-tasting kiss;
it is through their love that I am
sick.

Ná creid, is ní chreidfe mé,
  fear ar domhan tar éis cháich;
do chuala mé sgéal ó 'né,
  och, a Dhé! is géar rom-chráidh.

Do not believe, and I shall not,
one man in the world more than
another; I heard a story
yesterday – ah God, it torments
me cruelly!

Do bhéardaois airgead is ór,
  do bhéardaois fós agus maoin,
do bhéardaois pósadh is ceart
  do mhnaoi, nó go teacht an laoi,

They would offer silver and
gold, they would offer treasure
too; they would offer marriage,
as is right, to a woman – till
morning comes.

Ní mise amháin do mheall siad,
  is iomdha bean riamh do chealg
grádh an fhir nách bia go buan,–
  och, is mairg do chuaidh rem cheird.

Not me alone have they
deceived, many a one has been
tricked before by the inconstant
love of men; och, woe to her
who has gone my way!

Author unknown; fifteenth–sixteenth century?

Moladh Ban

Mairg adeir olc ris na mnáibh!
  bheith dá n-éagnach ní dáil chruinn;
a bhfuaradar do ghuth riamh
  dom aithne ní hiad do thuill.

Binn a mbriathra, gasta a nglór,
  aicme rerab mór mo bháidh;
a gcáineadh is mairg nár loc;
  mairg adeir olc ris na mnáibh.

Ní dhéanaid fionghal ná feall,
  ná ní ar a mbeith grainc ná gráin;
ní sháraighid cill ná clog;
  mairg adeir olc ris na mnáibh.

Ní tháinig riamh acht ó mhnaoi
  easbag ná rí (dearbhtha an dáil),
ná príomhfháidh ar nách biadh
  locht;
  mairg adeir olc ris na mnáibh.

Agá gcroidhe bhíos a ngeall;
  ionmhain leó duine seang slán, –
fada go ngeabhdaois a chol;
  mairg adeir olc ris na mnáibh.

Duine arsaidh leathan liath
  ní hé a mian dul 'na dháil;
annsa leó an buinneán óg bocht;
  mairg adeir olc ris na mnáibh!

                    Gearóid Iarla

Against Blame of Women

Speak not ill of womankind,
  'Tis no wisdom if you do.
You that fault in women find,
  I would not be praised of
  you.

Sweetly speaking, witty, clear,
  Tribe most lovely to my
  mind,
Blame of such I hate to hear.
  Speak not ill of womankind.

Bloody treason, murderous act,
  Not by women were
  designed,
Bells o'erthrown nor churches
  sacked.
  Speak not ill of womankind.

Bishop, King upon his throne,
  Primate skilled to loose and
  bind,
Sprung of women every one!
  Speak not ill of womankind.

For a brave young fellow long
  Hearts of women oft have
  pined.
Who would dare their love to
  wrong?
  Speak not ill of womankind.

Paunchy greybeards never more
  Hope to please a woman's
  mind.
Poor young chieftains they
  adore!
  Speak not ill of womankind.

                    Gerald, Earl of Desmond

Envoi

Aoibhinn, a leabhráin, do thriall
  i gceann ainnre na gciabh gcam;
truagh gan tusa im riocht i bpéin
  is mise féin ag dul ann.

A leabhráin bhig, aoibhinn duit
  ag triall mar a bhfuil mo ghrádh;
an béal loinneardha mar chrú
  do-chife tú, 's an déad bán.

Do-chífe tusa an rosg glas,
  do-chífir fós an bhas tláith;
biaidh tú, 's ní bhiad-sa, fa-raor!
  taobh ar thaobh 's an choimhgheal
  bhláith.

Do-chífe tú an mhala chaol
  's an bhráighe shaor sholas shéimh,
's an ghruaidh dhrithleannach mar ghrís
  do chonnarc i bhfís a-réir.

An com sneachtaidhe seang slán
  dá dtug mise grádh gan chéill,
's an troigh mhéirgheal fhadúr bhán
  do-chífe tú lán do sgéimh.

  An glór taidhiúir síthe séimh
  do chuir mise i bpéin gach laoi
cluinfir, is ba haoibhinn duid;
  uch gan mo chuid bheith mar taoi!

Brian Ó Nolan 1911–66

Delightful, book, your trip
to her of the ringlet head,
a pity it's not you
that's pining, I that sped.

To go, book, where she is
delightful trip in sooth!
the bright mouth red as blood
you'll see, and the white tooth.

You'll see that eye that's grey
the docile palm as well,
with all that beauty you
(not I, alas) will dwell.

You'll see the eyebrow fine
the perfect throat's smooth
  gleam,
and the sparkling cheek I saw
latterly in a dream.

The lithe good snow-white waist
That won mad love from me –
the handwhite swift neat foot –
These in their grace you'll see.

The soft enchanting voice
that made me each day pine
you'll hear, and well for you –
would that your lot were mine.

Brian Ó Nolan 1911–66

217

Poems by Daibhí Ó Bruadair

Adoramus Te, Christe

Adhraim thú, a thaibhse ar gcrú,
a mhaighre an mhúir neámhdha,
d'athraigh le searc ón Athair go neart
dár gcabhair i gceart Mháire;
mar ghréin tré ghloin do léimeadh libh
d'aonscrios oilc Ádhaimh,
go rugais le crann duine 's a chlann
a hifearn ceann Cásca.

A choinneall an chuain do chuireas
chum suain
siosma na nguas ngáifeach,
achainim ort anam an bhoicht
caigil, is coisc Sátan;
gé mise do thuill briseadh do thaoibh
is tuilg na dtrí dtairne,
ná dún do dhearc lonnrach leasc
riom, acht fear fáilte.

Tinnede ár spéis id bhuime, a Mhic
Dé,
gur fionnadh de phréimh Dháibhí:
maighdean bhleacht do dheimhnigh
reacht,
radharc is rath máthar;
an fhinnegheal úr do ionaghair thú,
a linbh, i gcúil chrábhaidh,
gloine mar í níor gineadh i gclí
is ní thiocfa go fuíoll mbrátha.

Adoramus Te, Christe

Ghost of our blood, I worship
    You,
    Hero on Heaven's rampart,
Who left for love a mighty
    Father
    – by Mary's grace – to save
us.
You made a leap like sun
    through glass
    to abolish Adam's evil
and saved with a cross Man and
    his tribe
    at Eastertime from Hell.

Harbour-candle that lulls to rest
    the quarrel of deadly dangers,
the poor man's soul, I beg of
    You,
    save, and restrain Satan.
Your broken side is all my fault,
    and the tracks of the three
    nails,
but do not shut your calm bright
    eye
    upon me – make me
    welcome.

We regard Your nurse the more,
    God's son,
    that she was of David's line:
a virgin with milk, to prove the
    Law,
    with a mother's looks and
    grace,
bright, noble and fair to nurture
    You,
    Child, in a holy nook.
Pure like her never grew in
    womb
    nor will till the end of time.

*Is mairg nár chrean le maitheas
  saoghalta
do cheangal ar gad sul ndeacha in
  éagantacht,
's an ainnise im theach ó las an
  chéadluisne
nach meastar gur fhan an dadamh céille
  agam.*

*An tamall im ghlaic do mhair an
  ghléphingin,
ba geanamhail gart dar leat mo
  thréithese –
do labhrainn Laidean ghasta is Béarla
  glic
's do tharrainginn dais ba cleas ar
  chléireachaibh.*

*Do bheannachadh dhamh an bhean 's a
  céile cnis,
an bhanaltra mhaith 's a mac ar
  céadlongadh;
dá ngairminn baile is leath a
  ngréithe-sean,
ba deacair 'na measc go mbainfeadh éara
  dhom.*

*Do ghabhainn isteach 's amach gan éad
  i dtigh
is níor aistear uim aitreabh teacht aréir
  's aniogh;
dob aitheasc a searc fá seach le chéile
  againn
'achainghim, ceadaigh blaiseadh ár
  mbéile-ne'.*

Woe to that man who leaves on
  his vagaries
without busying himself tying
  up some worldly goods.
There is misery in my house
  from the first dawn-light,
and no one believes I've got one
  tatter of sense.

For as long as the shining penny
  was in my fist
my ways were charming and
  cheerful, you would think.
My speech was fluent Latin and
  cunning English!
I could describe a flourish to
  dazzle the scribes!

Wives and the mates of their
  flesh saluted me
and mothers and their boys
  before their breakfast.
If I were to ask for a village,
  with half its contents,
I'd find it hard to get a refusal
  among them.

I could enter and leave a house,
  and no complaint;
turn up at the same house night
  and day – it was nothing.
Jointly and several, the burthen
  of their love
was: 'Deign, I implore you, to
  take a taste of our meal!'

D'athraigh 'na ndearcaibh dath mo
   néimhe anois
ar aiste nach aithnidh ceart im
   chéimeannaibh;
ó shearg mo lacht le hais na
   caomhdhroinge,
d'aithle mo cheana is marcach mé dem
   chois.

Is annamh an tansa neach dom
   éileamhsa
is dá n'agrainn fear ba falamh a
   éiricsin;
ní fhaiceann mo thaise an chara
   chéibheann chlis
dar gheallamhain seal 'is leat a
   bhféadaimse'.

Gé fada le sail mo sheasamh
   tréithchuisleach
ó mhaidin go feascar seasc gan
   bhéilfhliuchadh,
dá dtairginn banna sleamhain séalaithe
ar chnagaire leanna, a casc ní bhéarainn
   sin.

Is tartmhar mo thasc ag treabhadh im
   aonarsa
le harm nár chleachtas feacht ba mhéithe
   mé;
d'atadar m'ailt de reath na crélainne
is do mharbh an feac ar fad mo
   mhéireanna.

A Athair na bhfeart do cheap na
   céidnithe,
talamh is neamh is reanna is
   réithleanna,
earrach is teaspach, tartha is téachtuisce,
t'fheargain cas is freagair m'éagnachsa.

But I've taken a different colour
   now in their eyes
so that they see no right in my
   procedures,
To judge by this gentry now,
   my milk has turned
and after my time of respect I
   must ride on foot.

It is seldom anyone seeks my
   services,
while if I press them on people
   the pay is poor.
I find no more that cunning and
   sweet companion
who promised me once: 'All I
   can do, it is yours.'

I could stand at the counter long
   and wearily
from morn till night – arid, with
   unwet lips –
and not if I offered a surety
   sealed and shining
for a naggin of beer, could I lure
   it out of the cask.

It's a thirsty task, ploughing this
   lonely furrow,
with a weapon I never employed
   when I was rich:
this sword-play into the earth
   has swelled my ankles
and the shaft has martyred my
   fingers totally.

Father of Miracles, Who madest
   the first things
– Earth and Heaven and
   constellations and stars,
Spring and warmth, fruit and
   freezing water –
avert Thy wrath and answer my
   lamentation!

Seirbhíseach Seirgthe Íogair Srónach Seasc

*Seirbhíseach seirgthe íogair srónach
  seasc
d'eitigh sinn is eibear íota im scornain
  feacht,
beireadh síobhra d'eitill í gan lón tar
  lear,
an deilbhín gan deirglí nár fhóir mo
  thart.*

*Dá reicinn í is a feileghníomh
  dogheobhadh ceacht,
is beirt an tí go leigfidís im scórsa casc;
ó cheisnimh sí go bhfeirg linn is beoir
  'na gar
don steiling í nár leige Rí na glóire i
  bhfad.*

*Meirgíneach bheirbhthe í gan cheol 'na
  cab
do theilg sinn le greidimín sa bpóirse
  amach;
cé cheilim ríomh a peidigraoi mar
  fhógras reacht,
ba bheag an díth dá mbeireadh sí do
  ghósta cat.*

*Reilgín an eilitín nach d'ord na mban
is seisce gnaoi dá bhfeicimíd sa ród re
  maith;
a beith 'na daoi ós deimhin di go deo na
  dtreabh
san leitin síos go leige sí mar neoid a
  cac.*

A Shrewish, Barren, Bony, Nosey Servant

A shrewish, barren, bony, nosey
  servant
refused me when my throat was
  parched in crisis.
May a phantom fly her starving
  over the sea,
the bloodless midget that
  wouldn't attend my thirst.

If I cursed her crime and herself,
  she'd learn a lesson.
The couple she serves would
  give me a cask on credit
but she growled at me in anger,
  and the beer nearby.
May the King of Glory not leave
  her long at her barrels.

A rusty little boiling with a
  musicless mouth,
she hurled me out with insult
  through the porch.
The Law requires I gloss over
  her pedigree
— but little the harm if she bore a
  cat to a ghost.

She's a club-footed slut and not
  a woman at all,
with the barrenest face you
  would meet on the open
  road,
and certain to be a fool to the
  end of the world.
May she drop her dung down
  stupidly into the porridge!

Poems by Aogán Ó Rathaille

An Ceangal

Mo threighid, mo thubaist, mo
  thurainn, mo bhrón, mo dhíth!
an soilseach muirneach miochairgheal
  beoltais caoin
ag adharcach foireanndubh mioscaiseach
  cóirneach buí,
's gan leigheas 'na goire go bhfillid na
  leoin tar toinn.

The Knot

Pain, disaster, downfall, sorrow
  and loss!
Our mild, bright, delicate,
  loving, fresh-lipped girl
with one of that black, horned,
  foreign, hate-crested crew
and no remedy near till our lions
  come over the sea.

Do Shiúlaigh Mise An Mhumhain Mhín

Do shiúlaigh mise an Mhumhain mhín
's ó chúinne an Doire go Dún na Rí;
mo chumha níor briseadh cé'r shúgach
*   sinn,*
*   go feicsint brugh Thaidhg an Dúna.*

Do mheasas im aigne 's fós im chroí
an marbh ba mharbh gur beo do bhí,
ag carabhas macra, feoil is fíon,
*   punch dá chaitheamh is branda.*

Feoil de bhearaibh is éanlaith ón
*   dtoinn,*
ceolta 's cantain is craos na dí,
rósta blasta 's céir gan teimheal,
*   conairt is gadhair is amhastrach.*

Drong ag imeacht is drong ag tíocht,
is drong ag reacaireacht dúinn go binn,
drong ar spallmaibh úra ag guí,
*   's ag leaghadh na bhFlaitheas go*
*   ceansa.*

Nó go bhfuaras sanas ó aon den chúirt
gurb é Warner ceannasach séimh glan
*   subhach*
do bhí sa mbaile gheal aosta chlúil,
*   flaith nárbh fhann roimh dheoraí.*

I Walked All Over Munster Mild

I walked all over Munster mild,
and from Doire corner to Dún
    na Rí,
my grief unchecked (though
    cheerful once)
    – to Tadhg an Dúna's
    mansion.

There to my mind and heart it
    seemed
that the vanished dead returned
    to life:
young men revelling, meat and
    wine,
    punch being drunk, and
    brandy;

meat from spits, birds of the
    wave,
music, singing, great thirst for
    drink,
tasty roasts, clean honeycombs,
    hound-packs, dogs and
    barking;

people leaving, people arriving,
people pleasantly chatting with
    us,
people praying on the cool flags
    meekly melting the heavens.

Till one in that court reminded
    me
it was lordly Warner – mild,
    chaste, gay –
dwelt now in that ancient
    famous house,
    a prince not mean to the
    wanderer.

'S é Dia do chruthaigh an saoghal slán,
's thug fial in ionad an fhéil fuair bás,
ag riar ar mhuirear, ar chléir, ar
    dháimh,
    curadh nach falsa, mórchroí.

God, Who created the world
    aright,
gave a generous man for the one
    who died
to serve his household, scribes
    and poets
    – a true, great-hearted hero.

Gile Na Gile

Gile na gile do chonnarc ar slí in
*   uaigneas,*
criostal an chriostail a goirmroisc
*   rinn-uaine,*
binneas an bhinnis a friotal nár
*   chríonghruama,*
deirge is finne do fionnadh 'na
*   gríosghruannaibh.*

Caise na caise í ngach ribe dá
*   buí-chuachaibh,*
bhaineas an cruinneac den rinneac le
*   rinnscuabadh,*
iorra ba ghlaine ná gloine ar a broinn
*   bhuacaigh,*
do gineadh ar ghineamhain dise san tír
*   uachtraigh.*

Fios fiosach dom d'inis, is ise go
*   fíor-uaigneach,*
fios filleadh don duine don ionad ba
*   rí-dhualgas,*
fios milleadh na droinge chuir eisean ar
*   rinnruagairt,*
's fios eile ná cuirfead im laoithibh le
*   fíor-uamhan.*

Leimhe na leimhe dom druidim 'na
*   cruinntuairim,*
im chime ag an gcime do snaidhmeadh
*   go fíorchrua mé;*
ar ghoirm Mhic Mhuire dom fhortacht,
*   do bhíog uaimse,*
is d'imigh an bhruinneal 'na luisne go
*   bruín Luachra.*

Brightness Most Bright

Brightness most bright I beheld
    on the way, forlorn.
Crystal of crystal her eye, blue
    touched with green.
Sweetness most sweet her voice,
    not stern with age.
Colour and pallor appeared in
    her flushed cheeks.

Curling and curling, each strand
    of her yellow hair
as it took the dew from the grass
    in its ample sweep;
a jewel more glittering than glass
    on her high bosom
– created, when she was created,
    in a higher world.

True tidings she revealed me,
    most forlorn,
tidings of one returning by royal
    right,
tidings of the crew ruined who
    drove him out,
and tidings I keep from my
    poem for sheer fear.

Foolish past folly, I came to her
    very presence
bound tightly, her prisoner (she
    likewise a prisoner . . .).
I invoked Mary's Son for
    succour: she started from me
and vanished like light to the
    fairy dwelling of Luachair.

Rithim le rith mire im rithibh go
  croí-luaimneach,
trí imeallaibh corraigh, trí mhongaibh,
  trí shlímruaitigh;
don tinne-bhrugh tigim – ní thuigim cén
  tslí fuaras
go hionad na n-ionad do cumadh le
  draíocht dhruaga.

Brisid fá scige go scigeamhail buíon
  ghruagach
is foireann de bhruinnealaibh sioscaithe
  dlaoi-chuachach;
i ngeimhealaibh geimheal mé cuirid gan
  puinn suaimhnis,
's mo bhruinneal ar broinnibh ag
  broinnire broinnstuacach.

D'iniseas dise, san bhfriotal dob fhíor
  uaimse,
nár chuibhe di snaidhmeadh le slibire
  slímbhuartha,
's an duine ba ghile ar shliocht chine
  Scoit trí huaire
ag feitheamh ar ise bheith aige mar
  chaoin-nuachar.

Ar chloistin mo ghutha di goileann go
  fíor-uaibhreach
is sileadh ag an bhfliche go life as a
  gríosghruannaibh;
cuireann liom giolla dom choimirc ón
  mbruín uaithi –
's í gile na gile do chonnarc ar slí in
  uaigneas.

Heart pounding, I ran, with a
  frantic haste in my race,
by the margins of marshes,
  through swamps, over bare
  moors.
To a powerful palace I came, by
  paths most strange,
to that place of all places, erected
  by druid magic.

All in derision they tittered – a
  gang of goblins
and a bevy of slender maidens
  with twining tresses.
They bound me in bonds,
  denying the slightest comfort,
and a lumbering brute took hold
  of my girl by the breasts.

I said to her then, in words that
  were full of truth,
how improper it was to join
  with that drawn gaunt
  creature
when a man the most fine, thrice
  over, of Scottish blood
was waiting to take her for his
  tender bride.

On hearing my voice she wept
  in high misery
and flowing tears fell down from
  her flushed cheeks.
She sent me a guard to guide me
  out of the palace
– that brightness most bright I
  beheld on the way, forlorn.

Mac An Cheannaí

Aisling ghéar do dhearcas féin
ar leaba 's mé go lagbhríoch,
an ainnir shéimh darbh ainm Éire
ag teacht im ghaor ar marcaíocht,
a súile glas, a cúl tiubh casta,
a com ba gheal 's a mailí,
dá mhaíomh go raibh ag tíocht 'na gar
a díogras, Mac an Cheannaí.

A beol ba bhinn, a glór ba chaoin,
is ró-shearc linn an cailín,
céile Bhriain dár ghéill an Fhiann,
mo léirchreach dhian a haicíd:
fá shúistibh Gall dá brú go teann,
mo chúileann tseang 's mo bhean
ghaoil;
beidh sí 'na spreas, an rí-bhean deas,
go bhfillfidh Mac an Cheannaí.

Na céadta tá i bpéin dá grá
le géarshearc shámh dá cneas mhín,
clanna ríthe, maca Míle,
dragain fhíochta is gaiscígh;
gnúis ná gnaoi ní mhúsclann sí
cé dubhach fá scíos an cailín –
níl faoiseamh seal le tíocht 'na gar
go bhfillfidh Mac an Cheannaí.

The Redeemer's Son

A bitter vision I beheld
  in bed as I lay weary:
a maiden mild whose name was
  Éire
  coming toward me riding,
with eyes of green, hair curled
  and thick,
  fair her waist and brows,
declaring he was on his way
  – her loved one *Mac an*
  Cheannaí.

Her mouth so sweet, her voice
  so mild,
  I love the maiden dearly,
wife to Brian, acclaimed of
  heroes
  – her troubles are my ruin!
Crushed cruelly under alien flails
  my fair-haired slim
  kinswoman:
she's a dried branch, that
  pleasant queen,
  till he come, her *Mac an*
  Cheannaí.

Hundreds hurt for love of her
  – her smooth skin – in soft
  passion:
kingly children, sons of Míle,
  champions, wrathful dragons.
Her face, her countenance, is
  dead,
  in weariness declining,
and nowhere near is there relief
  till he come, her *Mac an*
  Cheannaí.

A ráite féin, is cráite an scéal,
  mo lánchreach chlé do lag sinn,
go bhfuil sí gan cheol ag caoi na ndeor,
  's a buíon gan treoir gan
  maithghníomh,
gan fiach gan feoil, i bpian go mór,
  'na hiarsma fó gach madaí,
cnaíte lag ag caoi na ndearc
  . go bhfillfidh Mac an Cheannaí.

A fearful tale, by her account
  – her weakness my heart's
  ruin!
She, musicless and weeping
  tears,
  her faint troops leaderless;
no meat or game; she suffers
  much
  – a scrap for every dog;
wasted, weak, with mourning
  eyes,
  till he come, her *Mac an
  Cheannaí.*

Adúirt arís an bhúidhbhean mhíonla
  ó turnadh ríthe 'chleacht sí,
Conn is Art ba lonnmhar reacht,
  ba foghlach glac i ngleacaíocht,
Críomhthainn tréan tar toinn tug géill,
  is Luighdheach Mac Céin an fear
  groí,
go mbeadh sí 'na spreas gan luí le fear
  go bhfillfeadh Mac an Cheannaí.

The sweet mild woman spoke
  again:
  her former kings being fallen
– Conn and Art of violent reigns
  and deadly hands in combat;
strong Críomthainn home with
  hostages,
  Luighdheach Mac Céin the
  sturdy –
dried branch she'll stay, with no
  man lie,
  till he come, her *Mac an
  Cheannaí.*

Do-bheir súil ó dheas gach lá fá seach
  ar thráigh na mbarc an cailín,
Is súil deas-soir go dlúth tar muir,
  mo chumha anois a haicíd,
a súile siar ag súil le Dia,
  tar tonntaibh fiara gainmhe;
cloíte lag beidh sí gan phreab
  go bhfillfidh Mac an Cheannaí.

Her eye looks South day after
  day
  to the shore for ships
  arriving,
to sea Southeast she gazes long
  (her troubles are my grief!)
and a Westward eye, with hope
  in God,
  o'er wild and sandy billows
– defeated, lifeless, powerless,
  till he come, her *Mac an
  Cheannaí.*

A bráithre breaca táid tar lear,
  na táinte shearc an cailín;
níl fleadh le fáil, níl gean ná grá
  ag neach dá cairdibh, admhaím;
a gruanna fliuch, gan suan gan sult,
  fá ghruaim is dubh a n-aibíd,
's go mbeidh sí 'na spreas gan luí le
  fear
    go bhfillfidh Mac an Cheannaí.

Her dappled Friars are overseas,
  those droves that she held
  dear;
no welcome, no regard or love,
  for her friends in any quarter.
Their cheeks are wet; no ease or
  sleep;
  dressed in black, for sorrow
– dried branch she'll stay, with
  no man lie,
    till he come, her *Mac an*
    Cheannaí.

234

Cabhair Ní Ghairfead

Cabhair ní ghairfead go gcuirthear mé i
gcruinn-chomhrainn –
dar an leabhar dá ngairinn níor ghairede
an ní dhomhsa;
ár gcodhnach uile, glac-chumasach shíl
Eoghain,
is tollta a chuisle, 'gus d'imigh a bhrí ar
feochadh.

Do thonnchrith m'inchinn, d'imigh mo
phríomhdhóchas,
poll im ionathar, biora nimhe trím
dhrólainn,
ár bhfonn, ár bhfothain, ár monga 's ár
mínchóngair
i ngeall le pinginn ag foirinn ó chrích
Dhóbhair.

Do bhodhar an tSionainn, an Life, 's
an Laoi cheolmhar,
abhainn an Bhiorra Dhuibh, Bruice
'gus Bríd, Bóinne,
com Loch Deirg 'na ruide 'gus Toinn
Tóime
ó lom an cuireata cluiche ar an rí
coróinneach.

Mo ghlam is minic, is silimse
síordheora,
is trom mo thubaist 's is duine mé ar
míchomhthrom,
fonn ní thigeann im ghaire 's mé ag
caoi ar bhóithre
ach foghar na Muice nach gontar le
saigheadóireacht.

No Help I'll Call

No help I'll call till I'm put in
the narrow coffin.
By the Book, it would bring it
no nearer if I did!
Our prime strong-handed prop,
of the seed of Eoghan
– his sinews are pierced and his
vigour is withered up.

Wave-shaken is my brain, my
chief hope gone.
There's a hole in my gut, there
are foul spikes through my
bowels.
Our land, our shelter, our
woods and our level ways
are pawned for a penny by a
crew from the land of Dover.

The Sionainn, the Life, the
musical Laoi, are muffled
and the Biorra Dubh river, the
Bruice, the Bríd, the Bóinn.
Reddened are Loch Dearg's
narrows and the Wave of
Tóim
since the Knave has skinned the
crowned King in the game.

Incessant my cry; I spill
continual tears;
heavy my ruin; I am one in
disarray.
No music is nigh as I wail about
the roads
except for the noise of the Pig
no arrows wound.

Goll na Rinne, na Cille 'gus chríche
    Eoghanacht,
do lom a ghoile le huireaspa ar díth
    córach;
an seabhac agá bhfuilid sin uile 's a
    gcíosóireacht,
fabhar ní thugann don duine, cé gaol
    dó-san.

Fán dtromlot d'imigh ar chine na rí
    mórga
treabhann óm uiseannaibh uisce go
    scímghlórach;
is lonnmhar chuirid mo shruthasa
    foinseoga
san abhainn do shileas ó Thruipill go
    caoin-Eochaill.

Stadfadsa feasta – is gar dom éag gan
    mhoill
ó treascradh dragain Leamhan, Léin is
    Laoi;
rachad 'na bhfasc le searc na laoch don
    chill,
na flatha fá raibh mo shean roimh éag
    do Chríost.

That lord of the Rinn and Cill,
    and the Eoghanacht country
– want and injustice have wasted
    away his strength.
A hawk now holds those places,
    and takes their rent,
who favours none, though near
    to him in blood.

Our proud royal line is wrecked;
    on that account
the water ploughs in grief down
    from my temples,
sources sending their streams out
    angrily
to the river that flows from
    Truipeall to pleasant Eochaill.

I will stop now – my death is
    hurrying near
now the dragons of the
    Leamhan, Loch Léin and the
    Laoi are destroyed.
In the grave with this cherished
    chief I'll join those kings
my people served before the
    death of Christ.

Poems about Places

A Blue Eye Will Look Back

A Blue Eye Will Look Back

Fil súil nglais
fégbas Érinn dar a hais;
noco n-aceba íarmo-thá
firu Érenn nách a mná.

There is a blue eye which will
look back at Ireland; never
more shall it see the men of
Ireland nor her women.

Colum Cille (about to leave Ireland, A.D. 563)

The Shannon

A Shionann Bhriain Bhóroimhe,
  iongnadh is méad do gháire,
mar sguire dod ghlóraighe
  ag dol siar isin sáile.

Gluaise láimh ré Bóroimhe,
  téighe láimh ré Ceann Choradh,
ag moladh Mheic mhórMhuire,
  go bráth bráth is binn t'fhoghar.

An port asa dtéighisi,
  ó Shliabh Iarainn 'ga neimhcheilt;
lór a luaithe téighisi
  tré Loch Ríbh, tré Loch
  nDeirgdheirc.

Ag dol tar Eas nDanainne
  nocha nfhéadthar do chuibhreach:
is ann do-ní an ramhaille,
  ag dola láimh ré Luimneach.

Ó Luimneach an mhearsháile
  go dtéighe i nInis Cathaigh,
láimh ré port ar Seanáinne,
  caidhe th'imtheacht 'na dheaghaidh

The Shannon

Shannon! King Brian's native
  river,
– Ah! the wide wonder of thy
  glee –
No more thy waters babble and
  quiver
As here they join the western
  sea.

By ancient Borivy thou flowest
And past Kincora rippling by
With sweet unceasing chant thou
  goest,
For Mary's babe a lullaby.

Born first in Breffney's Iron
  Mountain
– I hide not thy nativity –
Thou speedest from that
  northern fountain
Swift through thy lakes, Loch
  Derg, Loch Ree.

Over Dunass all undelaying
Thy sheer unbridled waters flee;
Past Limerick town they loiter,
  staying
Their flight into the western sea.

From Limerick, where the tidal
  welling
Of the swift water comes and
  goes,
By Scattery, saintly Seanán's
  dwelling,
Thou goest and whither then
  who knows?

Fa imlibh ar bhfearainne
  meinic théighe in gach ionam,
ar ais tar Eas nDanainne,
  ag dul san bhfairrge, a Shionann.

Bóinn is Siúir is seinLeamhain
  agus Suca nach sriobhmall –
adeirid na deighleabhair
  gurab uaisle tú, a Shionann.

Thomond is clasped in thy
  embraces
And all her shores thou lovest
  well,
Where by Dunass thy cataract
  races
And where thy seaward waters
  swell.

Boyne, Siuir and Laune of
  ancient story,
And Suck's swift flood – these
  have their fame;
But in the poet's roll of glory
Thine, Shannon, is a nobler
  name.

Contae Mhuigheo

Ar an loing seo Phaidí Loinsigh sea
nímse an dobhrón,
ag osnaíl ins an oíche is ag síorghol sa
ló,
muna mbeadh gur dalladh m'intleacht,
is mé i bhfad óm mhuintir,
dar a maireann is maith a chaoinfinnse
Contae Mhuigheo.

An uair a mhair mo chairde ba bhreá
mo chuid óir,
d'ólainn fíon Spáinneach i gcomhluadar
ban óg,
muna mbeadh síoról na gcartaí
is an dlí a bheith ró-láidir,
ní i Santa Cruz a d'fhágainn mo
chnámha faoin bhfód.

Tá cailíní na háite seo ag éirí rómhór
faoi chnotaí is faoi hair-bag gan trácht
ar bhúclaí bróg,
dá maireadh damhsa in Iar-Umhall
do dhéanfainn díofa cianach
muna mbeadh gur thagair Dia dhom
bheith i gcianta faoi bhrón.

The County of Mayo

On the deck of Patrick Lynch's
boat I sat in woeful plight,
Through my sighing all the
weary day and weeping all
the night.
Were it not that full of sorrow
from my people forth I go,
By the blessed sun, 'tis royally
I'd sing thy praise, Mayo.

When I dwelt at home in plenty,
and my gold did much
abound,
In the company of fair young
maids the Spanish ale went
round.
'Tis a bitter change from those
gay days that now I'm forced
to go,
And must leave my bones in
Santa Cruz, far from my own
Mayo.

They're altered girls in Irrul
now; 'tis proud they're
grown and high,
With their hair-bags and their
top-knots – for I pass their
buckles by.
But it's little now I heed their
airs, for God will have it so,
That I must depart for foreign
lands, and leave my sweet
Mayo.

Dá mbeadh Pádraig Lochlainn ina iarla
in Iar-Umhall go fóill
Brian Dubh, a chliamhain, ina thiarna
ar Dhuach Mhór
Aodh Dubh MacRiada
ina choirneál i gCliara –
is ansin a bheadh mo thriallsa go
Contae Mhuigheo.

Tomás Ó Flannghaile

'Tis my grief that Patrick
Loughlin is not Earl in Irrul
still,
And that Brian Duff no longer
rules as Lord upon the Hill;
And that Colonel Hugh
MacGrady should be lying
dead and low,
And I sailing, sailing swiftly
from the county of Mayo.

George Fox

Thomas Flavell (Attributed. Late 17th century)

Cill Aodáin

Anois teacht an Earraigh beidh an lá
dul 'un síneadh
Is taréis na Féil' Bríde ardóidh mé mo
sheol:
ó chuir mé im cheann é ní stopfaidh mé
choíche
Go seasa mé síos i lár Chontae
Mhuigheo.
I gClár Clainne Muiris bheas mé an
chéad oíche
Is i mBalla taobh thíos de thosós mé ag
ól;
Go Coillte Mach racha mé go ndéana
mé cuairt míosa ann,
I bhfoisceacht dhá mhíle do Bhéal an
Átha Mhóir

Ó fágaim le huacht é go néiríonn mo
chroíse,
Mar éiríonn an ghaoth nó mar
scaipeann an ceo,
Nuair chuimhním ar Chearra is ar
Ghailean taobh thíos de,
Ar Sceathach-an-Mhíle is ar phlandaí
Mhuigheo:
Cill Aodáin an baile a bhfásann gach
ní ann
Tá an sméar 's an sú-chraobh ann is
meas ar gach sort,
Is dá mbeinnse im sheasamh i gceartlár
mo dhaoine
D'imeodh an aois díom is bheinn arís
óg

Anthony Raftery (1784–1835)

Killeadan

Now with the springtime the
days will grow longer,
And after St Bride's Day my
sail I'll let go;
I put my mind to it and I never
will linger
Till I find myself back in the
County Mayo.
It is in Claremorris I'll stop the
first evening;
At Balla beneath it I'll first
take the floor;
I'll go to Kiltimagh and have a
month's peace there,
And that's not two miles
from Ballinamore.

I give you my word that the
heart in me rises
As when the wind rises and
all the mists go,
Thinking of Carra and Gallen
beneath it,
Scahaveela and all the wide
plains of Mayo;
Killeadan's the village where
everything pleases,
Of berries and all sorts of
fruit there's no lack,
And if I could but stand in the
heart of my people
Old age would drop from me
and youth would come back.

Frank O'Connor

Poems by Seán Ó Ríordáin

Seanmóintí

Sagart ag scréachaigh gach Domhnach,
Glór i gcóitín ins an teampall,
Seanmóintí iad gan amhras,
Fothram focal le clos.

Caithfidh a shamhail bheith ann leis,
Ó tharla sé caithfidh sé labhairt linn,
Fuair sé a ionad sa teampall,
I lár an phobáil istigh.

Pé acu searbh nó binn linn a chlampar
Bhí sé le bheith ann d'réir dealraimh,
Ceapadh ó thosach an domhain dó
Go mbeadh a thamall aige.

Cé nach ceolmhaire é ná an gandal,
Cé nár mheasa linn éisteacht le srann
  muc,
Is binne ná téada ag labhairt é,
Mar tá cláirseach an Mháistir aige.

Sermons

On Sundays priests start
 shrieking,
  Church petticoats give voice,
Sermons are surely speaking,
  Heard is a wordy noise.

He has to get a hearing
 when circumstances prod,
Over the pulpit peering
 amid the Church of God.

Be it sweet or bitter to the ear,
 whether we frown or smile,
Since the world began it's
 ordered here
  for him to talk a while.

Though ganders' voices are less
 sharp
  and pigs' grunts be preferred,
Yet still he holds the Master's
 Harp,
  and music tunes each word.

Na Leamhain

Fuaim ag leamhan leochaileach, iompó
* leathanaigh,*
Bascadh mionsciathán,
Oíche fhómhair i seomra na leapa, tá
Rud leochaileach á chrá.

Oíche eile i dtaibhreamh bhraitheas-sa
Peidhre leamhan-sciathán,
Mar sciatháin aingil iad le fairsingeacht
Is bhíodar leochaileach mar mhná.

Dob é mo chúram lámh a leagadh orthu
Is gan ligean leo chun fáin,
Ach iad a shealbhú gan sárú tearmainn
Is iad a thabhairt chun aoibhnis iomlán.

Ach dhoirteas-sa an púdar beannaithe
'Bhí spréite ar gach sciathán,
Is tuigeadh dom go rabhas gan
* uimhreacha,*
Gan uimhreacha na fearúlachta go
* brách.*

Is shiúil na deich n-uimhreacha as an
* mearbhall*
Is ba mhó ná riamh a n-údarás,
Is ba chlos ciníocha ag plé le
* huimhreacha,*
Is cách ba chlos ach mise amháin.

The Moths

A fragile moth-sound, a page
     turned, a pair
  of tiny wings to bruise
One autumn night I in my
     bedroom dare
  a fragile thing misuse.

So then another night I saw in
     dream
  a pair of moth's wings shine
Wide as an angel's wings while
     yet they seem
  fragilely feminine.

I try with hands as gentle as can
     be
  to fence them and decoy
Without encroachment of their
     privacy
  and bring them to full joy.

But I spilt the sacred powders
     that were spread
  on either tender wing,
And realized my manliness was
     fled
  for lack of numbering.

Then the ten digits picked out
     from the haze
  a fresh restatement and define
With numbers every race and
     nation plays
  and every voice is heard but
     thine.

Fuaim ag leamhan leochaileach, iompó
  leathanaigh,
Creachadh leamhan-scannán,
Oíche fhómhair is na leamhain ag
  eiteallaigh
Mór mo bheann ar a mion-rírá.

A fragile moth-sound, a page
  turned by me,
with little filmy wings thus
  made a prey,
Moths on the wing one autumn
  night I see
and strive to heed the tiny
  thing they say.

Tulyar

A Tulyar, a Stail
A cheannaigh De Valéra ón Aga
  Khan,
Tír mhór geanmnaíochta tír mo shean,
Tír maighdean, tír ab,
Tír saltar is soiscéal,
Is bráithre bochta ar mhórán léinn,
A Tulyar, sin stair:
Ach cogar, a Stail,
Nach dóigh leat é bheith ait
Ceardaí ded cheird, ded chlú, ded
  chleacht,
Ded chumas breise thar gach each,
A theacht
Ag cleachtadh a cheirde anseo inár
  measc
I dtír na n-ollamh, tír na naomh,
An tír a bheannaigh Pádraig féin?
Ní hé gur peaca cumasc each,
Ach suathadh síl ab ea do theacht;
Ní soiscéal Phádraig thugais leat
Ach intinn eile
'Thuigfeadh Eisirt;
Is lú de pheaca peaca, a Stail,
Tú bheith i mbun taithí inár measc,
Id stail phoiblí, lán-oifigiúil,
Thar ceann an rialtais ag feidhmiú.
    An é go rabhamar fachta seasc,
    Gur theastaigh sampla stail' inár
    measc?
    Nó an rabhamar dulta eiriciúil
    Mura ndéanfaí tusa oifigiúil?

Tulyar

Tulyar, you Stallion, you whom
  Dev was man
enough to purchase from the
  Aga Khan,
my father's land's a land of stern
  chaste habits,
  an ancient land of Virgins and
  of Abbots,
a land of Psalm and
  Gospel-books are we,
  a land of Friars, who have
  come to be
as great in learning as in
  poverty,
  Such now, O Tulyar, is our
  history.
Suppose you blew a whisper in
  my ear
  fresh from the horse's mouth
  would I not hear
you say a Stallion thinks it
  somewhat queer
  that one, like you, with such
  a reputation
for strength and expertise in
  your vocation
  of unartificial fertilization
should be
  invited to exercise it publicly
here in the land of Saints and
  Scholars though
  St Patrick came and blessed it
  long ago?
I'm not suggesting it's a sin
  indeed
  for mares to mate like that,
  or you to breed
since you come specially to
  purvey seed.
  Yet it's not Patrick's Gospel
  you present,

your Ideology is different,
  it's something Eisirt would
  have understood
in Rabelaisian mood.
  Sex seems less sinful, Stallion,
  now that you
may ply your trade amongst us
  as you do,
  The Government has
  sponsored you in fact
to work officially in every act.
  Were we convicted of
  sterility?

A Theanga Seo Leath-Liom

Cé cheangail ceangal eadrainn,
A theanga seo leath-liom?
Muran lán-liom tú cén tairbhe
Bheith easnamhach id bhun?

Tá teanga eile in aice leat
Is deir sí linn 'Bí liom,'
Do ráinig dúinn bheith eadraibh,
Is is deighilte sinn ó shin.

Ní mór dúinn dul in aice leat
Go sloigfí sinn ionat
Nó goidfear uainn do thearmann,
Is goidfear uaitse sinn.

Ní mheileann riamh leath-aigne,
Caithfeam dul ionat;
Cé nach bog féd chuid a bhraithim tú,
A theanga seo leath-liom.

O Language Half-Mine

Who caused this our
    conjunction,
    O language but half-mine?
If you refuse to function
    let's choose a selling line.

Another language twits me
    and wants to be my wife,
I'm Schizophrene, it splits me,
    I lead a double life.

O with you we must go and
    dwell
    to be absorbed and won,
Or we will lose our citadel
    and you your garrison.

Half minds are unabrasive,
    and won't grind rough or
    fine;
You're tough and you're
    evasive,
    and are so far half-mine.

An Lacha

Maith is eol dúinn scéal na lachan,
Éan nár gealladh riamh di
Leabhaireacht coisíochta:
Dúchas di bheith tuisleach
Is gluaiseacht léi ainspianta
Anonn is anall gan rithim,
Is í ag marcaíocht ar a proimpe:
Ba dhóigh leat ar a misneach
Gur seo chughat an dán díreach
Nuair is léir do lucht na tuigse
Gur dícheall di vers libre.

The Duck

We all know all about the Duck
    absurd bird, damned by her
    ill-luck
from paces long and strong and
    free
    It is her fallen nature now to
    be
An awkward stumbler that goes
    bumping all
    her way broken and
    unmetrical
rocking and rolling on her
    posterior,
    yet looking so determinedly
    superior
that marvelling at such courage
    you must say
    See how heroic couplets stalk
    this way,
Yet how obvious it is
    to the discerning
that the best she can do
    is vers libre.

Catchollú

Is breá leis an gcat a corp,
Is aoibhinn léi é shearradh,
Nuair a shearr sí í féin anocht
Do tharla cait 'na gceathaibh.

Téann sí ó chat go cat
Á ndúiseacht as a ballaibh,
Fé mar nár chat í ach roth
De chait ag teacht is ag imeacht.

Í féin atá sí ag rá,
Is doirteann sí slua arb ea í
Nuair a shearrann an t-iomlán,
Á comhaireamh féin le gaisce.

Tá na fichidí catchollú
Feicthe agamsa anocht,
Ach ní fichidí ach milliúin
'Tá le searradh fós as a corp.

Catchollú

Its body to a cat is a delight
    and to stretch it is a great
    pleasure too,
and every time it stretched itself
    tonight
    out wave on wave the
    showers of cats flew.

It goes from cat to cat, for it can
    feel
    them waking from its
    members, till it grow
Into no single cat, but a whole
    wheel
    of cats, that come as quickly
    as they go.

It is of course its mode of
    self-expression
    made every cat of that
    unending host,
and every stretch adds on to the
    procession
    of which its cat-creativeness
    can boast.

Already I've seen scores of cats
    attain
    Felinization with success this
    night
while yet not scores but millions
    yet remain
    for yawns and stretches to
    bring yet to light.

Poems by Máirtín Ó Direáin

Fuaire

Luí ar mo chranna foirtil!
Céard eile a dhéanfainn féin
Ó tá mála an tsnáith ghil
Follamh i do pháirt go héag,
Ach tá a fhios ag mo chroí,
Cé goirt le roinnt an scéal,
Go bhfuil na cranna céanna
Chomh fuar leis an spéir.

Chill

Stand fast by my protective
   props!
Is there an alternative?
Since, in your regard
The horn of plenty is empty till
   death.
Yet I know in my heart –
Bitter and all as it is to say –
That these same props
Are as cold as sky.

Gearóid Ó Crualaoich

Mothú Feirge

Feic a mhic mar a chreimid na lucha
An abhlann a thit as lámha na dtréan,
Is feic fós gach coileán go dranntach
I bhfeighil a chnáimh ina chró bréan
Is coinnigh a mhic do sheile agat féin.

Anger

See, boy, how the vermin gnaw
The holy host that fell from
  mighty hands.
See too how every snarling pup
In his foul kennel guards his
  stinking bone,
And buddy! keep your spittle to
  yourself.

Gearóid Ó Crualaoich

Eala-Bhean

Deireann gach cor is gotha
Deireann do cholainn uile:
'An bhfuil sibh réidh faoi mo
    chomhair?'
Is ní túisce cos leat thar dhoras
Ná is leat an duais ó mhná,
Is nuair a théir go héasca thar bráid:
Is stáitse agat an tsráid,

Ná ni háibhéil dúinn a rá
Nach siúl do shiúl ach snámh,
Is tráth scaoilir gatha do scéimhe
Ni thagaid ó leanbh go liath slán.

Swan-Woman

Every twist and gesture
Every point of your bodily
    person asks:
'Are you ready for my coming?'
And no sooner your foot
    out-of-doors
Than, among women, the prize
    is yours;
While, as you lightly pass along
Street for you is stage.

We could even deign to say
That your carriage is more glide
    than walk,
And when you project your
    beauty's arrow
Neither child nor old grey head
    is safe from you.

Gearóid Ó Crualaoich

Cranna Foirtil

Coinnigh do thalamh a anam liom,
Coigil chugat gach tamhanrud,
Is ná bí mar ghiolla gan chaithir
I ndiaidh na gcarad nár fhóin duit.

Minic a dhearcais ladhrán trá
Ar charraig fhliuch go huaigneach.
Mura bhfuair éadáil ón toinn
Ní bhfuair guth ina héagmais.

Níor thugais ód ríocht dhorcha
Caipín an tsonais ar do cheann,
Ach cuireadh cranna cosanta
Go teann thar do chliabhán cláir.

Cranna caillte a cuireadh tharat:
Tlú iarainn ós do chionn,
Ball éadaigh d'athar taobh leat
Is bior sa tine thíos.

Luigh ar do chranna foirtil
I gcoinne mallmhuir is díthrá,
Coigil aithinne d'aislinge,
Scaradh léi is éag duit.

Props

Soul! Stand your ground;
Clutch at every rooted thing
Be not like a beardless youth
When your friends have failed
    you.

You've often seen a red-shank
Solitary on a washed rock;
If he got no titbit from the sea
That was no reproach.

Your head came without a lucky
    caul
From your own obscure
    dominion,
But the wood of your cradle was
    confidently hung
With protective timbers.

The props they used for you
    were perished props:
Iron tongs above you
Your father's garment beside
    you
And a poker stuck in the fire.

Stand fast by your staunch
    moor-poles
That shore you up against all
    tides,
And maintain your vision's
    spark;
To let that go is death for you.

Gearóid Ó Crualaoich

260

Poems by Somhairle Mac Gill-Eain

Calbharaigh

Chan eil mo shùil air Calbharaigh
no air Betlehem an àigh
ach air cùil ghrod an Glaschu
far bheil an lobhadh fàis,
agus air seòmar an Dùn-éideann,
seòmar bochdainn 's cràidh,
far a bheil an naoidhean creuchdach
ri aonagraich gu 'bhàs.

Calvary

My eye is not on Calvary
nor on Bethlehem the Blessed,
but on a foul-smelling backland
   in Glasgow,
where life rots as it grows;
and on a room in Edinburgh, a
   room of poverty and pain,
where the diseased infant
writhes and wallows till death.

Hallaig

'Tha tìm, am fiadh, an coille
    Hallaig'

Tha bùird is tàirnean air an uinneig
troimh 'm faca mi an Aird an Iar
's tha mo ghaol aig Allt Hallaig
'na craoibh bheithe, 's bha i riamh

eadar an t-Inbhir 's Poll a' Bhainne,
thall 's a bhos mu Bhaile-Chùirn:
tha i 'na beithe, 'na calltuinn,
'na caorunn dhìreach sheang ùir.

Ann an Screapadal mo chinnidh,
far robh Tarmad 's Eachunn Mór,
tha 'n nighean 's am mic 'nan coille
ag gabhail suas ri taobh an lóin.

Uaibhreach a nochd na coilich ghiuthais
ag gairm air mullach Cnoc an Rà,
dìreach an druim ris a' ghealaich –
chan iadsan coille mo ghràidh.

Fuirichidh mi ris a' bheithe
gus an tig i mach an Càrn,
gus am bi am bearradh uile
o Bheinn na Lice f'a sgàil.

Hallaig

' *Time, the deer, is in the wood of*
    Hallaig '

The window is nailed and
    boarded
through which I saw the West
and my love is at the Burn of
    Hallaig,
a birch tree, and she has always
    been

between Inver and Milk Hollow,
here and there about
    Baile-chuirn:
she is a birch, a hazel,
a straight, slender young rowan.

In Screapadal of my people
where Norman and Big Hector
    were,
their daughters and their sons are
    a wood
going up beside the stream.

Proud tonight the pine cocks
crowing on the top of Cnoc an
    Ra,
straight their backs in the
    moonlight –
they are not the wood I love.

I will wait for the birch wood
until it comes up by the cairn,
until the whole ridge from Beinn
    na Lice
will be under its shade.

<table>
<tr><td>

Mura tig 's ann theàrnas mi a Hallaig
a dh' ionnsaigh sàbaid nam marbh,
far a bheil an sluagh a' tathaich,
gach aon ghinealach a dh' fhalbh.

</td><td>

If it does not, I will go down to
    Hallaig,
to the Sabbath of the dead,
where the people are
    frequenting,
every single generation gone.

</td></tr>
<tr><td>

Tha iad fhathast ann a Hallaig,
Clann Ghill-Eain 's Clann MhicLeòid,
na bh' ann ri linn Mhic
    Ghille-Chaluim:
Chunnacas na mairbh beò.

</td><td>

They are still in Hallaig,
MacLeans and MacLeods,
all who were there in the time of
    Mac Gille Chaluim
the dead have been seen alive.

</td></tr>
<tr><td>

Na fir 'nan laighe air an lianaig
aig ceann gach taighe a bh' ann,
na h-igheanan 'nan coille bheithe,
dìreach an druim, crom an ceann.

</td><td>

The men lying on the green
at the end of every house that
    was,
the girls a wood of birches,
straight their backs, bent their
    heads.

</td></tr>
<tr><td>

Eadar an Leac is na Feàrnaibh
tha 'n rathad mór fo chòinnich chiùin,
's na h-igheanan 'nam badan sàmhach
a' dol a Chlachan mar o thùs.

</td><td>

Between the Leac and Fearns
the road is under mild moss
and the girls in silent bands
go to Clachan as in the
    beginning,

</td></tr>
<tr><td>

Agus a' tilleadh as a' Chlachan,
á Suidhisnis 's á tir nam beò;
a chuile té òg uallach
gun bhristeadh cridhe an sgeòil.

</td><td>

and return from Clachan
from Suisnish and the land of
    the living;
each one young and
    light-stepping,
without the heartbreak of the
    tale.

</td></tr>
<tr><td>

O Allt na Feàrnaibh gus an fhaoilinn
tha soilleir an dìomhaireachd nam beann
chan eil ach coimhthional nan nighean
ag cumail na coiseachd gun cheann.

</td><td>

From the Burn of Fearns to the
    raised beach
that is clear in the mystery of the
    hills,
there is only the congregation of
    the girls
keeping up the endless walk,

</td></tr>
</table>

A' tilleadh a Hallaig anns an fheasgar,
anns a' chamhanaich bhalbh bheò,
a' lìonadh nan leathadan casa,
an gàireachdaich 'nam chluais 'na ceò,

's am bòidhche 'na sgleò air mo chridhe
mun tig an ciaradh air na caoil,
's nuair theàrnas grian air cùl Dhùn
    Cana
thig peileir dian á gunna Ghaoil;

's buailear am fiadh a tha 'na thuaineal
a' snòtach nan làraichean feòir;
thig reothadh air a shùil 'sa' choille:
chan fhaighear lorg air fhuil ri m'
    bheò.

coming back to Hallaig in the
    evening,
in the dumb living twilight,
filling the steep slopes,
their laughter a mist in my ears,

and their beauty a film on my
    heart
before the dimness comes on the
    kyles,
and when the sun goes down
    behind Dun Cana
a vehement bullet will come
    from the gun of Love;

and will strike the deer that goes
    dizzily,
sniffing at the grass-grown
    ruined homes;
his eye will freeze in the wood,
his blood will not be traced
    while I live.

Conchobhar

Chan fhàg mi 's an aon uaigh iad
fad fìn-shuaineach na h-oidhche,
a broilleach cìoch-gheal
ri uchd-san mór geal
tré shìorruidheachd na h-oidhche,
a bhial-san r'a bial, r'a gruaidh
air cho fliuch 's bhios ùir an tuaim:
b' fhaide 'n oidhche na 'n Gleann Da
   Ruadh,
bu luasgan cadal Gleann Eite;
bidh 'n oidhch seo fada, 'n cadal fòil,
gun dìth shùilean air na doill.

Conchobhar

I will not leave them in the same
   grave
for the whole long night,
her fair breasts
to his great fair chest
throughout the night's eternity,
his mouth to her mouth, to her
   cheek,
for all the wet earth of the
   tomb:
the night would be longer than
   in Glen Da Ruadh,
sleep in Glen Etive was unrest;
this night will be long, the sleep
   tranquil,
the blind will need no eyes.

Eadh Is Féin Is Sàr-Fhéin

Chaidh na samhlaidhean leis a'
bhearradh
agus na h-ìomhaighean thar na creige
is chailleadh iad air machair fharsaing
air cabhsair an rathaid dhìrich
o'm faic an reusan an fhìrinn.

Chan eil a' mhachair idir farsaing
agus tha an rathad lùbach
is ged a tha sgurrachan a' bhearraidh
corrach do threibhdhireas'an t-seallaidh,
chan fheàrr a' choille throm dhùmhail
's i fàs a mach á cnàimh an rathaid,
as mo chluasan, as mo shùilean,
as mo bhial, as mo chuinnlein
's as gach bìdeig de m' chraiceann,
eadhon as an roinn bhig sin
a tha blàth os cionn mo chridhe.

Tha imcheist na machrach móire
cho doirbh ri sgurrachan na dórainn.
Chan eil buaidh air a' mhachair
's chan eil bhith beò anns a' choille.

Id, Ego And Super-Ego

The symbols went over the
escarpment
and the images over the cliff
and they were lost on a wide
plain,
on the causeway of the straight
road
from which reason sees the
truth.

The plain is not at all wide
and the road is twisty,
and though the peaks of the
escarpment are
unsteady for sincerity of vision,
the thick heavy wood is no
better,
growing out of the bone of the
road,
out of my ears, out of my eyes,
out of my mouth, out of my
nostrils
and out of every little bit of my
skin,
even out of that little part
that is warm above my heart.

The perplexity of the great plain
is as difficult as the peaks of
grief.
The plain has no grace
and there is no living in the
wood.

Chan fhuirich an cridhe air a'
   mhachair;
's mór as fheàrr leis a' chridhe
('s e cho càirdeach do'n spiorad)
bhith 'n crochadh air piotan ris an stalla
is fear mór 'na cheannard ròpa,
Calvin no Pàp no Lenin
no eadhon bragairneach bréige,
Nietzsche, Napoleon, Ceusair.

Tha Freud 'na bhàillidh air a' choille
(tha'n oifis aige àrd air uirigh)
's air gach oighreachd nach tuigear.
Cha mhoth' air-san fear an ròpa
(an ròp e fhéin 'na bhalg-séididh):
sùil saoi air friamhaichean céine;
uirigh 'san chreig chais uaibhrich
a' toirt neor-thaing do choille 'n
   luasgain,
do 'n choille fhìrinnich ìochdraich,
do 'n choille iriosail 's i air laomadh
le luibhean searbha dathte mìlse.

The heart, which is such a close
   relative
of the spirit, will not wait on the
   plain;
it much prefers
to hang from a piton against the
   rock-face
with a big man as rope-leader,
Calvin, or Pope or Lenin,
or even a lying braggart,
Nietzsche, Napoleon or Kaiser.

Freud is factor of the woodland
(his office is high on a ledge)
and of every incomprehensible
   estate.
He doesn't much regard the
   ropesman
(the rope itself a bellows);
sage eye on distant roots,
his ledge in the steep proud rock
defying the restless wood,
the truthful subject wood,
the humble wood that teems
with bitter variegated sweet
   plants.

A' Bheinn Air Chall

Tha bheinn ag éirigh os cionn na coille,
air chall anns a' choille th' air chall,
is bhristeadh sinn air clàr ar gréine
on a tha na speuran teann.

Air chall ann an aomadh na coille
ìomhaighean iomadhathach ar spéis
a chionn 's nach téid na sràidean ciùrrte
's a' choille mhaoth an cochur réidh.

A chionn 's gu bheil Vietnam's Uladh
'nan torran air Auschwitz nan cnàmh
agus na craobhan saoibhir ùrar
'nam prìneachan air beanntan cràidh.

Dé 'n t-sìorruidheachd inntinn 's an
    cuirear
Ameireaga mu Dheas no Belsen,
agus a' ghrian air Sgurr Urain
's a bhearraidhean geàrrte 'san
    t-sneachda?

Tha 'm bristeadh cridhe mu na
    beanntan
's anns na coilltean air am bòidhche
ged tha 'n fhuil mhear gu luaineach
air mire bhuadhar' san òigridh.

The Lost Mountain

The mountain rises above the
    wood,
lost in the wood that is lost,
and we have been broken on the
    board of our sun
since the skies are tight.

Lost in the decline of the wood
the many-coloured images of
    our aspiration
since the tortured streets will not
    go
in the wood in a smooth
    synthesis.

Because Vietnam and Ulster are
heaps on Auschwitz of the
    bones,
and the fresh rich trees
pins on mountains of pain.

In what eternity of the mind
will South America or Belsen be
    put
with the sun on Sgurr Urain
and its ridges cut in snow?

Heartbreak is about the
    mountains
and in the woods for all their
    beauty,
though the restless sportive
    blood
rages triumphantly in the young.

Sìorruidheachd Dhante is Dhùghaill
'na seann solus ùr aig beagan
agus neoini ghlas na h-ùrach
'na comhfhurtachd chrìon phrann aig
    barrachd.

The eternity of Dante and of
    Dugald Buchanan
an old new light to a few,
and the grey nonentity of the
    dust
a withered brittle comfort to
    more.

Pàrras gun phàrras a chuideachd,
imcheist a' ghiullain Shaoir-Chléirich
a ghearan is a dhiùltadh sàmhach
'nan toibheum an amhaich Sineubha;

Paradise without the paradise of
    his own people,
the perplexity of the little Free
    Presbyterian boy:
his complaint and silent refusal
blasphemy in the throat of
    Geneva;

agus an amhaich na Ròimhe
– ged·tha Purgadair nas ciùine –
an robair eile air a' chrann
is Spartacus le armailt chiùrrte.

and in the throat of Rome
– though Purgatory is gentler –
the other robber on the tree
and Spartacus with his tortured
    army.

Aig Uaigh Yeats

Tha leac mór leathann na h-uaghach
ort fhéin 's air Deòrsa do bhean
eadar a' mhuir is Beinn Ghulbain,
eadar an t-Sligeach's Lios an Doill;
's tha do bhriathran mìorbhaileach
a' tigh'nn le osaig o ghach taobh
le dealbh na té òig àlainn
ann an teilifis gach raoin.

An guth binn air slios Beinn Ghulbain
o'n aon bhial cuimir òg
a thug a chliù o Dhiarmad
on chualas e air Grìne
's e air fàs 'na sgread le bròn
agus leis an fheirg uasail
is leis na h-euchdan còire
bu bhinn an cluais O Conghaile
's an cluasan a sheòrsa.

Fhuair thusa 'n cothrom, Uilleim,
an cothrom dha do bhriathran
on bha a' ghaisge 's a' bhòidhche
's an croinn bhratach troimh do
*   chliathaich.*
Ghabh thu riutha air aon dòigh,
ach tha leisgeal air do bhilean,
an leisgeal nach do mhill do bhàrdachd
oir tha a leisgeal aig gach duine.

At Yeats's Grave

The big broad flagstone of the
    grave
is on yourself and George your
    wife
between the sea and Ben Bulben,
between Sligo and Lissadell;
and your marvellous words are
coming in the breeze from every
    side
with the picture of the young
    beautiful one
in the television of each field.

The sweet voice on the side of
    Ben Bulben
from the one shapely young
    mouth
that took his fame from Dermid
since it was heard on a Green,
become a screech with grief
and with the noble anger
and with the generous deeds
that were sweet in the ears of
    Connolly
and in the ears of his kind.

You got the chance, William,
the chance for your words,
since courage and beauty
had their flagpoles through your
    side.
You acknowledged them in one
    way,
but there is an excuse on your
    lips,
the excuse that did not spoil
    your poetry,
for every man has his excuse.